I0635678

A Sunday Kind of Love

by

Lynna Banning

Dedication

For my niece, Leslie Yarnes Sugai

Chapter One

Maple Shade, Oregon
1873

Of the four women gathered on the wide front porch of the Maple Shade boardinghouse, only Leah Rydell had thought to bring out a pitcher of cold lemonade. She plunked it down on the low table and watched as a plate of sugar cookies and four tall glasses also appeared. Sally and Martha then settled onto straight-backed wooden chairs, and Leah took her place on the porch swing next to Belle, who grudgingly swept her ruffled dimity skirt aside to make room.

"Lemonade!" Belle exclaimed. "Oh, Leah, I am simply parched! Whatever would we do without you?"

Leah surveyed the tall, elegant woman beside her. "Maybe bring the lemonade pitcher yourself?"

Sally laughed aloud. "Lord love you, Belle, you've managed to avoid carrying a blessed thing this afternoon. As usual," she added under her breath.

"Why, of course," Belle said blithely, twirling a long blonde curl around her index finger. "I'm the only one of us who gets dressed up for our afternoon refreshments. You wouldn't want me to spill anything on my dress, would you?"

Sally snorted. "Honey, I wouldn't want to ruffle any of your bloomin' ruffles."

Belle merely smiled. "Oh, don't get your Irish up, Sally. I was already sitting out here on the porch swing before you all came out. There was nothing left for me to carry."

Leah watched Martha roll her eyes and hide a smile. As usual, Belle had an excuse for not lifting a single ring-laden finger to carry anything heavier than a volume of poetry. And Martha, who was used to the shenanigans of her schoolroom students, saw right through her.

Oh, it didn't matter, Leah thought. Nothing mattered on this hot, still, honeysuckle-scented Sunday afternoon here in the prettiest town in Oregon. All contentious thoughts drifted away from her overheated brain. All she wanted to do was gulp down some cool lemonade, and thank God she was no longer standing behind the cash register at Nanetti's mercantile.

Sally splashed lemonade into the four glasses, added a sprig of mint, and passed the cookie plate. "Drink up, ladies. Monday morning'll be here quicker than you can say an Irish blessing."

Belle smoothed her skirt. "Whoever in the world would want to say an Irish blessing?"

"An Irishwoman, of course!" Sally countered. She caught Leah's eye and winked.

"None of us is Irish except you, Sally," Belle remarked.

"Well, then," Sally said without a trace of warmth, "I'm feelin' truly sorry for you."

Leah laughed and settled back to enjoy her lemonade. She loved summer afternoons like this, especially Sunday afternoons when she didn't have to work. Sunday was the only day Mr. Nanetti closed the mercantile. "Is Sabbath," he often reminded her. "God say we should rest."

And pray, no doubt. That was something she had given up on her thirteenth birthday, the day after both her parents had died of cholera. She and Johnny, who was only ten years old at the time, had been taken in by their aunt and uncle, but Johnny hated them both. On his twelfth birthday, he'd run away from home.

Months later, when Aunt Irma and Uncle Sherman had come out West, Leah had come with them. When they decided they didn't like the frontier after all and returned to Ohio, fifteen-year-old Leah decided to stay. Which is how she came to live in Maple Shade, Oregon.

"I," Belle now pronounced carefully, "am definitely not Irish. The name Fontaine is French."

Sally pursed her lips. "Ye could still do with an Irish blessing, Miss Fontaine. Who knows, it might make your hair curly."

Belle smoothed one hand over her blonde ringlets. "*My* hair is already curly."

Leah crunched into a sugar cookie to keep from laughing. They all knew Belle rolled her hair up in rags every night; her bouncing curls were the envy of schoolgirls all over town. Leah had no use for long, swirly curls and wore her dark hair in a single thick braid that hung down her back. It kept her hair out of the candy jars and away from the bushel baskets of ripe, sticky peaches and apricots in front of the mercantile.

She sipped her lemonade and let her mind drift as Martha began her usual litany of amusing anecdotes about the antics of her students. Sally hummed "The Irish Washerwoman" under her breath, and Belle…well, Belle sat poking her foot out from under her skirt, admiring her new leather shoes.

All four of them had lived at Mrs. Swerdlow's boardinghouse for the last four years, and despite their foibles, Leah liked her three friends. Martha marched off to the Maple Shade schoolhouse every weekday morning to teach reading and writing and arithmetic and geography to a roomful of wriggly children. Sally spent evenings singing at the Shady Lady Saloon, though Leah knew she was no shady lady. Irish, yes. A singer, yes. A saloon girl, yes. But a real lady for all that.

Belle, of course, did not work. Belle had inherited a bank account full of money from her widowed father, and she had stepped off the eastbound train when it stopped at Maple Shade, liked what she saw, and decided to stay.

Leah often wondered why the well-to-do southern belle was content to stay in a small town in the wilds of Oregon. What, exactly, did Belle want out of life? Was she waiting for a rich, unmarried cattle rancher, a man who could buy her all the fancy dresses and leather shoes she could possibly wear in one lifetime?

Leah sighed and closed her eyes. What did it matter? Nothing would bother her on this lovely, lazy Sunday afternoon. She didn't even open her eyes at the sound of hoofbeats coming down the road. But she was startled when Belle sucked in her breath, jerked forward, and plunked her lemonade down on the table before them.

"*Who* is that man?"

"What man?" Sally asked.

"*That* man. The one on that black horse coming down the street."

****

Cal kept his eyes focused straight ahead, maintaining the gelding's steady, unhurried pace and trying not to notice the four women sitting on the verandah of the only boardinghouse in town. Young women. Pretty, too. One was all fluffed out in something pale green and sheer-looking with lots of ruffles. The one on the chair wore her hair in a tight bun and was buttoned all the way to her chin. Spinster, maybe. The blowsy-looking redhead next to her stared at him with a look that said *Interested.*

They were all drinking something, probably lemonade. He licked his dry lips. He'd ridden all the way from Silver City without a single drop of the whiskey in his canteen. Must be getting old. Or maybe he was getting religion. *Better make it religion, Cal, since preaching is partly what brought you here.*

The fourth lady, rocking in the porch swing next to the blonde with the ruffles, didn't even look up. She had a soft look about her, not over-refined, just nice somehow. Maybe she was dozing. The other three women were giving him a careful once-over, but this one didn't seem to care who was clip-clopping past her porch on this warm Sunday afternoon. Probably married with three kids.

A dart of remorse niggled into his brain. *Forget it, Zander. You've got other things to do here.* He started to walk Star on past, feeling three pairs of female eyes follow his every step. At the last moment, Miss Sleepyhead snapped her lids open, and her gaze met his head-on. Not bold or anything, like the redhead or Miss Ruffles, just calm and steady. And only mildly interested.

Her eyes were blue, so clear they looked like pools of brook water. Like bluebonnets. Did Oregon have bluebonnets?

Did he care? He didn't need bluebonnets. What he needed was a place to sleep.

Chapter Two

Nanetti's Mercantile had a just-scrubbed-looking white storefront and two big windows with a display of ladies' hats in one and an assortment of rakes and hoes in the other. Cal dismounted, looped the reins over the hitching rail, and tramped past the overflowing bushel baskets of peaches and green beans.

Inside, it was quiet and half a degree cooler. The proprietor was hunched over a newspaper next to the cash register. "Mr. Nanetti?"

The man didn't look up. "Yah?"

"I'm Callahan Zander. I wrote you from Texas, remember?"

"Yah, I remember. You want job?"

"Uh, no. I already have a job. What I need is a place to sleep."

"You gonna maybe stay in Maple Shade, huh?"

"Yes, if...if my job works out."

Mr. Nanetti gave him a slow, deliberate once-over, the man's eyes moving from his battered gray Stetson to his trail-dusty jeans. He even leaned over the counter to inspect Cal's boots. When the man's soft brown eyes returned to Cal's face, he wished he'd shaved that morning.

"What job you got, Mr. Zander?"

"At the church," Cal said quickly.

"Ah." The proprietor nodded. "Good. Church empty

for long time. Need dusting. Need maple trees trimmed, too, maybe."

Cal waited.

"I got cabin out back," Nanetti said at last. "My wife and me, we live there until the babies come. Now we live in big house on Spruce Street."

Cal waited some more.

"Okay, you come with me. I show you." The proprietor led the way through the store and out the back door.

Like the church, the cabin had obviously been empty for a long time. A dust-covered table and two chairs sat opposite a blackened iron stove, a wooden counter, and a dry sink. A narrow bed covered with a threadbare quilt sat in one corner, flanked by a nightstand and a battered-looking chest of drawers. Wooden shelves held an assortment of cups and mismatched china. The walls were studded with various-sized pots and iron skillets. A dented teakettle and a blue speckleware coffee pot perched on the stovetop.

"Is right for you?" Nanetti asked. "I build myself." He tried hard to look disinterested, but Cal could see how proud he was of the little cabin.

"Sure, Mr. Nanetti, your cabin is just right for me."

The older man beamed. "Good. Is good. You have questions?"

"Just one," Cal answered. "Uh…where is the church?"

****

Leah took the long way from the bank back to the mercantile so she could smell the roses in Mrs. Hardesty's front yard. The yellow ones smelled sweet and spicy at the same time, and the scent always reminded her of Ohio. When she walked back into the store, Mr. Nanetti was dancing with excitement.

"Miss Leah, you never guess what!"

"Another bushel of peaches from the Litvaks?"

"Ah, no."

"The Crawley twins ate all the caramels again?"

Mr. Nanetti laughed. "No peaches. No caramels. Is something good about my cabin behind store!"

"What about it?" She knew that cabin was Mr. Nanetti's pride and joy. It had stood empty for the past three years, ever since the Nanetti family had moved to their large white house with the big backyard. He had offered the cabin to her, but she hadn't wanted to give up her room at the boardinghouse. She also didn't want to live that close to the mercantile.

"Someone is come to live in my cabin!" Mr. Nanetti crowed.

"Who? Who is coming?"

"Mister Zander is come. He has job at the church."

"Zander? He must be new to Maple Shade."

"Yes, is new. Come from Texas."

"Texas! Why? Does he have relatives in town?"

"This I do not know. But he is nice man. I hope you will like."

Leah shrugged and turned her attention to straightening up the candy jars on the counter. It was obvious Jamie and Flora Crawley had been at the caramels again. She hid a smile, reached for the feather duster, and thought no more about this Mr. Zander."

But the next morning, when she arrived at the mercantile, there he was—the man on the black horse who'd ridden past the boardinghouse on Sunday afternoon.

Mr. Nanetti grinned at her. "Miss Leah, I like you to meet Mister Zander."

He was tall, his face lean and tanned. His Levis looked worn, and the sleeves of his blue chambray shirt were rolled up to reveal forearms browned by the sun. He extended his hand, and when she shook it, she noted he had long, well-shaped fingers.

"Callahan Zander," he said.

Ah, he is Irish. Sally will be pleased. "Leah Rydell, Mr. Zander."

"Call me Cal," he murmured.

She looked up into steel-gray eyes. "Call me Miss Rydell," she said clearly. She decided she did not like him. He was too sure of himself. Too polished. Too…good-looking. She didn't like him one bit. She couldn't say why, exactly; he just made her uneasy.

Cal didn't speak for a long minute. Leah Rydell was pretty in a quiet kind of way, but still pretty enough to stop a man's breath. She had clear, expressive blue eyes which darkened to purple-blue as he watched, hair the color of dark molasses she wore caught in a loose braid that hung over one shoulder, and skin the color of cream, smooth and unblemished with a soft sprinkle of tiny freckles over her nose. He knew he was staring, but he couldn't help it.

But her name was Rydell, and that reminded him of the real reason he'd come to this small Oregon town. He had a message for her. And a warning.

Chapter Three

Leah decided there was definitely something odd about Callahan Zander. For one thing, he spent hours at Sheriff Mankewicz's office, which she knew because the sheriff's office was right across the street from the mercantile. And on top of that, Sally reported that Callahan Zander was a regular visitor at the Shady Lady Saloon. A poker-playing visitor.

Early Wednesday morning, the bell over the mercantile door sounded, and in swept a large woman with the hands of two wriggling children clutched in each of hers.

"Ah, Miz Crawley," Florio Nanetti said loudly. He smiled and tousled the hair of one of the children. "What I can do today for you?"

"You can get Miss Leah to help me pick out a new hat," the harried woman replied. "Stop pulling, Timothy!"

"Aw, Ma, I dowanna look at dumb old hats," her son whined. "I wanna look at rifles."

"You're too young for a rifle," Mrs. Crawley said with finality. "You take Daniel and find some shirts in your size. Go on, scoot!"

The two eight-year-old twins disappeared down the apparel aisle, and Mr. Nanetti conducted their mother to the millinery section. "Leah?" he called. "You come, please. Help Mrs. Crawley find new hat."

Leah emerged from the back storeroom, wiping her hands on her apron. "A new hat, Mrs. Crawley? What would be the occasion?"

"Why, church, of course! Come Sunday morning I intend to be decked out proper to meet the new preacher."

"Oh? I hadn't heard that Maple Shade has a new preacher."

The older woman nodded decisively. "One of them circuit-riding preachers. You know, they preach the Good Book for six or seven months and then move on. Maybe this one'll stay permanent."

Leah pursed her lips. Most likely not. She had no use for preachers, circuit or otherwise. Most of them spouted sanctimonious nonsense, and none of them had a lick of common sense about life in a frontier town because they came from big cities like Portland or Omaha.

She guided Mrs. Crawley to the ladies hat aisle. "Did you have a style in mine? Or perhaps a color?"

"Purple," the woman replied. "Gonna get gussied up in my good purple silk. Never get to wear it out on the farm, see. Gonna pop my Harvey's eyes out."

"I'm sure your husband will admire you in…um, purple, Mrs. Crawley. Now here's one that might suit." She lifted a concoction of feathers and fake fruit off the top shelf.

"Ah," the woman sighed. "Perfect." She plopped it on her graying hair and turned to Leah. "How do I look?"

The minute Mrs. Crawley rescued the garden tools from her twin sons and swept out with two boys' plaid shirts and one purple hat, the bell over the door rang again. Another woman, the wife of a wheat rancher,

12

plunked down seventy-five cents for a pink straw creation with a veil that tied under her chin.

And it didn't end there.

Mr. Nanetti beamed and encouraged, and all day long Leah gave millinery advice to a stream of ladies until her throat went dry. *What* was going on? Surely one circuit-preacher was the same as all the others?

"But Miss Leah," Mr. Nanetti pointed out. "Does not matter what preacher preaches. The ladies, they don' go to see him. They go to see each other!"

Of course, she acknowledged. The women of a ranching community like Maple Shade had few occasions to dress up and show off their finery. Even the barn dances out at the Janson ranch didn't rate Sunday silks and outlandish hats. Barn dances meant calico skirts and starched shirtwaists.

By Friday afternoon, Mr. Nanetti's supply of millinery was growing sparse, and by Saturday, grumbling ranchers and business owners, even Sheriff Mankewicz, had depleted the aisles of men's shirts and new white handkerchiefs.

That night, supper at the boardinghouse raised Leah's eyebrows. Belle was in a perfect fizz about something, and it took only a few minutes to grasp that whatever it was, it was happening on Sunday morning.

"But I simply *must* have the sadiron to myself tonight. After all, church is tomorrow!"

"I didn't know you were so religious," Martha remarked dryly.

"Well, you wouldn't want to wear something *wrinkled* on the Sabbath, would you?"

Martha sighed and spooned out another helping of mashed potatoes while the landlady, Dora Swerdlow, flitted in and out of the kitchen with more creamed peas and another platter of fried chicken.

"What about you, Leah?" Belle queried. "What will you be wearing tomorrow?"

"Just my usual denim skirt and a shirtwaist. It's my day off, and I don't plan to go to church."

"But honey, you can't be serious! The whole town is buzzing about the new preacher. I hear he's not only learned but eloquent."

"Pooh," Leah scoffed. "How would anyone know? No one's ever heard him preach before. We don't even know his name."

"True," Martha added. "None of the announcements at the bank or in the barbershop window mentioned a name. It could be a woman, for all we know."

Belle and Mrs. Swerdlow gasped. "A woman!" The landlady's free hand went to her ample bosom. "Land's sake, what is the world coming to?"

"Women," Belle inserted, "know nothing about—"

Martha snorted. "You can bet your best petticoat that whatever a man knows, a woman knew it first."

Mrs. Swerdlow gasped again, and Leah had to laugh. She wished Sally were here to join the fray, but Sally was working late at the Shady Lady, and anyway, Sally wasn't much of a church-goer.

"So, Leah?" Belle queried. "Does that mean you are not going to attend church tomorrow?"

"I am not," she said with finality. "The ladies of Maple Shade bought out Mr. Nanetti's supply of millinery, and therefore…" She caught Martha's eye and smiled. "I'm afraid I have no hat to wear."

They were still laughing when Mrs. Swerdlow brought out the apple pie.

Around midnight, when Sally arrived home from the Shady Lady, Leah was still sitting in the front parlor with a copy of *Ivanhoe* on her lap.

Sally stopped dead just inside the front door. "Why, Leah, what are you doing up at this hour?"

"I couldn't sleep," Leah replied.

"Too much coffee?"

"Too much church talk."

"I'm not going to church tomorrow, either," Sally admitted. "I listen to men talk every single night. I certainly don't need to hear more talk on Sunday morning!"

"Exactly," Leah agreed. Still, she had to admit she was curious. No one seemed to know anything about this new preacher, yet everybody was going off to church tomorrow to hear him. And to show off their new hats, she added.

But on Sunday morning, lying in bed listening to Belle and Martha and Mrs. Swerdlow rattle up and down the staircase offering each other advice on ribbons and reticules, Leah had had enough. Oh, all right, she *was* curious, she admitted. Besides, with all the thumping and bumping, now she was wide-awake.

Oh, bother. She might as well get dressed and peek in at the church to see what all the fuss was about.

****

A wriggly line of wagons and horses and buggies clogged the tree-lined road up Snapdragon Hill where the Maple Shade Community Church stood. Painted a blinding white, the small, square structure was surrounded by maple trees and a tangle of rosebushes someone had planted years before Leah had come to town. It was pretty in a Sunday-ish sort of way. She hadn't set foot in the place except once, when Elsa and Sammy Madsen were married. She couldn't recall who had conducted the ceremony, but he had talked far too much. Preachers were like that, she sniffed.

She arrived late on purpose. Tentatively she approached the double door at the back of the church, which stood wide open, and positioned herself unobtrusively behind the seated congregation. She spied Belle in the first pew, the ribbon on her pale blue straw hat streaming down her back. Martha sat next to her, her head tipped down, reading the Bible. Belle was sitting bolt upright, apparently prepared to find the preacher's words riveting.

The preacher, whoever he was, had not yet entered the church, and people sat coughing and shushing their children and rustling the pages of their hymnals. Then the side door opened, and a tall, lean, dark-haired man in a plain blue shirt and jeans stepped forward.

Oh, my stars. It was that man, Callahan Zander! But he was just Mr. Nanetti's helper...

Wasn't he?

****

Cal swept his gaze over the sea of upturned faces before him and took a deep breath. It was now or never. He'd thought about this moment often over the past seven years, but now that he found himself actually standing with a dry mouth and pounding heart before the townspeople gathered before him in the church, he wasn't so sure.

He drew in another long breath and hoped to God he knew what he was doing. Before he opened his mouth to speak he caught sight of a slim figure in a simple blue skirt and gingham shirtwaist standing at the back of the church.

Leah Rydell.

Don't think about her. Just say what you walked out here to say.

He sucked in another gulp of air and opened his lips. "Good morning, folks. My name is Callahan Zander."

A muttered response greeted him.

"I guess you haven't had a preacher in a while, judging from the thickness of dust on the pews and the state of the rosebushes outside."

Murmurs of assent rose. He swallowed and took another breath.

"So you might say I've come to…uh…prune the roses and dust off the pews."

Laughter.

"And I've come to talk about some things. Things I've learned the hard way. Things you might find make some sense."

He paused and swallowed again. Unable to help himself, his gaze traveled to the young woman standing in back. Her mouth was pressed into a firm line, and her eyes, so clear and blue they looked like a summer sky, looked downright challenging. Right at that moment he knew this was going to be uphill all the way.

"This morning," he began, "I thought I'd talk about…about families. We all have a family. Whether we communicate with them, or whether we even like them, doesn't matter. We all have a mother and a father. We all came from a family."

A long sigh traveled around the room.

"Maybe you haven't spoken to them in years," Cal continued. "Maybe they moved away or maybe they're dead and gone. But at some time, somewhere, all of us had a family."

He cast his eyes over the upturned faces before him, steeling himself for what would come next. "So," he said with more confidence than he felt, "this morning I decided I wanted to say something about families."

He stopped speaking, and Leah watched his chest expand as he took three deep breaths. Well, how interesting! Was the preacher nervous? Fascinated, she found she couldn't take her eyes off him.

He opened his mouth, closed it, and then opened it again.

"We all had mothers," he said in a low voice. "And fathers. Maybe we have a sister or a brother. Maybe more. And maybe you love all of them, or just one or two of them, or even none of them. But because they are your family, we owe them something."

He stopped and looked hard at the congregation. No one made a sound. The people crowding the pews sat like stone statues, barely breathing, their faces upturned. Waiting.

In spite of herself, Leah was spellbound. The man spoke well, and his voice…He was a magician. A conjurer. Callahan Zander was intriguing. And a little frightening.

She shook herself and looked away. What nonsense! Why should a preacher in a church she never attended make her feel…humbled, in a way. No, that wasn't right. Not humbled. Unsettled.

She shook herself again. Hard. She hadn't thought of her parents in years. When they had both died within a week of each other, she'd been numb. She lived through the terrible months that followed only by closing off her feelings, and now she no longer knew if she had any feelings left. Mostly she still felt numb. At least she tried hard to keep herself that way, because if she could avoid feeling things, then she could avoid pain.

She clenched her hands. But her brother Johnny was another matter. When he was twelve years old, Johnny had disappeared and never returned. At first, she thought something had happened to him. The sheriff and a posse of townsmen searched for weeks, but they found nothing, not a trace. Finally, the sheriff confided that Johnny had most likely run off to be a cowboy or join a circus or some such.

That made her purely mad. She was furious with her brother for months and months. Years, even. Then she felt hurt. Why would he have left her? After Mama and Papa died, she and Johnny had only each other. *Why, why would Johnny leave her all alone?*

The preacher was speaking again, but Leah was no longer listening. His words stirred up something inside her, something she didn't want stirred up. She closed her ears and shut off her mind. Then, without really thinking, she unclenched her fists, straightened her hat, and without sparing a glance at the man standing before the assembled townspeople of Maple Shade she slipped out the back of the church and headed across the grassy meadow and down the hill.

She needed a calming cup of tea. And she wondered if Mrs. Swerdlow kept any whiskey in the house.

Cal saw a flash of blue gingham disappear through the door at the back of the church and realized that Leah Rydell had walked out. Well, he couldn't blame her. He wasn't an experienced preacher. Probably he was a long, long way from being eloquent. The congregation had listened, though. Maybe he'd said something that spoke to them in some way.

Or maybe not. Maybe the people of Maple Shade were just being polite. They hadn't had a preacher, even a circuit preacher such as he was, for a long time. They were probably starved for some "Sunday" words, and he had to admit he was kind of glad about that. Still, he also had to admit he'd wanted to stir up Leah Rydell, and he had purposely chosen "family" as his topic this morning with her in mind.

But Leah...Leah had looked more than stirred up. She had looked mad as a hornet.

Well, there was always next Sunday. And he would see Leah at the mercantile every day.

And if there is one thing you've learned over the years, Callahan Zander, it's that you are a patient man who is very good at waiting.

Chapter Four

Leah tramped all the way back to the boardinghouse, brewed herself an extra-strong cup of tea, and plopped down on the front porch swing. Imagine, a sermon on being a family. How presumptuous!

But the entire congregation had sat in rapt silence until she bolted out the back of the church and plodded across the meadow, her fists clenched at her sides.

Why, *why* was he so outspoken on a subject that was none of his business? A subject that had nothing to do with the Ten Commandments or the teachings of Jesus. What do we owe family members indeed, she sniffed. She owed her brother Johnny a good talking to, that's what. How dare her brother abandon her and not send a single word all these years?

She didn't sleep that night, and she blamed it all on Callahan Zander's Sunday sermon. The next morning, she felt as wrung out as Mrs. Swerdlow's damp laundry hanging on the clothesline.

She opened the front door of the mercantile, and Mr. Nanetti beamed at her from behind the cash register. "Ah, good morning, Miss Leah."

She acknowledged his greeting with a short nod. It wasn't a good morning at all. She felt tired and out of sorts, but she worked up as much of a smile as she could muster.

"Good morning, Mr. Nanetti. I see the Crawley

twins have been at the candy jars again." She pointed to the two glass jars perched haphazardly on the counter. "I'll put these to rights, shall I?"

Without waiting for an answer, she pulled the jars forward and started to unstick the lemon drops from the jelly beans. She had her back to the rear door, so the sound of Cal Zander's voice startled her.

"Good morning, Florio. Good morning, Leah."

Leah swung around to face him. "Good morning, *Mister* Zander," she pronounced carefully.

He reached to pluck a gummy lemon drop from her fingers. "Good morning, Leah," he said again. He smiled at her, and a little jolt of awareness shot through her. Awareness of *what*, she didn't know. She would ignore it. And him, she decided. She marched out to the storeroom for a damp cloth to wipe the fingerprints off the candy jars.

Suddenly she heard Mr. Nanetti's tense voice. "Miss Leah, come quick! Something is happen."

When she returned to the store, the first thing she saw was a young cowhand dressed in dusty jeans and a worn sheepskin vest. He clutched a battered brown Stetson in one hand and he was breathing hard.

"Miss Leah," Mr. Nanetti began, "he say he have message for you."

"Message? What message?"

"I'm real sorry to barge in on you like this, Miss," the young man stammered. "But this here's important."

Her entire body went cold. "What is it?"

He turned a tired, dust-streaked face toward her. He was maybe 17 or 18, and he'd obviously ridden a long way. He was covered in dust, and the red bandana around his neck was damp with sweat.

"If you're Leah Rydell, I got a message for you." He stopped to suck in a breath. "I'm sorry, Miss. I been ridin' four days to reach you, and I'm pretty well played out."

Cal Zander produced a battered wooden chair from behind the counter, and the young cowhand dropped into it and sent him a grateful look.

"Where did you ride from, son?" Cal asked.

"The Circle M Ranch, up near Boise. Caleb Martindale's the owner. I'm one of the ranch hands."

"And?" Cal questioned.

The boy sucked in two deep breaths. "We got a line shack up in the mountains, see. A few days back two of us rode up to check on it, and we found—" He withdrew a folded sheet of paper from his vest pocket and thrust it at Leah. "If you're Leah Rydell, this here note's for you."

Cal watched her slowly unfold the scrap of grimy paper and turn away to read the contents. Then he heard a strangled cry.

Florio Nanetti was no stranger to hysterical females, Cal observed. The diminutive storekeeper motioned the cowhand out of the chair, took Leah by the shoulders, and sat her down in his place.

Her face had gone white as milk, but she wasn't crying. She was shaking pretty bad, though. Cal fished the bottle of brandy from under the counter, uncorked it, and held it to her lips.

"Take a swallow," he ordered.

She shook her head. "I n-never touch spirits," she said in a shaky voice.

"You never get messages from somewhere up in Idaho, either," he said. "Swallow!"

Obediently she tipped the bottle up, took a small

23

mouthful, and coughed until tears came to her eyes. He was halfway sorry he'd urged the brandy on her, but Florio was nodding his approval so he guessed he'd done the right thing.

"What does letter say?" the storekeeper asked.

She held it out without answering. Nanetti lifted his hands, indicating he wouldn't take it. "You read, Cal. I know not English words enough."

Cal lifted the note out of Leah's trembling hand and read it.

Dear Sis,

I was coming to find you but I got hurt bad.

I need help so please come.

Johnny

He spun to face the cowhand. "You got a doctor up there in Idaho?"

"Oh, yessir. Doc came out to the ranch, and right away he sent me ridin' to reach Miss Rydell."

"You know how he got hurt?"

"No, sir. Just that he took a bullet in his chest and his leg's been shot up pretty bad. Doc says he's runnin' a fever."

Without a word, Cal stepped down the clothing aisle. When he reappeared, he piled two plaid boy-sized shirts and a pair of jeans on the counter. Next came a pair of boots, two pairs of socks, and a blue bandana. Last he laid a revolver from Mr. Nanetti's gun case and a box of shells on top of the stack.

Leah watched him dully. "What are you doing?" she asked.

"Getting ready."

She sat up straighter. "Ready for what?"

24

"For going to Idaho. It's a long trip on horseback. You'll need to dress differently."

Chapter Five

Leah stared at Cal for a long minute, then covered her face with her hands. "I haven't heard a single word from my brother in almost ten years. I thought he was dead."

"Hate to say it, Miss," the young cowhand said, "but he's gonna be dead pretty quick 'less Doc can pull him through."

She looked up at him. "When are you heading back?"

"Soon as I can, I reckon. You comin'?"

Cal stepped forward and settled his hand on her shoulder. "She's coming, but not with you. You ride on back to your ranch, and make it as fast as you can. Tell Johnny she's coming. We'll start as soon as we can get packed up."

Leah stared at him. "We?"

"Yeah. Alone you won't make it more than half a day. Together we can cover some ground." He glanced at Mr. Nanetti. "Florio, is it okay if this kid—What's your name, son?"

"Anthony. They call me Slim."

"All right, Slim. Okay if Slim here loads up some coffee and tinned goods?"

"Sure, sure," the mercantile owner said. "Take anything you need."

"Thanks, mister. I'll start back soon as I load up my

saddlebag." He started to stand, but Leah reached out and stopped him. "Wait. Tell my brother I'm coming. And-and tell him I l-love him. Will you do that?"

"Shore will, Miss. It's a lucky man that's got a pretty sister who cares about him. Wish I did."

Cal motioned him out to the storeroom, and Leah heard the low murmur of voices. Mr. Nanetti gathered up tinned corn and beans, added a small sack of coffee beans, and set them on the counter next to the pile of jeans and shirts.

"Leah, you want I should pack supplies for you?"

Before she could answer, Cal and Slim stepped back into the store and surveyed the items on the counter. "Thanks, Florio," Cal said quietly. "Take it out of my rent for the cabin."

"Rent! I no charge you rent, Mister Cal."

"I think you should. Might not be back right away, and I'd like to be sure the cabin's still here for me."

"Cabin will be here," Mr. Nanette said decisively. "You go, help Miss Leah."

Cal helped Slim load up his saddlebags, then walked the cowhand out to the hitching rail where his horse stood. "My name's Cal Zander, son. You tell young Johnny I'm bringing his sister and he better the hell be alive when we get there."

"Yessir, I sure will."

Cal swung the loaded saddlebag up and secured it behind the saddle, then watched the young man mount and clatter off down the road. When he returned to the mercantile, Leah had disappeared.

"She in back room," Nanetti explained. "Trying on boots."

Cal was half-way surprised. Not many young

women would pull up her socks and get ready to ride out of town on a moment's notice. And not many would think to wear boots that fit. He gestured to the pile of garments on the counter. "Put those things on my tab, too."

"And the revolver?" Nanetti asked. "Miss Leah, she never like guns."

"And the revolver. She might need it before this is over."

The storekeeper shot him a puzzled look. "This is dangerous?"

"Might be. You never know."

"But…but you will be with her, is true?"

Cal smiled at the older man. "I will be with her, yes." He'd stick to Leah like a damned cocklebur. He'd waited years for this. He'd finally tracked down Johnny Rydell's sister, and when he found her, he knew all he had to do was wait for Johnny to turn up. Never expected he'd have to ride all the way to Idaho to see him.

Leah stepped back into the store carrying the pair of boots she'd plucked from Mr. Nanetti's counter.

"Make sure they fit tight," Cal advised. "Too loose and you'll raise blisters."

She nodded. "These are fine." He noticed she didn't try on the shirts or the jeans he'd selected. Instead, she began bundling them up in brown wrapping paper.

"Leave the revolver with me," he said.

"I'm not taking it. I am leaving it here."

Cal caught Florio's eye and shook his head. He'd slip the revolver into the bottom of her saddlebag before they left.

All at once he had an unexpected moment of misgiving. "Leah, you can ride, can't you?"

"Of course."

Not many women could last more than a few hours on horseback, especially when riding hard, as they would be. "You own a horse?"

"Well, no. I will rent one from the livery."

"You go on back to your boardinghouse and change your clothes. I'll rent you a mount."

She nodded, then lifted the bundle of garments into her arms. When she walked out the door, Florio caught his arm.

"Miss Leah, she will be safe?"

"She will be safe," Cal assured him. He'd stake his life on it.

Half an hour later, Cal tied a pretty roan mare and his own black gelding to the hitching rail, loaded the saddlebags with tinned beans and tomatoes, bacon, a small sack of flour and one of coffee, then added two extra boxes of cartridges, one for his Colt and one for the small revolver he'd picked out for Leah. Just in case, he told himself. She probably couldn't hit the broad side of the church, but still...

He settled down inside the mercantile, helped himself to a lemon drop, and waited.

****

Belle clasped a delicate hand over her mouth. "You're going to *what*? Leah, ladies do not wear jeans. You look positively scandalous!"

"I am going to Idaho," Leah said again. "On horseback."

"But why?" Mrs. Swerdlow blurted. "This morning you were going to the mercantile!"

Leah hesitated. "Because my brother is in Idaho, and he's been hurt."

The landlady set her coffee cup onto its saucer with a sharp click. "Your brother that disappeared all those years ago? The one you haven't heard one bleeding peep from in all this time?"

"Yes," Leah said simply.

Belle's green eyes widened. "But…but you can't just sashay off to Idaho alone."

"I won't be alone. Cal Zander is going with me."

Belle's forehead puckered. "Whaaat? Why is *Cal* going?"

Leah paused with a cheese and bacon sandwich halfway to her mouth. "He doesn't think I will be safe on my own. And he volunteered."

Sally folded both hands around her coffee mug. "That sounds just like Cal Zander, Leah. I told you he was a good man."

"I pray to God you're right, Sally," the landlady muttered. "You will be careful, won't you, Leah?"

"Of course I will, Mrs. Swerdlow. But I really don't have a choice. Johnny is my only brother."

"Oh," Belle moaned. "Martha's not going to believe this. Couldn't you wait until she gets home from school this afternoon? Martha is always so sensible."

Leah sighed. "*I* am sensible, Belle. I have been sensible all my life. Apparently, my little brother has not."

Mrs. Swerdlow handed her a dishtowel-wrapped stack of sandwiches. "Here. Cheese and bacon and—" Her lips quivered. "We'll be praying for you, honey."

Belle stood up and laid a hand on Leah's arm. "Be sure to wash out your underclothes every night," she said.

Sally snorted. "Are you kidding? How are clean

drawers gonna help her ride all the way to Idaho?"

"Oh," Belle said, her voice combative. "Surely it would help her feel better during all those hours on horseback if her drawers were—"

Leah suppressed a laugh. "I will certainly try to wash out my underthings, Belle. But it might not be an easy task in the company of Cal Zander."

Sally shook back her red curls. "Oh, Cal won't mind, Leah. I bet he won't even look!"

The three women followed Leah out the front door and stood on the porch, waving as she went down the steps and opened the gate. As soon as she was out of sight she drew in a long, fortifying breath, squared her shoulders, and marched on toward the mercantile.

Never in her life had she been this frightened. Except, she reminded herself, during those awful days after Johnny had disappeared.

Cal saw her coming down the street, moving at a fast walk and looking straight ahead. She wore a red plaid shirt that swelled over her breasts and a pair of Levis with a leather belt that nipped in her waist. Oh, man, those boy's duds he'd picked out fit her like no boy's garments had ever clung to a boy's body.

He turned to secure her saddlebag and tied a sturdy sheepskin jacket behind her saddle, then set a black wide-brimmed hat and a blue bandana on top.

When she reached him, she studied the roan mare for a long moment, then handed him a sack of something. "Sandwiches," she said. "But before we leave, I must say goodbye to Mr. Nanetti."

"Sure." He waited while she stepped inside the mercantile. Through the front window Cal watched the storekeeper awkwardly pat her shoulder, then saw her throw her arms around the old man. When she rejoined him, her eyes were shiny.

"You ready?"

She nodded and turned toward the mare.

"Her name's Lady," he said.

"Oh." She approached the horse hesitantly, then smoothed her palm over the animal's nose. "Hello, Lady. My name is Leah."

Cal grinned. Not many riders would bother introducing themselves to their horse. He found her action touching.

When she picked up the reins and reached for the saddle horn, Cal clenched his jaw. The view of Miss Leah Rydell's rounded backside made his mouth go dry.

He turned away, mounted his gelding in one smooth motion, and watched her slip the toe of her new boot into the stirrup and tighten her grip on the saddle horn. He'd adjusted the stirrups by guessing; must have guessed about right. She hauled herself half-way up, tried again, and finally made it all the way into the saddle. Then she leaned forward and patted Lady's neck.

Good girl. She might not be an experienced rider, but she wasn't easily deterred. And she was kind to the horse. He liked that. Actually, he had to admit he liked *her*. Not because she was Johnny Rydell's sister, but because…

Well, he wasn't exactly sure why. She was darned pretty, but she seemed unaware of it. There was more to Leah Rydell than just a pretty face and dark, lustrous-looking hair and a softly curved body that made his knees feel funny.

He'd have to give that some thought over the next four days.

Chapter Six

After three hours in the saddle, Leah suspected she wasn't the horsewoman she'd thought she was. After five hours, she was certain of it.

Cal had set a steady pace, but hour after hour passed and it never slackened. When they stopped to water the horses, she managed to slip off into the woods to take care of personal business, but each time she remounted she had to admit that pulling herself back into the saddle was like climbing a mountain.

She didn't dare complain, or even ask him to slow down. She wanted to press on as fast as possible and reach Johnny, but oh, how her backside ached! An hour ago, she had devoured one of Mrs. Swerdlow's bacon sandwiches and offered one to Cal. He refused to slow down, so they had eaten their lunch in the saddle.

The sun was merciless. She dampened her blue bandana and draped it around her neck, but it was dry within ten minutes, and under the plaid cotton shirt her camisole was sticky with perspiration. She had to laugh, remembering Belle's advice about washing out her undergarments every night. By evening she wouldn't have the strength to lift her arms, let alone launder her underdrawers.

To take her mind off her aching thighs and tight shoulders, she tried to focus on the countryside. Leafy sugar maples and box elders bordered the trail, and the sun hung like a big copper ball in a sky so blue and cloudless it looked as if it were painted.

Only when they rode through the few shady glades near mountain streams was there any relief from the relentless heat. These little oases, thick with a tangle of willows and lush green ferns, were life-restoring. Harebells grew along the stream banks. She gulped in the cooler air, mopped the sweat from her face, and resolved to hold on until they reached the next willow-shaded patch of greenery.

They rode on at the same relentless pace through meadow after meadow dotted with red and yellow wildflowers. She usually loved flowers. She never missed a chance to pick bouquets of scarlet daisies and Indian paintbrush for Mrs. Swerdlow's supper table, but for the past few hours she scarcely noticed anything other than the brown, dusty trail.

Gradually the trail wound through groves of Douglas fir and blue-tinged spruce, but the heat didn't abate. The next time Cal called a halt to water the horses, Leah was afraid to dismount for fear she wouldn't be able to drag herself back into the saddle. But when Cal sent her a questioning look and tipped his head toward a copse of maples, she slipped out of the saddle and tramped unsteadily into the trees. When she managed to remount, after three unsuccessful tries, every single muscle in her body was screaming.

Their route bordered a steep canyon, at the bottom of which she glimpsed dappled sunlight and patches of shade. As she was admiring the wild roses on the canyon edge, Cal dropped back to ride beside her.

"How are you holding up?" he asked.

Unwilling to trust her voice at the moment, she

didn't answer. He sent her a sharp look. "Leah?"

"Yes," she managed. "I am holding up." Just barely, but he needn't know that.

He chuckled. "Ride on ahead of me. I don't want you to fall too far behind."

She nodded and moved her mare to the front. Cal watched her closely. She was trying hard to keep her back straight, but it was plain as pancakes she was close to exhaustion. He hadn't heard a single word of complaint from her, and he admired her for that. He also knew she'd be plenty sore when she climbed off that mare, and tomorrow…He dreaded tomorrow.

Better start looking for a good place to camp.

After another hour, he knew Leah had had enough. "Hold up in that grove of trees up ahead," he called.

She lifted one hand to signal she'd heard, but when she reached the circle of pines, she sat there on her horse without moving a muscle. He drew abreast of her, glanced at her face, and quickly slipped out of the saddle. She was gray with fatigue.

"Leah, can you dismount?"

She didn't even twitch. "I don't think so."

He walked over, reached his hands around her waist, and lifted her out of her saddle. He set her down next to a fallen log. "Stay here," he ordered.

Instantly she sank down, steadying herself with one hand on the downed tree. As fast as he could, he shoved some stones into a circle, cobbled together a fire, and then walked off to the creek and wet his bandana. When he returned, he handed the sopping cloth to her. She just sat there, so he lifted it out of her hand and mopped it across her face. She closed her eyes, but when he finished, she didn't open them.

Quickly he untied her bedroll, spread it out, then bent to pick her up. When he got his arms underneath her legs, she jerked, but she didn't open her eyes. He lowered her onto the blanket and she sighed, tipped onto one side, and lay still.

"Leah, are you all right?"

"Don't know," she murmured. "Ask me in an hour."

He chuckled in spite of himself. She was half dead, but she still had a sense of humor.

He busied himself unpacking the saddlebags and wiping the horses down with wisps of dry grass, then rustled up a supper of tinned beans and made a pot of strong coffee. Last, he walked to where she lay and leaned over her sleeping form.

"Leah? Leah, wake up."

"Dowanna," she muttered.

"Try. You have to eat something."

Leah opened her eyes and smelled coffee. Her stomach grumbled, and she sat up. Something in a tin can was heating on a flat rock near the fire. Beans, she guessed. Cal knelt next to the coals, dribbling thick-looking coffee into a tin cup.

"Hungry?" he asked.

"Thirsty," she replied, reaching for the cup. She gulped down two big swallows, paused for breath, then downed two more.

"Hey, go easy. We're sharing this."

"Oh." She held the cup out to him. "Sorry."

He waved it away and stuck a fork into the can of beans.

"I guess we're sharing that, too," she said.

"Yep. Only one fork, so I hope you're not…shy."

"Shy! Of course I'm shy. I have never shared supper

with a man."

"Guess there's always a first time."

"In fact," she said after another swallow of his surprisingly drinkable coffee, "I have never spent a whole day in a man's company."

"Or," he said with a laugh, "a whole night."

She almost choked. "Oh. I hadn't thought of that."

He said nothing, for which she was grateful. As tired as she was, she wasn't up to discussing such a potentially unnerving situation. More than unnerving, the situation was positively compromising! On the other hand, this was precisely the pickle she found herself in, traveling alone with a man for days. And nights.

That thought niggled at her while she drained the rest of the coffee from the tin cup. *Why is he doing this, taking me to Idaho to see Johnny? Is it because Cal Zander is a good man, as Sally insists, and he wants to help me reach my brother?*

Some part of her only half-believed that. The other part of her...

How did Johnny know I was living in Maple Shade?

He lifted the tin cup out of her hand and refilled it, then gestured at the can of beans near the fire. "Hungry?"

"Yes," she said. "And curious."

His eyebrows rose. "Oh, yeah? Curious about what?"

"I want to know about my brother. Why I didn't hear anything from him all these years. Not one single word."

"Well, he...might have been...uh...someplace where he couldn't write a letter."

"Yes, I thought of that," she said quietly. "And then I wondered about you."

He jerked, almost bumping the tin of beans into the

fire.

"About you," she repeated. "I wondered if you knew Johnny. I mean before you came to Maple Shade."

He righted the can and repositioned the fork he'd stuck in it. But he remained silent.

"Did you know Johnny before? Don't you dare lie to me, Cal Zander. I do not deserve to be lied to."

Cal focused on relaxing his hand, concentrated on uncurling his fingers from the hard fist he'd closed them into. *Don't lie to me.* She was right. She deserved the truth. At least part of it.

Hell's half acre, he didn't think this situation would rear its ugly head so soon. He'd known very few women who could see a situation clearly and unravel a knot so fast. Maybe none. Definitely none. Leah Rydell wasn't just any woman. Leah Rydell was…Leah Rydell.

"You're right," he said finally. "I knew your brother before I came to Maple Shade."

"Where? Where did you know him?"

To buy time he stirred the can of beans. *How much should I tell her?*

Just enough.

"I knew Johnny in prison." He kept his voice low and steady. To his surprise and relief, she sat perfectly still, her eyes on his face.

"Go on," she said quietly.

"Your brother joined a gang when he was real young. Just a kid, really. They robbed stagecoaches, and they used Johnny as a lookout. At some point, one of their robberies went wrong, and the gang got away, all except for Johnny. He ended up in prison in Illinois."

She sat staring into the fire. "What about you? Did you rob stagecoaches, too?"

"Nope."

"Then why were you in prison with Johnny?"

Cal studied the flames dancing in the firepit. He'd never told anybody about his past before. But Leah wasn't just anybody. She was Johnny Rydell's sister, and she deserved the truth. At least as much of the truth as he could tell her right now.

"Look, Leah." He swallowed hard. "When I was sent to prison, I ended up sharing a cell with your brother. He talked a lot about you, about finding you when he got out. He heard you'd gone out West, and I knew he'd find out where."

"Why were *you* in prison, Cal?"

"I caught a man cheating in a card game. I ended up killing him."

That didn't seem to upset her as much as he'd feared it would. But her next question knocked the socks off him.

"So you and Johnny were friends in prison."

"Sort of, yeah."

"Is that why you wanted to find him? Because you were friends?"

He took a long, slow breath. "No. Johnny owes me some money."

"How much money?"

"Seven hundred dollars."

"Seven hun—!" She blanched. "In his entire life, Johnny never had as much as *seven* dollars. Where would he get seven hundred?"

"From me. He won it playing poker with me in prison. Problem was, Johnny was playing with a marked deck."

"And you weren't."

39

"No, I wasn't. I never cheat at cards. I don't have to."

"So," she said, her voice matter-of-fact, "you reasoned that if you found Johnny, you would find your seven hundred dollars." It wasn't a question, which told him she was smart enough to figure out the basics.

"Yeah."

"That's why you came to Maple Shade, isn't it? Because you thought eventually my brother would turn up there, and all you had to do was sit and wait. And pretend to be a preacher."

"Yeah. I'll tell you about being a preacher some other time."

She didn't trust him, but she did believe he was telling the truth. At least as far as it went.

"That's about it, Leah? Anything else you want to know?"

"No. But there is something I want to say to you. You are a snake, Cal Zander. You are dishonest and deceitful, and I wish I'd brought along that gun you picked out. But if I killed you, I would never find Johnny, so right now I don't have a choice. But hear this, *Mister* Zander: After I find my brother, I am going to push you off the nearest cliff!"

He stared at her. "Can't say I'd blame you, Miss Rydell. But right now, you're stuck with me, and whether you believe it or not, right now I'm on your side."

"Fiddlesticks! You're on the side of your seven hundred dollars."

She wobbled over to her bedroll, flopped down, and curled up in a tight ball.

"Leah, that tin of beans is hot now. You should eat

something."

She didn't answer.

"Leah. Miss Rydell. Listen, I'll make a bargain with you. I'll teach you how to fire my revolver, and when we reach your brother, you can shoot me."

"It's a deal," she snapped. She sat up and pointed to the beans. "And since there is only one fork for our supper, I get it first."

He couldn't help laughing at that. But he noticed Leah didn't even crack a smile.

Chapter Seven

Leah thought she knew what being tired felt like. She often felt tired working late at the mercantile reorganizing heavy bolts of calico and wool challis and scrubbing grimy fingerprints off the front windows. Now she was beginning to understand the difference between mere tiredness and bone-deep exhaustion. How could she have been so naïve?

No matter how desperately she wanted to crawl out of her bedroll this morning and stand up, she knew she could not. Everything hurt from her neck down to her ankles, and her derriere hurt most of all. When she moved even a few inches, pain screamed down her spine and bit into her thighs.

But this morning she *had* to get up. What on earth was she going to do?

She kept her eyes shut tight and tried to come up with a plan. And now, oh God, she could smell coffee! Her mouth watered. She could hear Cal moving around the campsite. Maybe he would bring her a cup of coffee if she asked him. But, she acknowledged, she hated Cal Zander so much she didn't want to send one civil word in his direction, even to ask for some coffee.

Still, she had to do *something!* She couldn't stay wrapped up in her bedroll all day. Besides, what was most pressing at the moment was the need to relieve herself. How embarrassing!

If she *could* manage to stand up, could she force her aching legs to carry her over behind a tree and drop her jeans? Worse, would she be able to pull them up again after she had done her business? She clenched her jaw against an overwhelming need to weep.

She heard the clank of a skillet, followed by a sizzling sound. Bacon! She suppressed a moan. After a moment, footsteps tramped toward her, and a hand touched her shoulder.

"Hungry?"

"No," she lied.

"Can you move your legs?"

"No," she said truthfully.

After a long silence she heard his low voice again. "I figure you're plenty stiff and sore, so I'm gonna help you out."

Oh, really? Exactly how are you going to do that?

The blanket lifted off her, and she felt his hands slip under her knees and her shoulders. Then he was carrying her...somewhere. He set her on her feet, and she smelled pine branches.

"You need help unbuttoning your jeans?"

She jerked. "Certainly not!"

"Suit yourself." She could hear him chuckling all the way back to the pan of sizzling bacon.

"Cursed man," she muttered under her breath. "Low-life. Liar." Well, no, he wasn't a liar. Exactly. But "liar" was close enough. She'd called him other names before she'd fallen asleep last night; there must have been twenty or more.

She unhooked the leather belt at her waist, fumbled with the buttons at the front of her jeans, and managed to shimmy them down over her hips. After a long moment, she even managed to pull them back up again, but she had to grit her teeth to do it.

She took a tentative step forward, then another, and moved slowly and very gingerly toward the enticing smell of frying bacon. Before she had covered ten steps, Cal approached, lifted her hand and wrapped her fingers around a tin cup of coffee.

"Don't drink it all," he instructed. "I haven't had any yet."

She swallowed three huge gulps, then remembered they were sharing this cup and fought the urge to dump the rest on the ground. He must have guessed what was in her mind because he suddenly lifted the cup out of her hand and walked her over to a fallen log he'd rolled in front of the fire.

"Sit," he ordered. He eased her down until her bottom met the wood. She managed not to cry out, but her eyes stung. The next thing she knew a tin plate of perfectly fried bacon appeared on her lap. And biscuits! How on earth had he managed to make biscuits?

"Eat slow, but leave some for me. Only got one fork, remember."

"I don't need a fork," she snapped. She popped a slice of bacon into her mouth and crunched it up. As she chewed, she surveyed the fire pit and noticed that small blobs of white dough were dotting a flat stone near the flames.

"Are those blobs biscuits? Is that how you—?"

"Yep. Old Indian trick. They use hot rocks to bake bread dough."

"How would you know that?"

He shrugged. "I grew up in Texas. Apache country."

"Is that really true?" she blurted in spite of herself.

"Swear to God."

"Preachers don't swear," she said.

He laughed and reached for the coffeepot. "This one does."

While she gobbled down her bacon and biscuits, he refilled the tin cup. "You still mad?"

She didn't answer, just sent him a steely look.

"Guess so," he breathed.

Sunlight began to filter through the pine branches, and Leah groaned. She was in for another scorching, sweaty day in the company of this man she hated. Well, she would stiffen her spine and endure what she had to endure until she reached her brother. And then she would point a revolver at Callahan Zander's black heart and pull the trigger.

Cal sent her an amused look. "Guess you're planning on how you're going to kill me."

Leah jerked, sloshing some coffee onto the ground. "How did you—? Why would you think that?"

"Because that's what I'd be doing if I was in your shoes."

She could think of nothing to say to that, so she finished the second biscuit, and he lifted the tin plate out of her hand. "Sure didn't leave me much," he observed.

"Exactly," she said icily. "There's more than one way to skin a polecat."

Cal laughed and forked three more slices of bacon out of the skillet, added three freshly baked biscuits off the hot rock, and grinned at her. There were a lot of ways to entertain oneself on the trail. Sparring with Leah Rydell was the best yet.

He gobbled his breakfast, slurped down the last of the coffee, and set about breaking camp, washing the tin plate and the cup in the creek, packing up the saddlebags, and tying both bedrolls behind the saddles. He noticed Leah hadn't moved from the log. Probably so stiff and sore she couldn't stand up.

When he'd fed the horses a handful of oats and kicked dirt over the fire pit, he walked over and offered her a hand. She just looked at him. *Okay, that's how you want it, is it?* He bent, snaked an arm around her waist, and lifted her to her feet.

She gave an unladylike screech, but he walked her over to the mare and lifted her into the saddle. Then he fished her black hat out of her saddlebag and handed it up to her. She glowered at him and jammed it on her head.

"Give me your canteen and your neckerchief," he said. He made another trip to the creek, and when he returned, she snatched both items out of his hand and kicked the roan into motion.

Cal watched her and smiled. It was pretty clear Leah was still plenty mad at him.

For the first two hours on the trail, he rode behind her, and when her pace faltered, he took the lead. As he moved past her, he noticed her mouth was pressed into a tight, angry line. But to her credit, he hadn't heard one word of complaint, not even when she limped off behind a bush to pee. And she even managed to pull herself back up into the saddle without his help. And she did it without groaning. Or grumbling.

He was learning things about Leah Rydell, and one of them was that she wasn't a complainer. She'd be good company if she wasn't so mad at him. Oh, hell, she was good company anyway. Actually, Leah was the only woman he'd ever known who didn't need to utter a single word to be good company.

As if the scorching heat wasn't bad enough, Leah discovered that swarms of mosquitos hovered near the streams, and whenever she knelt to fill her canteen, they attacked without mercy. After her second encounter with the whining little pests, Cal motioned for her to stand up. He walked back to her horse, snaked the bandana off her neck, and tied it over her mouth and nose. Then he reached up and snugged her hat down tight over her ears.

"Lots of mosquitos in Texas," he quipped.

An unexpected laugh burst out of her mouth. "Apache ones, no doubt," she said. She watched him tie his red bandana over his face, and when he turned to nod at her, she noticed his eyes. They were an odd shade of mossy gray-green, and they were definitely not smiling.

Suddenly she was short of breath. For the next few hours, she kept her head down, reminding herself that a liar and a cheat could have intriguing eyes and still deserve to be shot.

By midday, the broiling sun was straight up over their heads, and Leah forgot all about mosquitos. Her stomach growled, and she fervently wished she had one of Mrs. Swerdlow's sandwiches in her shirt pocket. She clenched her teeth and tried not to think about bacon or biscuits or anything remotely edible.

When she thought she couldn't ride another mile without something in her belly, Cal swung back toward her and veered off into the woods. When he emerged, he spurred his black horse right up to hers, grabbed her hand, and dumped a fistful of blackberries into her palm. Then he leaned forward and slipped a biscuit and a strip of cold bacon into her shirt pocket.

"No one can ride all day without food," he said.

"Not even you."

"Or you?" she shot back.

He patted his own shirt pocket. "Or me. I'm only human. Like you," he added.

She turned away with a sniff. Tomorrow morning, she would be sure to save an extra biscuit and a slice of bacon for her lunch. In fact…She smiled. Tomorrow morning, she would surprise Mister Know-It-All and make breakfast herself! Any idiot could fry bacon. She could hardly wait to see his face.

She had to remove the bandana over her mouth in order to eat, and when she did, she found the mosquitos had disappeared. How strange! An hour ago, they were as thick as netting around her face, and now…

A shadow fell over the trail, and when she looked up, huge roiling black clouds were obscuring the sun. The sky turned an eerie shade of green, and the wind began to pick up. As the first drops of rain splotted against her skin, Cal turned his horse and started back toward her.

"Thunderstorm coming," he shouted. "Gotta take cover!"

Chapter Eight

Rain spit out of a black sky, and Cal's heart skipped. "Leah," he shouted. She half-turned in the saddle and called out something, but an angry roll of thunder swallowed her words. He gestured for her to stay put, then realized her horse had stopped under a tree.

"Get out in the open," he yelled.

"Why?"

He motioned for her to move. "Lightning! Don't stay under a tree!"

She stepped her mare into the clearing, and he spurred his black forward. By the time he reached her, the heavens had opened. Sheets of rain slanted toward them, blown sideways by the wind. Already her hat was sodden, and her shirt was plastered to her chest so tight he could see the outline of the camisole she wore underneath. He dug his rain poncho out from his saddlebag, settled it over her head, and spread it around her shoulders.

"Keep your head down," he shouted. "Ride for those rocks ahead."

She wheeled her mare away from him and did exactly as instructed. Before she reached the tumbled mass of boulders lodged against the hillside, lightning bolts were dancing in her path.

He jammed his heels in the black's side, raced

forward, and dragged her off her horse. She sent him a furious look, but when a clap of thunder crashed overhead her face went white. He dropped her close to an overhanging hunk of granite half the size of a barn, slid off his mount, and pushed her down onto the ground. Then he dropped beside her, shoved her under the overhang, and wrapped both arms around her.

"Keep your head down, Leah. Stay as close to this rock as you can."

She pulled away slightly, wriggled to slip the rain poncho out from under her bottom and spread half of it over him. At her gesture Cal felt closer to crying than he'd felt since he was seven years old.

Rain slashed at his face. He shut his eyes, and through his closed lids he could see flashes of lightning. Deafening, unrelenting thunder crashed around them. Leah's trembling form pressed tight against him, and under the poncho they shared she was sopping wet and cold.

The storm was now directly overhead, and he pulled the poncho tighter over their bodies. "Leah, don't move around. Lie still. Lightning is striking all around us."

He felt her head dip in a nod. She might have said something, but he couldn't hear her voice over the noise of the pounding rain.

He didn't know how long they lay there while the storm raged overhead. It seemed like hours. And then, almost as suddenly as it had started, the rain stopped. He waited until he was sure the storm had leveled off, and jostled her. "I think it's over," he said. "Come on."

They crawled out from under the rock and got to their feet, both of them shivering with cold. They found their horses standing under a thick Douglas fir, mounted quickly, and then headed down the mountain to where the trail widened.

Cal dismounted, scrounged up an armload of dry twigs, and built a fire. When it was burning steadily, he removed his shirt and started to unbutton his jeans.

Leah watched him for a moment. "W-what are you doing?"

"Drying out my clothes."

"Oh."

"Go pull a blanket from your bedroll, Leah. You can wrap it around you when you take off your—"

"Clothes," she finished.

He tried not to look at her. "Yeah. Ought to dry them out before we move on."

She said nothing, just began to undo the buttons on her shirt. Cal turned away to gather more branches, which he poked into the ground next to the fire. He draped his shirt and jeans over them, and he didn't look up until Leah handed him her own wet garments.

"Won't take long," he said. "The sun will speed things up."

When she didn't respond he glanced up to find her perched under a spruce tree with a blanket draped around her shoulders. He scrabbled in his saddlebag for the bottle of whiskey he carried, uncorked it, and took a long pull.

"Leah, I know you don't touch liquor, but a sip or two would warm you up."

"I am warm enough," she assured him. "And look, the sun is coming out."

Sure enough, the area was flooding with warm sunshine. In a funny way he felt disappointed. He draped her shirt and jeans near the fire, took another swig of Old

Henry, and settled himself next to her.

"You realize," she said calmly, "that you are wearing nothing but your drawers, do you not?"

Under the circumstances that was the last thing he expected Leah Rydell to say. "Yeah."

"You realize that I have never before seen a man wearing only his drawers, don't you?"

That was even more unexpected.

"Well, yeah. And I've never seen a woman wearing nothing but a wool blanket before."

But the most surprising thing of all was when Leah looked straight at him and laughed.

When their clothes were dry, Cal kicked dirt over the fire, pulled on his jeans and his boots, and waited while Leah retreated to the other side of a sugar maple to dress.

For the rest of the daylight hours after that terrifying thunderstorm, Leah gave thanks to God that she hadn't been struck by lightning. And, she grudgingly admitted, she was grateful she was riding to Idaho to see her brother with a man who knew exactly what to do to keep her safe.

Even if Cal Zander *was* a snake and a liar, he was knowledgeable and capable and a reliable traveling companion. He had kept her from getting struck by lightning or washed away by sheets of rain during the worst storm she had ever experienced.

And she acknowledged, biting her lip, Cal acted like a gentleman even when she sat naked under a blanket while her clothes were drying by the fire. While he was sitting beside her wearing nothing but his drawers, Cal Zander hadn't looked at her twice.

At least she didn't think he had. Now, as shadows

lengthened across the trail, he was scanning ahead for a place to camp, and she felt grateful for his presence. She had never liked the dark. She particularly disliked it when she was not inside a cozy boardinghouse with a front door that locked.

At last, he reined up in a grove of aspens. Leah breathed a sigh of relief, slipped off her roan mare, and began working the kinks out of her muscles. Before she dropped her saddlebag and bedroll in the area, Cal was scraping out a firepit and encircling it with stones. While he fed the horses and rubbed them down, she splashed water from the trickling stream over her face and neck, smoothed back her hair, and refilled both their canteens.

When Cal tossed his bedroll down next to hers, Leah sucked in her breath. Last night, they had slept on opposite sides of the fire. The truth was she'd been so exhausted she scarcely noticed where he'd slept, but tonight she was *not* exhausted, and tonight she *did* notice. Surely he didn't intend to sleep right next to her. Or did he?

Of course he didn't. After two days of riding, she must smell like a sweaty hound dog.

Cal busied himself opening tins of corn and tomatoes, dumped them into the skillet and stirred the mess around with the fork. Meanwhile, Leah rolled a small log over near the fire and carefully lowered her tender backside onto the end closest to the flames.

"You like succotash?" he asked.

"Y-yes." She hadn't eaten succotash since coming out to Oregon on the wagon train, and then she'd been so hungry she didn't care what she ate. His question made her realize how civilized her existence had been over these past eight years. Mrs. Swerdlow would certainly sniff at a plain supper of canned corn and tomatoes. Belle Fontaine would refuse to even pick up her fork. Sally and Martha were more practical; as long as they didn't have to cook it, it made no difference to either one of them what they ate.

Cal's voice brought her thoughts back to their campsite. "Think you could manage to feed the horses?"

"Of course. Uh…"

"You'll find a sack of oats in my saddlebag. One double handful each, okay?"

She had just found the oats when she heard his voice again. "Bring that bottle of whiskey, too."

"Sure you wouldn't rather have some oats?" she called. "No doubt the horses would enjoy the whiskey."

He clunked the fork into the skillet of succotash and straightened to face her. "You're pretty feisty after a long day in the saddle. You been nipping at my hooch?"

"What?"

"Have you been drinking my whiskey?" he clarified.

"Certainly not. I told you, I—"

"Yeah, I remember. I thought after today you might be ready to fall off the wagon."

"One of us has to stay sober," she said in her best proper-young-woman voice.

"Why?"

She blinked. "Well, because…" She turned away, untied the sack of oats, dug out a double handful, and cupped her hands under Lady's nose. "Because I am a well-brought-up woman, and you are a preacher. That's why." She fed the other horse and hoped Cal would drop the subject.

He didn't. "No one ever said a preacher couldn't take a drink," he said. "So could a well-brought-up young woman."

"Well," she huffed. "I don't live my life according to what anyone *else* thinks is acceptable behavior."

He snorted. "You sound pretty sanctimonious," he said with a laugh.

"Well, I'm not."

"Sure you are, Leah. You're so proper you squeak."

She marched over to his horse and stuffed the sack of oats back in his saddlebag. "I. Do. Not. Squeak." She articulated each word with extra care.

He said nothing, turned back to the bubbling skillet, and ran the fork around and around in the mess. She resumed her perch on the log, and then his voice jarred her again.

"Where's my whiskey?"

"Oh, for heaven's sake, Cal. Get it yourself!"

"Okay," he said, his tone matter of fact. "You come on over here and stir our supper."

Instead, she stomped back over to his horse, rummaged around in the saddlebag until she found the whiskey, and stomped back to the fire pit. "Here!" She thrust the bottle at him.

Then she noticed he was trying not to smile, and that made her madder. He took one look at her, uncorked the whiskey, and held it out to her. "Go on, Leah, take a sip. Might make you a little less proper and a lot more human."

Purposely she stepped down hard on the toe of his boot, snatched the bottle out of his hand, and poured the contents onto the fire. Instantly the flames exploded.

Cal yelped and jumped back. "What in blazes did you do that for?" he shouted.

"I did it to teach you a lesson."

He thrust his face close to hers. "Oh, you did, did you? Anyone ever tell you that you're a real menace, Leah Rydell? A *sanctimonious* menace?"

Her expression changed. "Y-yes. My b-brother." Tears welled up in her eyes. They looked like dark sapphires under water, he thought irrationally.

"Ah, Leah, I'm sorry I said that. You're not really sanctimonious, you're—"

"Over-proper? Bossy? T-that's what Johnny used to say."

He hesitated. He'd hurt her. Hell's bells, he didn't know what to do now, so he just kept staring at those big dark blue eyes of hers. "Come on, kid," he said after a minute. "Let's eat supper."

She stiffened. "Don't call me *kid.*"

He kept staring at her. If he was honest about it, he couldn't help looking at her. Man, she could get under his skin in sixty seconds flat. He itched to paste her a good one, but he'd never hit a woman and he wasn't about to start now. A preacher was supposed to turn the other cheek. And besides…well, he didn't want to hurt her.

He yanked the skillet off the flames, gave the contents a final stir, and dumped it into the tin plate they were sharing. In silence he motioned for her to sit down, stuck the fork in the middle of their supper, and handed the plate to her.

She scooped up a bite. "It tastes scorched," she said.

Cal bit back a groan. "And whose fault is that?"

She said nothing, just chewed and swallowed and forked another bite past her lips. Then, while he watched, a big fat tear rolled down one cheek. Jehosephat, he couldn't stand to see a woman cry. He looked away and tried to think of something else.

But then she opened her mouth and blew his equilibrium to kingdom come.

"It would taste better," she said, "if we had some whiskey."

He goggled at her. He hadn't forgotten that she'd poured his bottle of whiskey into the fire, but he began to laugh.

"Give me that!" He lifted the tin plate out of her hand and plopped down beside her. "First town we come to, Leah, you're gonna buy us some more whiskey."

Chapter Nine

Leah didn't say another word until all the succotash on the tin plate they were sharing was gone. While Cal brewed coffee, she picked up the plate and walked off to wash it in the creek. When she returned she didn't wait for the coffee to boil but unrolled her blanket and shucked her boots. She laid her hat beside her and rolled herself up in her blanket like a sausage.

Cal sat by the fire until the coffee boiled, dumped in a cup of cold water to settle the grounds, and poured the tin mug full. Then he walked over and set it down beside the blanket-covered lump on the ground, banked the fire, and unrolled his own bedroll.

She must have smelled the coffee because after a moment a small hand reached out and hooked a thumb and forefinger through the handle of the tin mug.

"Cal?" came a small voice.

"Yeah?"

"Tell me something."

"Okay, if I can."

There was a long, long pause, and then he heard a muffled voice.

"How on earth did you become a preacher?"

Leah heard his indrawn breath, a long sigh, and another deep breath. She pushed the tin cup of coffee toward him and waited.

"Well, uh…" She heard him swallow once, but it

took two more swallows before he continued.

"I grew up in a real small town in Texas, down near the border. Cactus Flat. Went to school and everything, but when my folks were killed in an Indian raid I kinda went off the rails. That's when I learned to play poker. Good poker."

He paused to sip some coffee. "I started to make money at it. Lots of money. So naturally every saloon between Cactus Flat and the rest of Texas offered me a table and a deck of cards. That lasted until…"

He stopped to drink again. Leah thought about getting up and refilling the cup, but she didn't want to interrupt him.

"You can probably guess what happened next. One night I caught this greenhorn cheating. He pulled a revolver on me, shot me in the shoulder. So I wrestled the gun away from him, but it went off, and…to make a long story short, he ended up dead and I ended up in prison. You can figure out the rest."

She could guess the rest, but it didn't go far enough. She waited, scarcely breathing.

"In prison I met Johnny, like I said before. He was reading the Bible, so I started reading it, too. Guess it kinda got to me, because by the time I was released I'd seen some kind of light, and I felt like telling folks about some of the things I'd learned. So I started telling them."

"Just like that?" she queried.

"Yeah. I saw some things in prison that showed me the way I *didn't* want to go. So I made a sharp turn in my life and rode in another direction. Figured I understood some things I never understood before."

"What things?"

"Things about…families. Loyalty. About…" He

stopped and swallowed. "About how people should, well, love each other. Or if they can't do that, at least be kind to each other. And…some other things."

"The things you talk about in church," Leah said quietly.

"Yeah. It might sound kinda simple-minded, but that's why I became a preacher."

Leah lay for a long time without speaking because she didn't know what to say. The truth was she wasn't sure she believed him, but that morning when she'd listened to Cal preach at church she had to admit his words somehow bored into her brain. What he said had moved her. *I guess that's what preaching is all about. Moving people's hearts and minds.*

But a man who gambled for a living? Who spent his evenings playing poker at the Shady Lady Saloon? A man who had staked her out and waited like a spider for her brother to come to town?

No. No. *No.* Not in a million years would she trust such a man, no matter whether he called himself a preacher or what pretty, trumped-up story he told her.

But the very next day Leah had to eat every single one of those words.

Chapter Ten

Before the sun rose the next morning, Cal cracked one eyelid open to see Leah sitting on her blanket, finger-combing her dark hair. He watched her, afraid to move for fear he'd startle her, and he didn't want her to stop what she was doing. It made him feel unsettled somehow. Finally, she gathered up the shiny dark tresses, twisted them into a single thick braid, and tied the end with a blue ribbon.

A song sparrow started up in a nearby aspen tree, and he closed his eyes and let his thoughts drift. When he heard the clank of the iron skillet, he shot to a sitting position. "What the—?"

Leah was paring off thick slices of bacon with a puny-looking ladyfied pocketknife and laying them in the pan. While he watched, she poked at the fire with a stick, stirred up the coals, and added two small logs. Then she set the skillet over the flames and dug the tin plate out of his saddlebag, mixed up two handfuls of flour with a dribble of water, and squashed the mess into little sticky balls. She set them on the flat rock nearest the fire. Looked like she was making biscuits! He smiled in spite of himself.

When he could smell the frying bacon he rolled out of his blanket and quietly walked off into the woods. On his way back to camp he fed the horses, gathered up both bedrolls, and tied them behind their saddles. The smell of bacon drew him back to the firepit where Leah was crouched. She looked up and grinned.

"I'm making breakfast!" she announced.

She looked so pleased with herself it made him chuckle. "Yeah, I see that." She forked over a slice of bacon and gestured at the blobs of dough on the rock.

"Biscuits," she announced. The pride in her voice made him hide another smile. So far, the blobs of dough on the rock just looked like blobs of dough.

He dropped onto the log near the fire and waited. After some minutes, the bacon got crisp and the biscuits turned brown. Leah scooted down to the creek to scrub the biscuit mixture off the tin plate, and when she returned she laid four strips of bacon in it and reached to lift a browned biscuit off the stone.

Nothing doing. The biscuit was stuck to the rock. Finally, she pulled the pocketknife out of her jeans and cut the biscuits free.

"I don't understand," she moaned. "*Your* biscuits didn't stick! Why did mine stick and yours didn't?"

"Did you smear some bacon grease over your baking stone?"

Her mouth dropped open. "Oh. Should I have done that?"

"Yeah."

Her face fell.

"Why don't you cut the rest of them off the rock," he ventured. "They should still taste like biscuits."

She handed him the tin plate and turned toward the fire.

The biscuits looked kind of flat, but the bacon tasted okay. He crunched up two slices and bit into a biscuit. It was as hard as the rock it had sat on.

Leah was watching his face. When she saw his expression, she frowned, then took a bite of one herself. "Oh, dear, these are awful!"

"You use flour?"

She nodded.

"And saleratus?"

"Oh." Her eyes widened into two blue pools. "Saleratus? Should I have used saleratus?"

He couldn't help laughing. "And a bit of bacon grease," he added. He ate most of the bacon and choked down three of her biscuits. She didn't touch any of them, so he crumbled up the rest and sprinkled them on the ground for the birds. He was still chuckling when he wiped out the skillet and scrubbed off the tin plate.

In total silence Leah mounted and moved off down the trail. He felt halfway sorry for her, but she sure was fun to watch.

****

As they rode farther north, the landscape began to change. The occasional copse of sugar maples and Douglas fir trees now became dense stands of pines punctuated by wide green meadows and fields of bright yellow mustard rippling in the breeze.

But Cal got a shock when they reached the stream that cut through the valley ahead of them. Yesterday's thunderstorm had turned what had been a tame, gently trickling stream into a raging brown river. Whole tree branches swirled past, tossed by the current into a raging, debris-filled torrent.

Leah sat her horse beside him, a frown creasing her forehead. "Could we go around?"

"No," he said shortly. "That would take us thirty miles out of our way. The water might recede in the next twenty-four hours, but waiting will cost us a day. I don't think you want to delay an extra day to see your brother."

"No," she agreed. "Johnny could be dying. I want to reach him as soon as possible."

"Then it looks like we'll have to cross here."

Leah shuddered. The swift-flowing water looked dangerous, and she had never learned to swim. Could the swollen stream carry a horse and rider downstream? Worse, could it sweep a rider off into the water? She bit the inside of her cheek.

Cal reached over and grabbed her bridle. "Dismount," he ordered.

"What?"

"Get off your horse, Leah. We're gonna ride double."

"But my horse…?"

"I'll come back for it. Come on, hurry up."

She swung off the mare, and he leaned down to extend his hand. "Put your foot in my stirrup."

She tried, but after her third attempt he dismounted, lifted her into his saddle, and swung up behind her. "Hold on to the saddle horn," he instructed.

He walked the black down the muddy bank and waded into the swirling water. Leah clung to the pommel with both hands so tight her knuckled turned white. As far as he could tell she'd stopped breathing. He tightened his arm around her waist and concentrated on keeping the horse moving slowly and steadily forward.

The roiling brown water reached his boots, and all at once he felt the horse struggle for solid footing. The animal jolted, and Leah gasped and cried out.

"Sit still," he yelled.

Her head dipped in a nod, and her fingers tightened

on the saddle horn. "Don't let go," he instructed.

The horse lurched sideways, and Cal struggled to keep it moving forward. Muddy water splashed over his knees. He kicked away a floating log.

Icy cold water swirled over Leah's ankles and surged up to her knees. *If I survive this, I will never, never say another critical word to Callahan Zander. Were it not for him, I wouldn't have a prayer of hope slogging through this swirling river. Or seeing my brother again!*

When they reached the opposite bank, she slid down off Cal's horse and watched him plunge back into that brown, muddy water to lead her roan mare safely across. Cal Zander might be a great many things, but he was certainly not a coward. In fact, at times he could be…well, almost heroic.

Minutes later, both animals struggled up the creek bank, and he laid her horse's reins in her hand.

"Oh, Cal, thank you," she murmured, her voice unsteady.

"That cowboy from Idaho told me there's a town somewhere up ahead. Maybe we'll dry out by the time we reach it."

Leah was so cold she couldn't answer. Instead, she pulled herself into the saddle and kicked her roan into motion.

****

The town lay in a wide valley dotted with wheat fields and acres of corn and green beans. "Green Valley," the sign said. "Home of the Thimbleberry."

"Thimbleberry!" Leah scoffed. "What on earth is a thimbleberry?"

"It's kind of like a salmonberry," Cal explained.

She laughed. "Well, then, what is a salmonberry?"

He didn't answer, just pointed ahead to the town, which consisted of a few unpainted wooden buildings and empty boardwalks bordering the dusty road. They moved past a barbershop, the sheriff's office, a newspaper office, two saloons, and a mercantile. Bushel baskets of ripe cherries sat in front of the mercantile. Cal took one look, licked his lips, and reined up.

"Leah, I'll be back in a minute. I want some cherries."

"And some whiskey," she reminded.

He dismounted and disappeared inside the mercantile. While she waited, three unkempt-looking men stumbled out of the saloon next to the mercantile. One lurched toward her.

"H'lo there, pretty lady. Wha's yer name?"

She stiffened and said nothing.

Two younger men stepped up on the other side of her mare. "Gonna say somethin', honey?" one said, slurring his words. The other laid his hand on her bridle.

She tightened her grip on the reins and looked across the road to the sheriff's office where a bearded man sat on the boardwalk, his chair tipped back and his feet propped on the hitching rail. Asleep.

One of the men reached for the reins clutched in her hand. "Ya got a name, honey?"

Fear choked off her breath. She tried to knee the mare away from him, but the one with the bridle gripped in his grimy hand gave it a sharp tug. "Don' back away from me, honey. Why don'tcha get down an' be fren'ly?"

He was reaching one hand up to grab her reins when a low, hard voice stopped him. "Take your hands off the

66

lady's horse, cowboy."

The man leaned drunkenly against her mare's flank. "Yeah? Whyn't you try an' make me."

Cal settled a hand on the man's shoulder, spun him away from Leah's horse, and slammed a fist into his belly. He reeled away, holding his midriff.

"Hey!" The blond kid and the older, unshaven one both charged him. Cal met one with an elbow across the neck; the other launched himself at him, but Cal simply stepped aside and booted him in the rear end as he hurtled past.

The three men slunk off down an alley. Cal handed Leah a paper sack bulging with ripe, red cherries, hauled himself into the saddle, and leaned over to slap her mare's rump. The animal jolted forward.

Clutching the bag of cherries, Leah dug her heels in its side and heard Cal's horse right behind her. She didn't stop until they were well out of town, and then she reined up and sat motionless, unable to stop trembling. Cal dismounted beside her. He said nothing; just reached up, lifted her out of the saddle, and wrapped his arms around her.

"Good girl," he said into her hair. "You held onto the cherries."

Chapter Eleven

When Leah stopped shaking, she began to cry, and that's when Cal came undone. She could have been hurt, even manhandled. She was trying hard to calm down, choking back tears and squaring her shoulders, trying to be brave. The sounds she was making had him gritting his teeth.

Part of him wanted to ride back to Green Valley and shoot all three of those ruffians. Another part of him was more sensible. *Yeah, you shoot them, and then what? More years in prison? I'd probably be hung for murder.*

He gave himself a hard mental shake. Leah's warm tears were wetting his shirt front, and something inside him turned over. All at once *he* was the one shaking.

Leah stepped back out of his arms and looked up at him. "You know what I want to do?"

He shook his head. He knew what *he* wanted to do. He wanted to kiss her. *That makes no sense, Zander. Leah Rydell means nothing to you.*

But when he met her teary-eyed gaze, his insides jolted. *Or does she?*

Heck, no, she doesn't. She was Johnny Rydell's sister, and he was taking her to Idaho to see him and collect the $700 her brother owed him. Leah didn't mean a thing to him. She was the bait to catch up with Johnny.

At that moment, she sent him a shaky smile and held

the bag of ripe cherries out to him. His heart gave another lurch and somersaulted into his belly.

What was wrong with him? For a long minute, he stared at the sprinkling of freckles across Leah's nose and those purple-blue eyes with the glimmer of light in their depths, and gradually the cobwebs in his mind floated away.

Well, you damn fool, you're falling in love with Johnny's sister!

Numb, his mind reeling, he snagged a ripe cherry out of the sack and slipped it into his mouth.

"They taste wonderful, don't they?" she said with an odd, almost shy smile. "So sweet and...wonderful."

"Yeah," he breathed. "Wonderful."

"I don't think I've ever tasted anything so sweet."

"Yeah," he said again. "Real sweet. Real wonderful, too."

He couldn't stop staring at her.

She held the sack of cherries out to him again, but he just looked at it, then shifted his gaze to her tear-streaked face. After a long moment she looked up at him.

"Cal," she said, her voice quiet, "why are you staring at me like that?"

His heart flip-flopped. "To be honest, Leah, I'm not real sure."

"Do you want to know what else I want to do beside eat cherries?" she said slowly.

"Uh...sure. What else do you want to do?"

"I want you to teach me how to shoot that revolver you think I don't know you hid in my saddlebag."

"Why?" He swallowed hard. "Why?" he repeated.

"Because. If something should happen to you, I need to be able to protect myself." She sent him a long look.

"And, of course, if *you* were threatened by someone, I would want to protect you."

"Leah…"

She turned shiny eyes up to him. "Yes, Cal?"

He drew in a long breath, then said the first thing that swam into his mind. "Leah, you are one helluva woman. I've never known anyone remotely like you."

She sent him a wobbly smile. "And I have certainly never known a man who was tamed by a sack of ripe cherries." She popped another one into her mouth, chewed it up, and spit the pit into her palm. Then she again offered the bag of cherries to him.

One helluva woman.

****

After breakfast the following morning, Leah scrabbled in her saddlebag until she found the revolver Cal had hidden at the bottom. "I'm ready to learn how to shoot this thing," she announced.

He glanced at her across the saddle he was settling on her mare's back. "Now?"

"Of course I mean *now*. There can't be very much to it," she reasoned.

He snorted. "It's real easy to load bullets into a gun and pull the trigger. But if you want to *hit* anything, there's a bit more involved."

"How much time would it take to teach me?"

He tightened the cinch on the roan, straightened up, and gave her a long look. "A week. Maybe less if you did some target practicing every day."

"A week! But I need to know *now*. Today!"

"Today," he muttered. "What's the big rush?"

"Oh for heaven's sake, Cal, I should think that would be obvious after yesterday. I might need to protect myself."

"Listen, Leah," he said tiredly. "There's nothing more dangerous than a greenhorn with a gun in his hand. Or *her* hand."

"Well, then," she said in a matter-of-fact tone, "the solution is obvious. Teach me how *not* to be a greenhorn."

Cal folded his arms on top of her saddle and leaned across it. "Listen, Miss Gotta-Do-It-Now. Learning how not to be a greenhorn with a gun takes years. Besides, you've got me to protect you, and nothing's gonna to happen to me."

"How can you possibly know that? Even a greenhorn knows that life is unpredictable. Something could happen to you before we travel one more mile, and then where would I be?"

"Another mile down the trail to Idaho," he said dryly. "Closer to the Circle K Ranch and your brother. So come on, Leah, let's get on our way."

"Oh, no," she said, narrowing her eyes. "I am not going one single step unless I know how to fire this gun!" She waved the revolver around in a big loopy circle, and Cal ducked behind his horse. Then he crept stealthily around the animal's rear quarters, made a grab for the weapon, and knocked it out of her hand. Instantly he stepped on the barrel so she couldn't pick it up.

"Don't ever do that again!" he yelled, snatching up the gun. "Dammit, Leah, you're enough to drive a man to drink!"

Her eyes got real hot-looking. "Just exactly what did I do that's so terrible?"

He studied her scarlet-flushed cheeks and expelled a long sigh. "You're stubborn. You're pig-headed.

You're headstrong. And, God help us, you're always convinced you're right."

"Oh." Her cheeks flushed an even deeper crimson. The color reminded him of ripe raspberries, and he closed his eyes. *You're also a tough, brave lady who doesn't complain, and you're the most entertaining traveling companion I've ever had.*

He studied her a moment longer. God help him, right now she's so beautiful his jeans were starting feel too tight.

"Cal?"

He snapped to attention. "What."

"A shooting lesson would only take about an hour, wouldn't it?"

"Maybe."

She stepped out from behind her mare. "Then let's not waste any more time. I'm ready."

He groaned and fished a box of cartridges from his saddlebag. "Okay," he growled. "You get one hour."

She sent him a smile so dazzling he felt weak in the knees and danced up to him, brandishing the revolver. He grabbed it out of her hand.

"Lesson one," he yelled. "Always assume a gun is loaded. Waving a weapon around like that could get you killed."

Instantly she thrust her hands behind her back.

"Follow me," he ordered. He strode away from the horses to a clearing, and Leah followed, docile as a kitten. Close at his heels, he could hear her humming under her breath. Kinda funny that learning how to fire a revolver would make her so happy. But then, Leah wasn't like any other woman he'd ever known.

He stopped dead in his tracks. "What's the matter?"

she said at his back.

"Nothing." His throat felt thick. *Liar. Everything is the matter.*

"Oh, good," she said.

He moved farther into the clearing, found a silver dollar in his pocket, and propped it up on a fallen log. Then he walked off twenty paces, slipped five cartridges into the chamber of the revolver, and handed it to Leah.

"Now, I want you to put a hole right through the center of that silver dollar." Instantly she raised the gun and pulled the trigger.

"It won't fire," she complained.

"That's because you haven't cocked it. You have to pull the hammer back before you pull the trigger."

She did as he instructed and quickly raised the revolver again.

He caught her arm. "Leah, wait. Bring the gun up slowly, and sight along the barrel. *Slowly.*"

"It's heavy, Cal. My hand starts to shake."

"Use both hands, then." He moved behind her and positioned her hands on the butt of the revolver. Big mistake. He was way too close to her, so close he could smell her hair and feel the warmth of her body.

He stepped away. "Now, bring the gun up slowly and sight carefully. If your hand starts shaking, lower the gun and start over."

She did exactly as he instructed, and stood quietly, sighting down the barrel without moving. "Now what?"

"Keep your finger on the trigger. Now, take a breath, and let it out part-way. Then—"

The crack of the gun caught him off-guard. *Jumping Jenny!*

"I didn't hit the target," she said.

"Not so fast, Leah! Try it again, slowly. And this time just slowly squeeze the trigger until it—"

Again, the gun went off. Then she fired off two more shots in quick succession. One of them kicked up the dust near the log where the intact silver dollar rested, but all of them went wide. Without waiting, she fired off another shot. This time the bullet clipped the edge of the silver dollar and spun it off the log.

"I did it!" she crowed.

"Yeah," he said flatly. "That'll do until you meet up with an outlaw or two. That will be the real test."

"Oh? What would a 'real test' involve?"

He studied her animated face. "The real test isn't marksmanship, Leah. The real test comes when you're facing someone who's a threat and you have to make a decision about whether to shoot him. Maybe kill him. It sounds easy, but it's not. It isn't a matter of hitting a target. It's deciding whether you *should* hit that target. Do you understand?"

"Y-yes." She sounded much less cocky, thank God.

"Good." He emptied the chamber and handed the revolver back to her.

She practiced sighting down the barrel until he reached over and lifted the weapon out of her hand and shoved it as deep as he could in her saddlebag. "Don't load it unless you're facing a threat."

"I understand, Cal. Really I do."

He only half-believed her. He knew she was desperate to reach her brother. He'd bet she wasn't going to let anything short of an angry bear or a forest fire stand in her way. Leah Rydell would shoot first and ask questions later. A man had to admire that kind of determination. Not only that, even after an absence of almost ten years, he guessed she had some strong feelings for her brother. That trumped everything.

He envied Johnny Rydell. His sister Leah loved him, and nothing, absolutely nothing, was going to keep her from reaching him.

Johnny Rydell was a lucky man.

****

That night Cal found a pretty grove of aspens and vine maples for their campsite. After hours in the saddle, Leah was bone-tired and out of sorts. She was also apprehensive. Sometime tomorrow they would reach the Circle K ranch and the line shack where Johnny was hiding, but an awful thought kept slicing through her brain. *Was he still alive?*

Her throat closed. She watched Cal dismount, toss down the saddlebags and bedrolls, and turn toward her with a puzzled look.

"What's wrong? How come you're not getting off your horse?"

"I'm just…thinking."

"About Johnny?"

"Well, yes. It's been a while. He probably won't even know me."

"He'll know you. He talked about you all the time in prison."

"But I-I look so different. The last time he saw me I was only fifteen years old. I was young and pretty then, and my hair was long and curly and—"

"He'll know you," he said again. "Now get down from there and feed the horses while I rustle up some supper."

He fried the last of the bacon, stirred up some flapjacks, and sprinkled a handful of wild blackberries over them.

"Bacon and blackberries?" she exclaimed. "I didn't see any blackberries today. When did you pick these?"

"Back when we stopped to water the horses the last time. They were growing off in the woods, so I filled up both my shirt pockets when I went to—"

"Oh," she interrupted. "I see."

"There's a lot of things you don't see, Leah."

She clanked the fork onto the tin plate they were sharing. "What? Whatever does that mean?"

"Nothing," he said quickly.

Leah studied him for a long moment. There was something he wasn't telling her. For the past two days Cal had seemed preoccupied, downright thoughtful, and that wasn't like him. Most likely he was planning how to retrieve his $700 from her brother.

Botheration! She gave up trying to understand Cal Zander. Too many things about him didn't make sense. Part of him was a gambler, a person who had killed a man over a card game. Another part of him was the man who'd taught her to shoot her revolver and stuffed his shirt pocket with blackberries for their supper.

She knew he didn't like her. For the past two hours he'd scarcely said three words to her other than "feed the horses" and "get some water."

She watched him flip over another pancake in the skillet. Goodness, he did everything with such careless skill, as if only half his mind was on the task and the other half was somewhere far away. Maybe he was thinking about his next Sunday sermon.

And that was something else about him that puzzled her. This was a man who played poker at the Shady Lady Saloon every night and then preached a sermon in church on Sunday morning. She never would understand Cal Zander, or really come to know him. But since he didn't like her, she guessed it didn't matter much.

The funny thing was that *she* was beginning to like *him*.

Oh, well. She blew out a long breath and held out the plate for a golden brown flapjack. None of this would matter a whit once they reached her brother.

After stuffing down the last blackberry, she picked up the plate they'd shared and walked off to the creek to wash it. When she returned, Cal had poured some hot coffee into the tin cup.

He drank half of the first cup without speaking, handed it to her, and sat staring into the dying fire. After another half hour of complete silence, he tossed the dregs into the fire pit and stood up.

"I'm turning in." He rolled out his blanket, pulled his saddle into place at his head, and spread Leah's bedroll a few feet away. They lay side by side in silence while the fire died and an evening sparrow started to sing.

"Need to get an early start tomorrow," he said at her back. "Want to reach that Circle K line shack before dark."

Leah nodded, then realized he couldn't see her with her back to him. Anyway, he wasn't looking at her.

Or was he? She glanced over her shoulder to find Cal stretched out full-length on his bedroll, one arm folded under his head, and he *was* watching her. Something in his expression sent an odd flutter into her chest.

She sat up and leaned over him. "Cal?"

"Yeah?"

"You don't like me much, do you?"

He didn't answer for a long time. And when he finally spoke, she wondered if she was dreaming.

"You're right, Leah. I don't like you." He looked at her for a long moment, then reached up and pulled her down to him, and kissed her.

His mouth moved slowly under hers, and everything seemed to come to a stop, her breath, her brain, even her heartbeat. It went on for a long, long time, his lips warm and firm and her heart pounding inside her chest.

When he released her, he drew in an uneven breath and looked steadily into her eyes. "Must be plain as day I don't like you one bit," he murmured. "Now shut up and go to sleep."

Chapter Twelve

The Circle K ranch sat at the head of a wide green valley halfway between a small river and a thick forest of spruce, aspens, and scrubby looking pine trees. Ten or twelve cows were sprawled in the shade of a big sugar maple in the meadow, and a few horses grazed near a fenced corral.

When Cal and Leah rode across the cattleguard and through the iron gate, a large floppy-eared dog set up a racket, and almost instantly half a dozen cowhands poured out of the big white ranch house. One of them, an older man with silver-gray hair and new-looking jeans, met them on the bottom step of a wide porch that ran the length of the house.

"Howdy," he called. "You must be the gent Slim told us about. My name's Jason Halliday. I own the Circle K."

Cal dismounted and shook hands with the man, then exchanged a few words Leah couldn't hear, after which Cal waved an arm toward her. "Leah Rydell here is the sister of the man holed up in your line shack."

Halliday tipped his hat. "How-do, miss. Doc's up there now, so I expect you'd like to ride on up there straightaway."

Leah nodded and watched Cal remount. One of the cowhands clattered down the porch steps. "Hi-ya, Mr. Zander. 'Member me—Slim?" He tipped his hat and grinned at Leah. "Miss Rydell. I'll get my horse and take you up to the shack."

They waited while the tall, skinny cowboy called Slim climbed into the corral, and when he reappeared riding a handsome brown gelding, Leah released a sigh of relief. She didn't want to waste time being sociable with the ranch owner, but apparently Cal had forestalled that.

"The line shack's about six miles from here," Slim said. "Up in the timber a ways." He wheeled his gelding away and they fell in line behind his horse. When Leah looked back, Mr. Halliday and the other hands were still standing on the porch. Thank the Lord Johnny had ended up here, where a stranger wasn't shot on sight or arrested. And, she thought, where a doctor was not only available but going out of his way to help.

Slim set a fast pace, for which Leah was grateful. Still, she had to bite her lip to keep from urging him on even faster. Cal was riding behind her, and she could feel his eyes on her. For the past four hours they had spoken very little, and before that he'd had no words for her at all.

She had none for him, either, she admitted. Ever since last night and his puzzling, completely shattering kiss, she hadn't a clue about what to say, or do, or even what to feel.

Were all men so...what? Impulsive? Surprising? So...inexplicable? If that was true, she resolved to never allow herself to get close to another male. She had always thought she would like to have a child someday, but if the price was living with a man who would always be a mystery, she would pass.

After two hours of riding uphill into the trees, Slim

raised his hand and reined up. "Line shack's just ahead," he called. "You kin almost see it through the aspens."

Squinting into the sunlight, Leah could just make out a small, trim cabin with smoke puffing out the stovepipe on a weathered shake roof. It took all her restraint not to slide off her mare and race toward it.

Slim moved on ahead, and suddenly she found herself in the clearing where the cabin stood. Before she could drop to the ground, the cabin door opened and a tall, slightly paunchy man in a wrinkled shirt and striped trousers stepped out.

"You Leah Rydell?" he called.

"Yes!" she shouted. She dismounted and stumbled toward him. Just as she started into the cabin, he reached out and snagged her arm.

"Whoa, miss. Hold on a minute."

She tried to pull free. "That's my brother in there!"

"Yep, I know that, Miss Rydell. But before you go larruping on in there, you better hear me out."

Leah froze, and Cal stepped up behind her. "Yes?" she said. "What is it?"

"I'm Doc Calciano, folks. Lambert Calciano. I need to tell you a few things about your brother before you see him."

"What things? Tell me!"

The physician cleared his throat and glanced at Cal behind her. "Well, firstly, your brother's been shot in the leg and the chest. I dug one of the bullets out of his chest, but the other's lodged too close to his heart to mess with."

Leah sucked in her breath and felt Cal's hand settle on her shoulder. "Go on," he said.

The physician exhaled. "He's running a fever, and—

"

Cal broke in. "How long has he been running the fever?"

"More than a week. He's…well, he's plenty weak, and…"

Leah could not utter a single word.

"And?" Cal asked.

Dr. Calciano sighed. "I hate to tell you this, miss, but most likely your brother's not going to make it."

She gave a cry and started forward, but Cal stopped her. "What else?" he said quietly.

"I'd advise you to be as quiet as you can, and don't upset him. No crying or carrying on, if you take my meaning. He's conscious only about half the time, and he's hurting, so sleep is a blessing."

"Right," Cal said. He tightened his hand on her shoulder.

"Okay," the doctor said with a sigh, "you can go on in. I'm dead tired, and I'm going back down to the ranch house and get some sleep. I'll be back in the morning."

Leah nodded and started to move past the physician, then found Cal beside her. He touched her arm but didn't speak. She heard the jingle of a horse's bridle behind her and the sound of two horses moving off down the trail.

Cal slipped his arm around her shoulders. "Come on, Leah. Let's go in."

Inside the cabin it was dim and cool, even though a blue speckleware coffeepot and a basin of water sat warming on top of the potbelly stove in the center of the room. In one corner of the room, under the single window, stood a narrow cot, and on it lay a slim form with a shock of unkempt red hair. A wide white bandage stretched across his chest.

Leah tiptoed forward and dropped to her knees beside the cot. "Johnny?" she whispered.

Her brother groaned and opened his eyes. "H'lo, Sis."

Tears stung into her eyes. "Johnny," she said, her voice breaking. "When I got your message I came as soon as I could."

His eyelids closed, then flicked open and he looked up. "H'lo, Cal. Been long time."

"Yeah, kid," Cal said, his voice quiet. "Long time."

Johnny's gaze refocused on Leah. "I'm bad off, Sis. I know it."

Leah bit her lip. "Yes, Johnny. The doctor explained."

"Aw, heck, Sis, don't cry. Makes me feel worse."

Cal knelt beside her. "It took four days for Slim, that's one of the cowhands on this ranch, to reach your sister in Maple Shade, Johnny. And four more days for us to get here."

"Thanks, Cal," Johnny breathed. "Guess I owe you."

Cal said nothing. He couldn't bring himself to collect a gambling debt from a dying man.

"Johnny," Leah whispered, "is there anything you want? Are you hungry?"

"Water," he said, his voice raspy. "An' wanna look at you."

Cal rose and poured a cup of water from the pitcher on the counter and handed it to Leah, and she dribbled some of the liquid past her brother's parched lips.

"Golly, Sis, you turned out real pretty! Like I remember you, only better."

She swallowed. "Oh, J-Johnny. You look older, too. All g-grown up."

He tried to laugh and coughed instead. "All grown up an' dying. Kinda funny, isn't it, Sis? Haven't seen you in years an' years, and now I'm—"

"Johnny, don't talk. I can see that it tires you out."

Cal guessed at what she didn't say to her brother. She wanted to assure Johnny that he *wasn't* dying, but she couldn't do that because the truth was staring her in the face. Her brother *was* dying.

The most helpless feeling he'd ever experienced swept over him. He couldn't keep Johnny Rydell from dying. And he couldn't help Leah. But he couldn't look at her white, strained face without wanting to fold her into his arms and rock her.

He couldn't do that, either, because Johnny Rydell had no idea how Cal felt about his sister, and now sure wasn't the time to tell him. Right now wasn't the time for any of this. Just when you learned there might be something in one's existence to smile about after all, life had a way of kicking you in the teeth anyway.

"Sis?" Johnny reached for her hand.

"Yes, Johnny, I'm here."

"Sis, how come you're here with Cal?"

Cal saw her free hand close into a fist so tight her knuckles whitened.

"Well, you see…Cal is…he's the preacher at the church in Maple Shade. He…he offered to bring me to Idaho."

"Preacher?" The boy tried to laugh, but once again it ended in a hoarse cough. "You're kiddin', right? Cal's a preacher? Must be funnin' you folks down in Maple Shade."

Leah shot a look at Cal over her shoulder. "Oh, no, he's not funning, Johnny. He preaches about families and love and what we owe to each other."

Her brother's eyelids drifted closed and then opened wide. "I owe you a lot, Sis. Didn't treat you right after Ma an' Pa died."

With one hand Leah swiped moisture off her cheek. "D-don't think about that now, Johnny. Think about…"

Cal held his breath. *Don't lie to him, Leah. Don't give him hope when there isn't any.*

"…think about that old apple tree in our back yard, remember? Remember that summer when we built a swing and the rope broke and…"

Johnny's lids drifted closed again. "Yeah, I remember. I got a bloody nose. And you cried, remember?"

"Yes," Leah said softly. "I cried."

Johnny smiled. "I always liked swings, even if I did fall out of 'em."

Cal gently nudged Leah's arm with his elbow. "Look, Johnny," he began. "You don't have to talk any more right now. We're gonna camp right outside your cabin, so you can talk more later. Okay?"

"Okay," the boy breathed. "You're a good man, Cal. Thanks."

Cal rose, helped Leah to her feet and walked her quietly across the room to the porch outside. Purposely he turned her away from the cabin and pointed off to one side. "See that patch of camas grass? I'm gonna set up camp over there. And here's what I want you to do."

Very slowly she turned her head to look at him. Her eyes looked real shiny, and her lips were pressed together. "We'll watch over Johnny in shifts," he continued. "And in between times we'll get some rest, all right?"

She nodded.

"I'm gonna build a campfire and roll out your bedroll, and I want you to lie down and sleep if you can. I'll take the first shift."

"All right," she said dully. "You really are a good man, Cal."

"Huh. How do you figure that, Leah?"

She tried to smile. "Because Johnny said so."

****

Cal sat on the cabin floor next to Johnny Rydell's cot, watching him sleep. When the kid's face got sweaty Cal sponged it off with a cloth, and when his forehead felt hot he wiped it with cool water.

He and Leah traded off every few hours. The last time, around midnight, when she crawled out from under her blanket, she looked pretty well done in. But when he tried to convince her to rest some more, she just shook her head.

Now she quietly opened the cabin door and disappeared inside. Cal walked over to his bedroll, lay down, and closed his eyes. Just for a minute, he thought.

The next thing he knew the morning sun was peeking through the treetops, and Leah was standing on the porch. She looked strange somehow, her hands loose at her sides, her face dead white.

He stood up and started toward her, but when she didn't move he came to a stop.

"Leah?"

She looked at him and shook her head.

He reached her in two strides. "Leah, what's wrong?"

She tipped her head to look up at him. "He's gone, Cal. Johnny's gone."

Chapter Thirteen

She was swimming under water, except that she couldn't swim. And she couldn't breathe. She had to get to the surface. Had to tell someone...what? What did she have to tell someone? Tell who?

Oh, yes. Cal. She had to tell Cal. Now. She had to tell him now. Had to...

A hard, warm body lay next to her, holding her. She couldn't cry. So she reached toward that warmth and held on tight.

Horses approached. Two horses. She felt Cal stir, but he stayed where he was, holding her. He didn't even move when a voice called out.

"Mister Zander?"

"Yeah?" His breath ruffled her hair. It was that cowhand, Slim. And the other one had to be the doctor, what was his name? Something Italian.

"Is he—?" The doctor's voice.

"Yeah. Leah was with him."

The doctor moved closer. "Is she all right?"

"Not really. In shock, I think."

Leah heard rustling nearby and then the doctor's voice. "Here, son. Give her some of this."

"Got whiskey in my saddlebag," Cal said. "But I didn't want to get up and leave her."

"This is better," the doctor said. "I'll go on in and..."

"Yeah." Cal's voice. He lay without moving, holding her, just breathing in and out. He smelled of smoke and sweat, and she decided that she liked it. Him. She could feel his breath on her hair. She never dreamed a simple thing as being held could ease such an awful, empty feeling.

She heard the doctor's voice again, and then Slim's voice talking in low tones. Then Cal spoke near her ear. "Slim says the ranch owner, Jason Halliday, has offered his family's burial plot for…"

She buried her face against his neck. He didn't say anything else, and for a long time he didn't move. Finally, she drew away far enough to say something. "Tell him…thank him for me."

His voice rumbled against her ear, and she heard Slim move away. Fading hoofbeats told her a horse was moving away.

"Take a swallow of this, Leah." Cal's voice.

"What is it?"

"Laudanum, I think."

She drew back and eyed the bottle in his hand. "Oh, good. Not whiskey."

He chuckled, and she looked at him. Cal unscrewed the cap on the bottle of laudanum and held it out. Her tongue came out and touched the narrow rim, then she wrinkled her nose and glugged down a hefty swallow."

"Whoa," he cautioned. "You want sedation, not stupor."

"Oh, no, Cal," she said, her voice husky. "I want stupor." She raised the laudanum bottle again, but he lifted it out of her hand and screwed the cap back on.

"You think you're ready to ride some?"

"Ride where? I d-don't want to leave Johnny. He'll

be all alone, and…"

"Doc's with him, Leah. And Slim's gone to bring a…" He hesitated. "…a coffin. Mr. Halliday says we're welcome at the ranch house until—"

"No. I want to stay here."

"All right, Leah. We'll stay here."

She lay down beside him again and said nothing more until the doctor tramped over and squatted beside them. "Would Miss Rydell like to sit with her brother until Slim gets back with the wagon and a coffin?"

Leah nodded against his shoulder and Cal looked up into the physician's lined face. "Yes, she does. Thanks."

"Then I'll see you folks tomorrow. The Halliday burial ground's about a mile down this trail, in a real pretty area off to the right. You probably passed close by it on your way up here."

"Yeah. I wondered what that black iron fence was doing back in the trees."

"Well…" The physician coughed. "I'm sorry to say that now you know."

That day and all that night they sat next to the cot where Johnny's body lay covered with a sheet. Cal fed wood into the potbelly stove, and around midnight he brewed coffee and fried up some bacon and a couple of eggs he found in the pantry box in the corner.

"Feels kinda funny to be eating supper in the same room where Johnny is," he said.

"Not to me," Leah said, her voice quiet. "It feels…comforting."

"You want to move our bedrolls inside? Sleep on the floor?"

She thought for a long moment. "No," she said at last. "Let's sleep outside. I like hearing the birds sing when the sun comes up."

"Maybe you're feeling a little better?"

"I don't feel anything at all, Cal. I'm numb."

He nodded. "Want some more laudanum?"

"No. You wouldn't happen to have any, um, whiskey, would you? Or…" she sent him a crooked little smile. "…some cherries?"

****

Just past sunup the next morning Cal heard the rumble of a wagon coming up the trail. Leah was inside the cabin, sitting in the rocking chair beside Johnny's body, so he walked down the trail to meet the wagon. Slim was driving. The cowhand pulled the horse to a stop, set the brake, and jumped down.

"How's Miss Rydell?" he asked.

"Grieving," Cal answered. "Go easy when you bring him out, will you?"

"Sure thing. They're waitin' down at the Halliday family plot."

Cal stepped into the cabin to find Leah on her knees beside the shrouded body of her brother. He knelt beside her. "Slim's here," he said. "With the coffin."

Without a word, she rose, leaned over to touch her brother's motionless form, and walked unsteadily out to the porch. She stood without moving while he and Slim laid Johnny's corpse in the wooden coffin and loaded it into the wagon. Then she stepped off the porch and walked toward him.

"I'm ready," she said. "But I'm beginning to feel shaky. What I want to know is…"

Cal took her hand. "Yeah?"

"Would you stand next to me when they…?"

"Sure. Do you want anything before we start down?

Some laudanum? A shot of whiskey?"

"No. Well, maybe some ch-cherries."

He squeezed her hand.

****

The Halliday family plot was nestled in a grassy area bathed in sunshine and thickly carpeted with tiny yellow wildflowers. Four graves were marked with moss-covered gravestones, the names chiseled into the granite. Rosemary Halliday, age thirty-seven. Jason Halliday, Junior, age three years.

Leah couldn't bear to read any more. She watched Slim and Cal slide Johnny's coffin out of the wagon bed and gently set it down beside a freshly dug grave. Dr. Calciano and ranch owner Jason Halliday stood off to one side, along with a dozen or more ranch hands and an older Mexican couple.

Cal and three ranch hands lowered Johnny's coffin into the earth, and then she heard clods of dirt thud against the wood. All at once she couldn't breathe. Her vision blurred to gray, and then everything went black.

Cal felt Leah's body crumple. One minute she was standing next to him, her frame erect, and the next she dropped bonelessly onto the ground.

The Mexican woman cried out and started forward as Cal bent over her. "She is fainted," the woman kept saying. She knelt beside him and began to rub Leah's hand. Cal cradled her head and watched Dr. Calciano step up, squat beside him, and lift Leah's wrist to check her pulse. Her face looked white as milk.

Finally her eyelids fluttered open. "What happened?" she murmured.

The doctor released her wrist. "You fainted, my dear."

Cal picked her up in his arms and walked over to the wagon. "Okay if I lay her here?"

"Of course," Jason Halliday said. He peeled off his sheepskin jacket and spread it on the wagon bed. "Take her on down to the ranch house. My cowhands will bring your horses."

****

An hour later Leah stretched out luxuriously in the tub of warm, scented water the Mexican housekeeper had insisted on. The woman's two nephews had lugged it into the ranch house kitchen, and then the woman—her name was Maria—chased them out and set a washcloth and a cake of soap on the floor beside her.

"You scrub good," she ordered. "Then you have long nap upstairs."

Leah tried to smile at the woman, but her mouth wasn't working right. Tears flooded her eyes, and try as she might she couldn't stop them.

Maria touched her shoulder. "Is good you cry, *Senorita*. Not good to hold the sadness inside. This I know," she added. "I lose two daughters when they are babies."

"Oh," Leah breathed. The tears kept coming, and finally she covered her face with her hands and let them flow. She cried until her temples pounded and her eyes were so swollen she could scarcely close her lids.

The housekeeper hovered nearby but didn't try to stop her grieving, just kept murmuring soft words in Spanish which Leah understood were meant to soothe. She felt as if a dam had burst inside her, but letting it all out eased the knot of pain in her chest. She cried and soaped her body and cried some more with Maria um-humming in sympathy until finally—*finally*—her mind began to clear.

She lifted the washcloth, dribbled warm water over her soap-slicked skin, and closed her eyes. Where was Cal? An hour ago, when the wagon had arrived at the house, he had entrusted her to Maria's care and disappeared. Most likely he was off drinking that whiskey he kept in his saddlebag. The last two days must have been a real trial for him.

She remembered with a start that Johnny had owed Cal $700. Her brother probably spent it long before he reached that cabin. Whoever shot him, or why, she would never know, and it hadn't occurred to her to ask him. When he was fighting to stay alive, that question hadn't seemed important.

Idly she swished her fingers through the tepid water and decided to wash her hair. After days of trail dust and campfire smoke she must smell like a hibernating bear.

An hour later, after Maria had poured two buckets of warm water over her freshly shampooed hair, the housekeeper presented her with a towel and a silky dressing gown.

"But surely this is yours, Maria!" she protested.

"Ah, no, Miss Leah. Belonged to Miss Rosemary, boss's wife. He still keep all her clothes in a big chest upstairs."

The robe was dark blue, and when she wrapped it around her body it felt...calming. *What a silly goose I am, reveling in something as frivolous as a silk robe after burying Johnny just this morning.* But she had to admit she was feeling stronger. Almost human, in fact. And all at once she was hungry! She hadn't eaten anything since yesterday's midnight meal of bacon and scrambled eggs.

"You stay for supper, no? Mister Cal, he say is okay.

He is *muy cansado*. Very tired. Boss say you will sleep here in house tonight."

Leah was too tired to argue, and she knew she was too unfocused to climb on a horse and ride for hours and sleep on the ground wrapped in a scratchy wool blanket.

"Besides," Maria said with a grin, "I wash all your clothes because they smell bad, and they are now drying."

For the first time in days, Leah laughed. She put her arms around the tiny Mexican woman and hugged her. "*Muy gracias*, Maria. That is all the Spanish I know."

"Mister Cal, he know much more," the housekeeper said. "He tell me many things."

Leah caught her breath. "What things?"

Maria turned away to stir something on the stove. "Just…things. You will see."

Chapter Fourteen

The "things" turned out to be negotiating a soft bed for Leah in an upstairs bedroom with blue flowered wallpaper and ruffled curtains on the windows. Cal would occupy the bedroom across the hall.

Maria had produced a gored denim skirt and a dark blue shirtwaist. "You wear while your clothes dry outside," the Mexican woman advised. "Belonged to Miss Rosemary, but boss say is okay."

After a supper of chicken and dumplings and apple pie shared with Jason Halliday and a dozen of his cowhands, along with Dr. Calciano and Cal, Leah joined the others gathered on the front porch. One of the ranch hands, Miguel, produced a guitar. Leah had no idea what the words of the Spanish songs meant, but apparently Cal did; in the middle of one verse, he grinned and pointed to her. Maybe it was about a girl. Or maybe, she thought as a shard of pain bit into her chest, it was about a red-headed boy who had been shot in the chest.

She closed her eyes, and when she opened them again, she found Cal watching her. He had settled his tall, rangy form on the top porch step, near where she sat in the porch swing with Maria. She couldn't look at him very long because tears blurred her vision, so she sent him a trembly smile and looked away.

Cal's gut clenched. Leah was trying hard not to cry,

and she wasn't succeeding. He wanted to pull her out of that damn swing and hold her close.

He wanted to kiss her.

He wanted to…*Don't go there, Zander. You haven't earned it.*

An hour later, she pleaded a headache and retired inside the ranch house. Cal sat without moving, feeling helpless and angry. It sure didn't pay to care about anyone; you got your heart roped and tied, pounded to a pulp, and sliced into little bits, and then what?

You died. You either died badly or you died well, but you died. And maybe, like Johnny Rydell, you broke somebody's heart in the process. *Face it, Zander. Caring about anyone is not for you.* Oh, hell, he was half-hog-tied, but at least he had sense enough not to step any deeper into the quicksand.

In the middle of one of Miguel's syrupy ballads, he stood up and strode out to the corral to check on the horses, fed them both an apple he'd filched from Maria's kitchen, and talked to his black gelding for a long time. Finally, he decided he'd had enough of this day. He tramped back up the porch steps, said his goodnights, and climbed the staircase to his bedroom.

Leah's door was closed, and no light showed underneath. He hoped she was asleep, not lying awake crying or staring at the ceiling.

He tossed and turned for a couple of hours and finally drifted off to sleep. But he was jarred wide awake when his bedroom door opened, and a shadowy figure crossed to the bed, sat down on the edge, and then slipped under the blanket next to him.

"Leah! What the hell are you doing here?"

She snuffled. "I know you don't l-like me much,

Cal, but I can't sleep."

"Leah," he breathed. "You don't want this, Leah. Trust me."

"Yes, I do, Cal. I just need to be…close to someone. I feel lost and sad and sick inside, and I'm s-scared."

He rolled toward her. He couldn't help it, he wanted to touch her, hold her. Her body was soft and warm, and he gritted his teeth.

"Cal?"

He didn't answer.

"Cal, do you think Johnny is at peace now?"

"You mean now that he's…gone?"

"Yes."

He was afraid to answer. Maybe if she thought he'd fallen asleep,, she'd go back to her own bed.

"Cal? I know you're not asleep because you're holding your breath."

He almost groaned aloud. "You want to know what I did tonight?"

"Yes, I do. Tell me. Tell me anything at all, just talk to me."

"Well, after you went into the house, I walked out to the corral to visit our horses. Took them both an apple." He didn't add that he'd talked to his gelding for over an hour to restore his equilibrium.

"Why?"

"Because come morning my gelding and your roan mare are going to take us back to Maple Shade. And because my horse, Dusty, gets kinda antsy some nights." He waited for the obvious question, but it didn't come.

He drew in a slow breath and kept talking. "Your horse," he continued, "is a real sweetheart. She gobbled up that apple like she'd never tasted a treat like that, something sweet and crunchy and…"

He let his voice fade away to see if Leah was still awake. "…and red," he murmured. "…and round. And…"

He waited, afraid to breathe. Was she still awake? When he heard nothing, he lay still and listened to her soft, steady breathing. "Yes," he whispered into the dark. "I think Johnny is at peace."

An hour before dawn, he eased himself away from her, pulled on his jeans and a shirt, and very quietly took himself downstairs. Not even the housekeeper was stirring. He moved out onto the front porch and settled into the swing.

When the sun touched the bunkhouse roof, a songbird started up in the walnut tree in the front yard, and after some minutes, a puff of blue smoke drifted from the metal bunkhouse stovepipe, and he smelled coffee.

But the scent wasn't drifting from the bunkhouse. It came from the ranch house, and after a minute, Jason Halliday stepped through the front door. "Thought I might find you out here," the ranch owner said.

"Miss Rydell up yet?" Cal asked.

"Nope. Still sound asleep," Halliday responded. "In your bed."

Cal couldn't stop his groan.

Halliday just chuckled. "Don't fuss yourself, Zander. I figure she was only there for half the night, and I figure that wasn't the half that counted."

"She'd just lost her brother. I couldn't…"

Halliday nodded. "Thought as much." He stomped his boot twice on the porch floor, and almost immediately Maria appeared with two steaming mugs of coffee.

He and the ranch owner sat sipping the brew in companionable silence while the bunkhouse slowly came to life. One by one the ranch hands drifted up onto the porch, and at the clang of an iron dinner gong there was a general rush into the ranch house dining room.

Jason Halliday looked over at him. "You comin', son?"

Cal choked on a swallow of coffee. He was closer to the ranch owner's age than to Leah's, but lately he'd been feeling young and unsure of himself in ways he'd thought he'd grown out of years ago. Maybe not. He heaved a sigh, followed Halliday into the house, and got another shock.

Leah had donned a frilly blue apron over her jeans and red plaid shirt and was handing around a big platter of pancakes. The ranch hands were saying "please" and "thank-you, ma'am" like they'd all been to charm school back East. Cal dropped into an empty chair and let Maria top up his coffee. When Leah bent near him with the pancake platter, he caught her eye.

"Thought you didn't like cooking," he intoned.

"Only when camping out," she said.

"Miss Leah, she make the flapjacks!" Maria announced.

"Miss Leah is a surprising woman," Cal said. He caught Jason Halliday's eye, and when the older man winked at him, Cal choked on a swallow of coffee. Again.

"Oh, man," Slim breathed. "Miss Leah, you figure on maybe settling in these parts?"

Miguel, sitting next to him, jabbed him in the ribs. "You fixing to get hitched, Slim?"

Leah's cheeks turned the color of ripe raspberries. "Oh, no," she answered. "I live in Oregon, in a town called Maple Shade, and I don't ever intend to leave. And," she added, "I don't ever intend to get married."

Jason Halliday's salt and pepper eyebrows rose, and he sent Cal a slow, enigmatic smile.

Breakfast lasted way too long for Cal, but Leah dawdled over her fried eggs and bacon and stretched two cups of coffee out about as long as she could. When she was no longer being admired by all the ranch hands, she let down her guard, and Cal saw the sadness in her eyes. She was putting on as brave a face as she could manage, but when her gaze met his he could see the anguish she was hiding from everyone else. Leah was holding herself together with nothing but spit and backbone,

Get her out of here, Zander. She's gonna break down any minute.

After breakfast, the ranch owner took Leah aside. "Miss Rydell, I am truly sorry about your brother. I know it isn't easy to lose someone you care about, but don't let it turn you against attachments of the heart. You hear me?"

Leah kissed the older man's bristly cheek. "I do hear you, Mr. Halliday. And thank you for caring for my brother."

"You come back any time you want to visit his grave, Leah. You'll be welcome."

She pressed his hand and turned away to mount. Cal sat his horse, watching her, his gray Stetson tipped down to shield his eyes. Leah recognized the gesture. Cal often hid his expression under his wide-brimmed hat. She guessed finding her in his bed last night had embarrassed him. And now her need for solace was making him withdraw from her.

She gave Maria a final hug, pulled herself into the saddle, and turned the mare onto the trail heading south. They rode without speaking all morning and half the afternoon, and then Cal suddenly reined up. Leah came to a halt behind him.

"Cal? What's wrong?"

He guided his black gelding back to where she'd stopped. "Don't look around, Leah. Someone's following us."

Chapter Fifteen

Leah stared at him. "What? What makes you think that?"

Cal hesitated. He didn't want to scare her needlessly, but he needed to keep her safe. "When we slow down, whoever it is behind us slows down, too. Anyone else would just maintain his pace and eventually catch up."

She shuddered. "Could it be one of Mr. Halliday's ranch hands? Maybe we forgot something?"

Cal shook his head. "Can't know for sure, but I'm guessing not. Anyone who knows us wouldn't be acting so cagey. So, here's what we're gonna do."

He pulled his Colt out of his saddlebag, slipped cartridges into the chamber, and stuffed it into his waistband. At his signal, they proceeded down the trail as before, but Cal gradually reduced his pace, keeping one hand on the butt of his revolver.

"Ride on ahead of me, Leah. Keep going at the same pace, and don't stop no matter what."

By now he could hear a horse some distance behind them, and he continued to slow down. Every so often he reined up to listen. Leah was now a good distance ahead of him, and soon she would be out of sight. He prayed she would keep moving forward, away from him, because every time Cal reined up, whoever was behind them stopped as well.

Finally, he'd had enough. Abruptly he wheeled the gelding around and dug his heels into its side. The horse bolted forward. He glimpsed a figure ahead of him, disappearing into the trees. Cal pulled up and sat perfectly still, watching and listening, but before he saw the figure again, a guttural voice rang out.

"Throw down yer saddlebag, mister. An' don't try anything fancy cuz I've got a shotgun and yer dead center in my sights."

Cal said nothing, and he didn't move.

"You hear me, mister? Throw it down. Now!"

"There's nothing of value in my saddlebag," Cal called. "Just some jerky and coffee. You want that?"

"Sure do," came the voice. "Maybe some money, too, if ya got any."

"I've got just one silver dollar. Got a bullet hole in it, though." He spoke slowly and then waited, trying to locate the speaker.

"I said throw it down."

Cal gigged the black slowly forward a step, reached behind him, and flipped his leather saddlebag onto the ground. "There it is," he yelled. "Come and get it."

The brush rustled, and a large gray horse stepped out onto the trail. A scruffy-looking rider with a ragged beard reined up and pointed at the ground. "Pick it up, mister."

"No," Cal said calmly. "You wanted it. *You* pick it up."

The man's shotgun came up. "Gotta shoot you to get it, huh? Well, better get ready, mister, cuz in about two minutes you're gonna be dead." He bent his head and sighted down the barrel.

Cal waited a split second, then dove off his horse.

At that same instant a shot rang out, and suddenly the man was staring down at his shirt where a ragged hole had been torn into the sleeve.

What the—?

The stranger wheeled his horse around and spurred it back up the trail, and while Cal wondered what had just happened, Leah stepped out from behind a spruce tree, her revolver clutched in both hands.

"I hit him, didn't I?" she asked, her voice trembling.

"Looks like it. He sure high-tailed it out of here."

"Oh, my Lord," she moaned. "I just shot a man."

Cal dismounted, grabbed the revolver out of her hand, and pulled her hard against him. "You didn't kill him. You didn't shoot *him*, exactly. You just put a bullet hole in his shirt sleeve. Scared him off, though."

Her face looked odd. "I feel awful, Cal. Like I'm going to throw up."

He patted her back. "I'll get my canteen." He unscrewed the metal cap and pressed it into her shaking hands. "Take little swallows." Instead, she gulped down a big mouthful, then leaned over and spit it out, closed her eyes, and drank again.

"Who was that man?" she asked.

"Drifter, most likely. Didn't look prosperous enough to be a real thief. Not a very good one, anyway."

She guzzled some more water.

"You feel steady enough to ride on?" Cal asked. "We should stop at the sheriff's office in Green Valley, tell him about that fellow."

"Yes, I feel steady enough to ride. But I don't feel steady enough to stop in Green Valley. That's where those men—"

"Yeah, but now you're packing a loaded revolver.

That should make you feel better."

She didn't answer. But when she led her mare out of the trees and climbed into the saddle, she smiled. Cal shook his head. Who would think owning a revolver could make a woman happy?

****

The Green Valley sheriff, Matt McConnell, alternately grinned and scratched his head as he listened to their tale.

"Gray gelding, huh?"

"Yeah," Cal said. "Big horse, maybe sixteen hands."

"Older guy? Looks kind used up?"

"Yeah. Surly, too."

"Who shot him?"

"I did," Leah said. "I mean I didn't exactly hit him. I only hit his shirtsleeve."

The sheriff tipped his chair back on two legs and gave her a long, calculating look. "You shoot at strange men often, do you, Miss?"

"N-no," she stammered. "Only men that threaten me or my companion."

"You two traveling together?"

"We are," Cal answered.

"Now, that's real interesting, a pretty young woman and a handsome-lookin' gent. How do I know you two aren't robbing people and blaming it on some old-timer?"

Without a word Cal got to his feet and headed for the door. Leah got there ahead of him, and he slammed it shut behind them with a satisfying crack. They didn't slow down until they reached the mercantile across the street.

"Cherries," Cal ordered when they walked in.

"Oh, yessir," the proprietor said.

"Lots of them," Leah added.

"Yup. Just happen to have a fresh bushel basket out back."

They filled a brown paper bag with ripe cherries and gobbled them on the trail, passing the bag back and forth as they rode. An hour later they made camp beside a meandering stream. They had cherries and black coffee for supper and watched the sun wash the sky pink and orange. Later, when Cal rolled out their bedrolls, Leah insisted on sleeping with her revolver tucked under one corner of her blanket.

"Good way to shoot yourself in the foot," he observed dryly.

"Not *my* foot," she corrected. "Some ragtag robber's foot."

Cal figured this was as good a time as any to make his confession. "Leah, I have something to tell you."

"Oh?" She sat up half-way and spit a cherry pit into the campfire.

"It's about…about Johnny."

At that she shot bolt upright. "Oh? What about Johnny?"

"Before we rode out this morning, Jason Halliday gave me something. He said to give it to you when you'd recovered a bit."

"What is it?"

He got to his feet, walked over to his horse, and lifted a worn leather bag from behind the saddle. When he set it down in front of her, she recognized it.

"That's my mother's travel satchel!"

"Halliday found it after Johnny turned up at his line shack."

Tentatively she touched one finger to the dark leather. "What's in it?"

"I don't know. I didn't look inside because I figure after Johnny—I figure now it belongs to you."

Slowly she undid the buckle, slipped her hand inside, and withdrew a faded daguerreotype. Tears flooded her eyes. "It's a picture of me when I was about fourteen." She turned it so he could see. "Johnny must have carried it with him all these years."

The photograph was gray-brown with age, but Cal could still recognize Leah, especially her eyes. And her shy smile. Looking at it made his throat feel tight.

She reached back into the satchel and gave a little gasp. "Look!" She pulled out a thick roll of currency. "Cal, where on earth would Johnny get this much cash? Unless he robbed a bank or a train or—"

"How much is there?"

Quickly she unrolled the wad of bills and tallied up the amount. "Over a thousand dollars," she said in a whisper. "Where on earth—?"

"Maybe you shouldn't ask, since it now belongs to you."

"Me! Oh, you mean because Johnny is—"

"Yeah. There's two kinds of people in the world, Leah. Those who do the work, and those who take the credit. In this case, looks like Johnny did the work and you're getting the credit."

She said nothing for a long time, just sat without moving, her chin resting on her drawn-up knees, staring into the dying fire. "I don't want the credit," she said at last. "I don't want this money. I would rather have my brother."

He touched her shoulder and she lifted her head.

Tears sheened her cheeks. "Leah, that money belongs to you. You know Johnny would want you to have it."

She turned away, lay down on her bedroll, and pulled the blanket over her body. She didn't say anything, and Cal waited. Finally she fell asleep, and he quietly retrieved her revolver, removed the remaining cartridges, and cleaned the barrel.

The next day and from then on, Leah insisted on carrying her revolver, and each night Cal managed to surreptitiously remove all the cartridges. Every morning before she woke up, he replaced just one bullet.

But that single bullet worried him. On the trail he tried to stay behind her except when they had to cross a rain-swollen stream, and then he dismounted and walked her mare across holding onto the bridle. He didn't really think Leah would shoot him, not on purpose, anyway. But a firearm, especially in the hands of someone not used to carrying one, was dangerous.

As the hours on the trail passed, Leah grew quieter and more distracted. Cal guessed she didn't want to be here, at least not with him. She hadn't liked him from that first day when he'd shown up at Nanetti's Mercantile, and no doubt that feeling had grown stronger when she discovered he'd known her brother in prison. Worse, when she'd found out Johnny Rydell owed him $700.

That thought brought him up short. He snatched off his gray Stetson and ran one hand through his hair. Hell's bells, she wouldn't actually shoot him, would she?

****

The tension between them continued, and by the time they rode back into Maple Shade on a hot, dusty afternoon, Cal was convinced there was absolutely no

108

chance that the chilly atmosphere between them would ever warm up. Not only that, he had no hope of any kind of relationship with Leah Rydell because it was plain as pancakes she didn't want one.

At the edge of town, he watched her dismount in front of the livery, lift off her saddlebag, and walk the mare on into the stable. Cal followed her into the dim interior and heard her greet the owner, Ebenezer Yellen.

"Have a good journey?" the elderly man inquired.

"Yes," she said in a tired voice. "For the most part."

"Glad yer back home, Miss Leah."

"Thank you, Eb. I'm glad to be back."

The gray-bearded liveryman shuffled toward Cal, took the reins he handed over, and sent him a half-salute and a toothless grin. "I'll brush yer gelding down real good, Mr. Zander."

Cal flipped the man a silver dollar and headed for his cabin behind the mercantile. Halfway down the boardwalk Leah's voice stopped him.

"Cal? Cal, wait a minute."

He swung around to face her. "Yeah?"

She looked up and held his gaze for a long moment. "Cal, I…Thank you for taking me to see Johnny. And for showing me all the things you showed me about camping and firing a revolver and…how to bake biscuits on a hot rock."

In spite of his somber state of mine, he couldn't help laughing. "You're welcome, Leah. Sure glad you like biscuits."

She sent him a wobbly smile. "You have been very kind, Cal. About Johnny and…well, about everything."

She looked like she was about to cry, and he had to squash the impulse to put his arms around her. She swallowed and made an effort to control her voice. "Thank you, Cal."

He decided to make it easy for her. "You're welcome, Leah. And you be sure to turn that revolver over to Mr. Nanetti."

"Oh. Oh, yes, I will."

He half-turned away. "Maybe I'll see you in church on Sunday."

If she answered him, he didn't hear her. And by the time he walked into the mercantile, he'd gotten his emotions under control. But with his first question, Florio Nanetti raked them all open again.

"Ah, Cal, you are return. Miss Leah, she was good to travel with?"

His heart kicked. *Jumping Jehosephat. Yes, she was 'good to travel with.' Leah Rydell was good to do everything with.* He nodded at the store owner. "Yeah. She's bringing that revolver back to you, Florio, but I'll pay you for everything else."

Nanetti waved him off. "Was small amount only. Miss Leah very special, so we forget, okay?"

"Okay."

The man looked at him expectantly. "You like Miss Leah?"

Cal sucked in a breath. "Yeah, sure." He more than liked Leah, but it wasn't any of Florio Nanetti's business.

"And?" the mercantile owner looked at him expectantly.

"And what?"

Nanetti raised both arms and let them drop to his sides. "And...well, I want Miss Leah to get marry someday. Make family."

Cal flinched. "Miss Leah's not interested in

marriage, Florio."

The man's dark eyebrows waggled. "She say this?"

"Yes, she say this," Cal confirmed.

The store owner's shiny face sagged. "Ah."

Chuckling, Cal headed for the back door. Florio Nanetti understood Leah about as much as *he* did. Which wasn't a whole lot. He strode into his cabin, dropped his saddlebag and two bedrolls and his hat onto the floor, and fell full-length across the narrow bed.

Then he laid one arm across his eyes and tried to come up with a plan for getting Leah Rydell out of his system.

Chapter Sixteen

"A thousand dollars!" Belle screeched. "A whole thousand dollars?"

Leah nodded. "We found it in an old satchel of my brother's."

Mrs. Swerdlow set a platter of fried chicken on the dining table. "There's mashed spuds, too," the landlady said. "And gravy."

"Oooh, gravy!" Sally reached for the bowl of potatoes. "Have a double helping, Leah. You look emaciated."

"I'm not very hungry," Leah said, her voice quiet.

"Well, *I* am," Martha announced. "I just spent half a day refereeing a spelling bee, and that takes strength!"

"And potatoes," Sally added with a smile. "Martha, I don't know why you never seem to gain a pound no matter how many potatoes you eat."

"That," the schoolteacher said, "is because hammering reading, writing, and arithmetic into young skulls takes an extraordinary amount of energy."

Belle daintily lifted a small chicken drumstick onto her plate. "*I* never seem to gain an ounce," she bragged.

"*You*," Sally observed dryly, "never eat potatoes!"

Belle reached for the bowl of creamed peas. "Let's get back to your thousand dollars, Leah. What in the world are you going to do with all that money?"

"I don't know, really. I haven't given it much

thought."

"Well, what *have* you been thinking about?" Belle pursued. "That handsome Callahan Zander?"

"No," she said shortly.

"Well, honey-lamb, whyever not?" Belle murmured. "That man certainly deserves to be thought about. I know *I* would certainly be thinking about him."

"Maybe he was not nice to Leah." Martha set the chicken platter in front of her. "Was he?"

"Oh!" Belle spluttered. "Cal is a perfect gentleman. Isn't that right, Sally?"

Sally nodded and picked up her fork. "Isn't he, Leah?"

"Yes," Leah said in a low voice. "Cal Zander was a perfectly well-behaved gentleman every mile of the way."

Sally smirked. "Told you so. You learn a lot about a man when you drink whiskey with him every night."

Martha tsk-tsked. "Really, Sally, a saloon is not exactly the proper setting for honest disclosures."

"Ha!" Sally shot. "What would an upstanding schoolmarm know about what goes on in a saloon? I bet you've never set one foot in the Shady Lady."

"Of course she hasn't," Belle said. "No properly brought up young woman would enter a saloon."

Leah pushed her chair back from the dining table and stood up. She started to move toward the front porch when Belle caught her hand. "Leah, wait. Are you going to invite Cal Zander to the picnic?"

"What picnic?"

"The Sadie Sunday picnic," Martha supplied. "The sheriff's office is sponsoring it. It's the only event all year long where a lady can invite a gentleman instead of the other way around. However," she said in a bored tone, "I have never attended."

"Well," Belle sang, "I for one can hardly wait!"

Sally choked on a bite of mashed potato. "Who can you 'hardly wait' to invite, Belle?"

"Why, Cal Zander, of course! I think he is the handsomest man in the entire county."

A dull headache nagged in Leah's temple. She didn't want to think about the Shady Lady or Martha's day-long spelling bee or Mrs. Swerdlow's mashed potatoes or the Sadie Sunday picnic or anything else. Especially not Cal Zander.

****

On Sunday morning, Leah avoided going to church, but she couldn't avoid attending the picnic in the park that afternoon. All day Saturday Mr. Nanetti had begged her to please, *please* come to the event. Nina and Florio Nanetti had five young children and were expecting a sixth at any minute. "You come, Miss Leah? Help my Nina watch children?"

She had reluctantly agreed, but only because Mrs. Nanetti had been especially hospitable to her when she had first come to Maple Shade. It was Nina Nanetti who had convinced Florio to hire her at the mercantile.

Now she packed bacon sandwiches and potato salad and molasses cookies into a picnic hamper, brushed her hair and tied it at her neck with a blue ribbon, and walked the short distance to the pretty green park next to the river. The afternoon was sunny, the balmy air heavy with the scent of honeysuckle. Puffy white clouds floated overhead in a blue, blue sky.

Leah sighed, drew in a deep breath, and searched the shady grove of willow trees for the Nanetti family. She spied Nina sitting heavily in the center of a quilt, surrounded by a gaggle of small children. She had just started across the grass to join them when suddenly she was aware of Cal Zander.

He was sitting awkwardly on a small blanket beside Belle Fontaine, looking for all the world like a wild gray wolf trapped in a cage. Belle, on the other hand, looked like a fairytale princess in ruffled pink dimity complete with a wide-brimmed straw sunhat trimmed with a puffy pink ribbon.

As Leah walked by, Belle sent her an odd, triumphant smile, and that gave her pause. *Why is Belle looking at me so strangely, as if she's just lapped up a saucer of cream?*

In the next instant she understood. Cal Zander was the saucer of cream! And for some reason, Belle wanted to make sure Leah understood that. As she passed them, Belle tipped her head toward the man beside her and sent Leah a slow, triumphant smile. *Just look at what I've got!*

Leah felt a stab of pity for Cal. No man, especially not one as independent as Cal Zander, wanted to feel roped and hogtied by a woman.

Cal looked up to see Leah in a simple blue gingham skirt and a plain white shirtwaist coming across the grass toward him. Her dark hair was tied back with a narrow blue ribbon, and she was squinting against the sun, apparently because she wore no hat.

His first impulse was to offer his gray Stetson to keep the sun off her face; then he realized his hat would droop past her ears. Besides, she probably wouldn't appreciate the gesture. Leah Rydell wasn't the least bit forgetful. If she wasn't wearing a hat it was because she didn't *want* to wear a hat.

He had to smile at that. Something about her slightly pink nose looped a small tug about his heart. He watched her settle next to Mrs. Nanetti, saw her smile at the three older children playing mumblety-peg on the grass, and tuned out the chatter of Belle Fontaine beside him. At this moment he'd give anything to be over there, teaching Leah how to flip a jackknife into the ground.

"Cal?"

He dragged his gaze away from Leah and focused on the woman who had invited him to the picnic. "Hmmmm?"

"You haven't heard a word I've been saying, have you?"

"No," he said honestly. "Guess my mind was wandering."

"Well," she said sweetly, "it *is* a lovely summer day, just right for daydreaming. I'll tell you mine, if you'll tell me—"

"What?" Suddenly he realized he'd been daydreaming about things he couldn't share with anyone, much less Belle Fontaine.

Belle fluffed out her skirt. "I said…Oh, never you mind, Cal. It wasn't important." She reached out a pale, manicured hand and laid it on his shirt sleeve.

Leah's hands, he remembered, were tanned and purposeful-looking. A working girl's hands.

"I said," Belle continued, "you have an extremely serious look on your face. I'd certainly like to hear what you are thinking about."

When he said nothing, she scooted closer to him. She smelled good, like roses or something. All at once she reached over and began to unbutton his shirt cuff.

What the—? He stared at her long white fingers

undoing the buttons on his cuff, and when she began rolling up his sleeve he sucked in a breath. *What in God's name is she doing?*

In the next instant he put two and two together. Belle Fontaine was trying to seduce him. It was ladylike and subtle, but it was still seduction. The damnable thing was that it was half-way working. He let out a long, careful breath. *Well, face it, Zander. You're only human.*

Still, it was strange to have this woman trailing her cool fingers over his forearm, feeling the faint stirrings of physical interest while watching Leah playing mumblety-peg with the Nanetti boy 50 feet away. He averted his eyes.

"Cal," Belle murmured. "Are you getting hungry?"

He jerked. Instantly he understood. Belle wasn't asking whether he wanted a sandwich or a dill pickle. She was asking if he wanted *her*. Well, he did, and he didn't. A man would have to be made of stone to be unmoved by a female suggestively rolling up his shirt sleeve.

On the other hand, it was Leah's hands he wanted to feel on his skin, not Belle's.

But Leah wasn't interested in him. He caught Belle's hand, carefully detached her fingers from his shirt sleeve, and laid it in her lap.

"Yeah, guess I'm getting hungry after all. Got any fried chicken?"

Chapter Seventeen

Leah gazed across the expanse of lush green grass in Maple Shade's town park and watched Belle Fontaine gracefully arranging her skirts around her, her pink beribboned sunhat perched jauntily on her blonde curls. Next to her, Cal Zander stretched out his long legs.

But Cal wasn't looking at Belle. He was looking across the park to where Leah sat with young Tommy Nanetti, who was trying to flip the blade of his father's pocketknife into the ground.

Belle was watching Cal, and on her face was an expression that would have made Leah smile were it directed at anyone other than Cal. But it *was* directed at Cal. Even from here, Leah could see Belle's interest. In fact, Belle was surveying the man sitting next to her with a decidedly predatory look.

As Leah watched, Belle slowly began rolling up Cal's shirt sleeve, revealing his tanned forearms. At first, Cal kept his eyes trained across the park on Tommy's father's pocketknife, but when Belle started to roll back his other sleeve, his concentration began to waver.

Leah wanted to laugh. Belle looked so intent, so purposeful as she worked Cal's sleeve up his arm. And Cal looked so…at first annoyed and then incredulous. And then he began to look halfway interested. A dart of annoyance pinged into her chest.

Tommy Nanetti stopped flipping his pocketknife.

"What's the matter, Miss Leah? Your face looks all funny."

"What? Oh, I must be getting sunburned. I have forgotten my sunhat."

"You can have my hat," the boy offered. He clapped his boy-sized blue Stetson onto her head. "Looks good," he chortled. "You'd make a good cowboy, Miss Leah."

Under the brim of Tommy's hat, she watched the drama playing out across the park. Cal was now glancing at Belle with a puzzled look on his face, and apparently in response to his question, she began unpacking the picnic hamper. That hamper, Leah knew, was chock full of Mrs. Swerdlow's fried chicken, Sally's potato salad, and Martha's sugar cookies. Belle, she recalled, had announced long ago that didn't like to cook.

But Cal didn't know that. Leah watched him accept a chicken drumstick and wave away a proffered bread-and-butter pickle that Sally, not Belle, had put up last spring. While Cal devoured his drumstick, his gaze once again moved across the park to where Leah sat entertaining young Tommy Nanetti and his two twin sisters, Sofia and Sonia, who were busy cutting out paper dolls.

She glanced down at Sofia's busy scissors. "Be careful, honey. And give Sonia a turn." From under the brim of Tommy's hat she slanted a peek at Cal and Belle.

Sofia handed the scissors to her sister and gazed up at Leah with wide brown eyes. "How come you're looking all frowny, Miss Leah?"

"Oh. Am I?"

"Yes. And you're blushing, too."

"Surely not, Sofia. Why, I'm all grown up, and grownups never blush."

"They do, too!" the twins chorused.

Leah bit her lip. "Did you learn that in school?" she asked in an attempt to divert their attention.

"Nuh-uh," Sonia said. "We learned that from Mama."

Over the twins' heads, Leah met Nina Nanetti's twinkling dark eyes. "Is true, Leah. I tell them about when their papa was courting me back in Salerno. Oh, so young we were then. We knew nothing of life!"

Leah sighed. And now Nina and Florio had five and three-quarters children. That is what came from blushes!

"Only certain men make women blush," Nina went on. "So when cheeks get hot, you should notice!"

Leah studied the book of paper dolls in Sonia's lap. She didn't want to think about blushes or paper dolls or picnics. She especially didn't want to think about what Belle Fontaine was doing with Cal Zander's shirt sleeve.

She got to her feet. "Come on, children. I'll race you to the river. Last one there is a rotten apple!"

Cal had just taken a bite of potato salad when he spied Leah flying across the grass with three small figures galloping in her wake. They were all laughing. Cal lowered his fork, stuck it in the mound of potato salad on his plate, and settled back to watch.

Leah's skirt kicked up around her ankles, revealing a ruffled white petticoat and the occasional flash of a bare knee. Screaming with excitement, the children dashed after her, and she subtly slowed her pace so they could catch up. When she headed for the river, the children raced to catch up and then tumbled on past her, screaming, "I won! I won!"

Leah pantomimed surprise, and Cal laughed aloud.

"What is so funny?" Belle inquired.

"Nuthin' much. Just…sure is a real pretty day."

"It doesn't take much to please you, Cal," she remarked. "Just a pretty day and…" She paused and looked suggestively at the bare forearm revealed below his rolled-up sleeve.

"And a pretty girl," he said. But when he said it, he wasn't looking at Belle; he was looking at Leah Rydell. Fortunately Belle didn't notice.

If he lived to be a hundred, Cal would never forget the sight of Leah playing tag with the three young Nanetti children, darting this way and that to evade them. The blue ribbon tying back her hair came loose and fluttered to the ground. Finally, they started back to their picnic blanket, where Florio's wife, Nina, was unpacking their lunch. The sound of Leah's happy laughter carried to him across the park, and all at once Cal felt lonelier than he ever had in all his thirty-seven years.

"Cal?" Belle nudged his arm. "Maybe we could stroll down by the river?"

"What?"

"The river," she repeated. "Could we go for a walk by the river?"

"Oh, sure." With relief he stood up, rolled down his shirt sleeve, and headed for the path that wound along the river. Belle fluffed out her skirt and caught up with him.

Leah watched Cal and Belle disappear into the tangle of willow trees along the river bank, gritted her teeth, and accepted a cheese sandwich from Nina Nanetti.

"I wanna go down to the river," Tommy cried. Mr. Nanetti dutifully rose, took his son by the hand, and marched off. Leah watched them disappear into the trees.

"Tommy, he is like his papa," Nina mused. "He want to see everything. That is why we come to America, because Florio want to see what it look like."

"Nina, is that why *you* left your home in Italy?"

"Ah, no. I come to America for two reasons," Nina said. "One, because Florio want it, and two, so our son would be born here in big new country."

"Which has lots of room for a big family," Leah said with a grin. She busied herself handing out sandwiches, but she kept one eye on the path leading down to the river, waiting for Cal and Belle to reappear.

An hour passed with no sign of them. Tommy and Mr. Nanetti emerged from the willow grove, and Tommy sprinted across the grass toward them. "Guess what I saw!" the boy shouted. Out of breath, he threw himself down on the quilt.

"What?" Sofia clamored. "What didja see?"

By the time the boy regained his breath, his father was tramping across the park. Sonia punched her brother's arm. "Tell me what you saw!"

"I saw…" The boy surveyed his listening audience. "I saw…"

Sonia smacked his arm again. "Tell me!"

"I saw Mister Cal and that fluffy lady standing real close to each other, and…"

Leah drew in a careful breath.

"…and they were *kissing*!"

Mr. Nanetti plopped down beside his son. "That is what people do when they like each other, Tommy." He sent a long glance at his wife.

"People who like each other very strong," Nina added.

"You mean 'very much,' Mama," Sonia corrected.

"Ah, no, I do not," Nina replied. "I mean very *strong* like each other. Very strong, like your papa and me."

Sofia's eyes widened. "You mean you kiss Papa?"

"No," Florio corrected. "Papa kisses your mama."

"Like Mister Cal and the puffy lady?" Tommy inquired.

"I could not see exactly," Mr. Nanetti said with a frown. "Look to me like 'puffy lady' was doing the kissing."

Leah bit into her cheese-and-bacon sandwich, choked down a bite, and tried not to look across the park to the river bank to see Cal and Belle when they emerged from the trees.

But they didn't emerge. Long minutes passed, and still there was no sign of them. She wrenched her gaze back to her sandwich and determinedly took another bite. It was none of her business what Cal and Belle were doing down by the river. None at all.

But it was strange how flat her cheese sandwich tasted all of a sudden. She guessed she wasn't as hungry as she thought.

Cal had picked up enough of Belle Fontaine's broad hints about the box social next Saturday to make the back of his neck feel itchy. "I never make plans that far ahead," he lied. "Might have to...uh...write my sermon for church on Sunday."

"But it's a Saturday night," Belle protested. "Surely you could have your Sunday sermon all written by then."

Cal groaned inwardly. He didn't want to write his sermon on a Saturday evening. He didn't want to attend the box social, either, but Florio Nanetti had told him that ladies' suppers were to be auctioned off at this particular

Saturday's box social, which would raise money needed for new desks at the Maple Shade schoolhouse.

"Belle, the sun's about to go down," Cal pointed out. "Time to walk you back to your boardinghouse before it gets dark." He took her elbow and guided her back to the picnic blanket, rolled it up, and stashed it under his arm. Then he picked up the picnic basket and started back across the grass.

Chattering nonstop, Belle kept up with his long legs until he spied something on the grass and stopped suddenly. He motioned her on ahead, then bent and snagged a scrap of blue ribbon off the ground. Leah's hair ribbon! He curled the bit of silk up in his hand and stuffed it into his shirt pocket. When he caught up to Belle, he pretended interest in her endless chatter until at last he could deposit the picnic hamper on the boardinghouse porch and leave her at the front door.

Chapter Eighteen

Leah bumped the screen door open with her elbow, set the tray of teacups on the low wooden table, and claimed a seat in the swing. Martha was the first to join her, massaging her neck as she sat down beside her.

"I spent all day correcting essays and planning geography lessons while you and Belle were off picnicking in the park." She accepted the cup of tea Leah handed her, added a slice of lemon, and blew across the surface to cool it down. "A schoolteacher *never* has an afternoon free for a picnic."

Sally stepped out onto the porch, followed by Belle, and they both sank onto two carved oak chairs. "Leah, bless you for making tea," Sally sighed. "I could certainly use a cup!"

"Any particular reason?" Martha inquired.

"There certainly is," the red-haired Irish girl huffed. "A whole table of poker players waited for Cal Zander to show up this afternoon, which he never did, so they got to arguing somethin' awful. The bartender finally had to toss them out."

"Cal was with me," Belle said smugly. "At the Sadie Sunday picnic in the park." She accepted the cup of tea Leah had poured, added three spoonfuls of sugar, and smiled at Leah as she stirred them in. "You saw us, didn't you, Leah?"

Yes, I most certainly did see you. You made sure of that. "I was busy keeping track of the Nanetti children most of the afternoon. Tommy, Mr. Nanetti's oldest boy, says he wants to be just like Cal when he grows up."

Belle's eyebrows rose. "Oh? Why is that?"

"Because," Martha interjected, "boys that age admire men who are—"

"Dashing," Belle finished for her. "And handsome, and strong, and—"

"Actually," Leah said quietly, "Tommy saw you and Cal down by the river, and he wants to grow up and kiss girls!"

Everyone laughed but Belle. "You mean he was spying on us?"

"Oh, not spying," Leah explained. "You and Cal and Tommy just happened to be in the same grove of willow trees at the same time."

Sally studied Belle with narrowed eyes. "Do I detect an interest in Cal Zander?"

Leah was also studying Belle. *Why, she's practically gloating over her picnic with Cal, sitting close to him, rolling up his sleeve, and...kissing him.* She wondered suddenly how he'd liked it.

Sally tapped the side of her teacup with her fingernail. "Belle? What about Cal Zander?"

"Why don't you ask *him*, Sally," Belle said, her voice silky.

"Because," Sally explained patiently, "Cal would only know if *he* had an interest in *you*, Belle. He wouldn't know if *you* had an interest in *him*."

"Well, you see him every night at the Shady Lady. So...um, you could just ask him, couldn't you?"

Sally set her cup on the saucer with a sharp click.

"For pity's sake, Belle, I'm not going to pry into Cal's private thoughts about you or anybody else. Cal Zander and I have other things to talk about."

Belle's eyebrows again rose. "What other things?"

Martha laughed out loud, and Leah watched Sally's lips form a tight, straight line.

"You know something, Belle Fontaine?" Martha said. "You might be the prettiest peach in the basket, but has it ever occurred to you that some men prefer apples?"

"Well, Miss Smartypants," Belle shot. "Cal Zander prefers peaches!"

Both Sally and Martha groaned. Leah was silent. Did Belle really want to attract Cal? Or did she want to prove that she *could* attract him? She had her answer with Belle's next statement.

"I think a girl deserves some credit when a handsome man pays attention to her," Belle said loftily. "It shows that she knows how to present herself. How to act. How to say the right things to intrigue him."

"And," Martha interjected with a smirk, "how to drop a lasso over his head and pull it so tight he chokes. Belle, you are a menace to every man in Maple Shade."

"I am *not* a menace! I am...attractive. And I am clever and amusing and...well, attractive. I don't see why Cal Zander *shouldn't* be attracted to me."

Sally gave a very unladylike snort. "Cal Zander might have some thoughts on that topic. But if he does, his feelings are a private matter."

Belle looked ready to scream. "Oh, Sally, please. Just *ask* him about me."

"No, I won't do it, Belle."

Suddenly Leah realized that she, too, wanted to know whether Cal was attracted to Belle. And, she thought with an inward groan, she had a sneaking suspicion about *why* she wanted to know.

She liked Cal Zander.

Her next thought sent a shiver of apprehension up her spine. She liked Cal Zander better than any man she'd ever known, and that sent fear coursing through her body. She never wanted to care about anyone. If you did, eventually they would abandon you, as her father and mother and even her brother had, and that ripped your heart in shreds. If you cared about anyone, you were sure to get hurt.

But Cal didn't deserve to be tracked down by a predatory female, even if she did gussy herself up in ruffles and ribbons. Belle Fontaine would never get hurt because Belle was looking at the wrong end of the stick; Belle cared only about Belle.

All at once Leah stood up, plunked her teacup on the tray, and walked into the house. She marched across the parlor and up the stairs to her bedroom, where she crawled under the blue patchwork quilt and lay without moving with a cool washcloth over her eyes.

Something was roiling around in her brain like a bubbling pot of applesauce. Something she did not want to think about.

Something that had to do with Cal Zander.

Chapter Nineteen

The minute Cal walked in the back door of the mercantile, he knew something was wrong. Florio grinned at him as usual, but Leah looked up from the yardage aisle where she was stacking bolts of fabric, nodded briefly at him, and quickly dropped her head.

He watched her for a full minute. She left the fabric aisle and puttered back and forth along the next aisle, poking rakes and shovels back into place, then straightening a display of flower seeds. She looked industrious as all get out, but somehow she didn't look natural. Her shoulders looked stiff, and when he caught a glimpse of her face, her mouth was tight and unsmiling.

He had never seen Leah look this tense. Not even when her brother lay dying had her face looked this white and set. *What in God's name has happened?*

"Leah?"

"Good morning, Cal." And that was all. She didn't look at him. She didn't smile. She didn't even turn around!

Florio bustled to and fro, unloading a bushel of ripe tomatoes into smaller baskets, humming something operatic as he always did. Apparently he was unaware of Leah's standoffish demeanor.

"Cal, you bring three bushels of apricots from storeroom, please?"

"Sure, Florio. You want 'em out front?"

"Yah, sure. Out front on boardwalk."

He retrieved the fruit, balanced the basket on his shoulder, and made his way toward the mercantile entrance. On his way he glanced down the fabric aisle where Leah was now bending over a bolt of red calico. She kept her back to him, and with a sigh he moved on out the front door.

When he reentered the store, she had disappeared. "Florio, where's Leah?"

"Eh? She was right here a minute ago. Maybe she go out to back storeroom."

But she wasn't in the storeroom. Cal hoisted another bushel of apricots onto his shoulder and made his way back through the mercantile to the front door. Suddenly he spied Leah hot-footing it down the boardwalk as fast as she could go.

What the—? Where was she off to in such a fizz? Had Florio sent her on some errand?

Or…He frowned as a thought surfaced. Leah was obviously avoiding him, but why? Yesterday afternoon he'd seen her at the picnic, but they hadn't spoken. He'd done a good deal of looking at her, but he'd never gotten close enough to talk to her. In fact, she acted like she didn't even notice him.

Now he watched her slip into the Lark and Peahen restaurant next to the Excelsior Hotel, and without thinking he strode down the boardwalk and followed her in. She sat down at a corner table next to the front window, spoke briefly to the waitress, and started to unfold her napkin. Before she could spread it on her lap, Cal slid into the chair across from her.

"Good morning," he said. "Again."

"Oh, hello, Cal. How are you?"

"Damn puzzled," he admitted.

The waitress set a cup of coffee down in front of her. "Do you care for something, sir?"

"No," he growled. "On second thought, yes. Coffee."

The girl flitted away to the kitchen, and Leah took a small sip of the dark brew in her cup.

"Puzzled about what?" she asked.

He hesitated. If he came right out and said he was puzzled about *her*, he knew she'd clam up. On the other hand, one thing he could never do with Leah Rydell was lie.

"I'm wondering why you seem so downright unfriendly this morning."

"Oh."

When she said nothing further, he decided to joggle her a bit. "Leah, we rode over two hundred miles together, slept next to each other for ten nights, and..." He lowered his voice. "...even spent one of those nights in the same bed."

"Yes," she said quietly. "I remember."

"Maybe we're not the best of friends, Leah, but at least we could be civil to each other."

"Yes," she said just as quietly, "we could."

He blew out a long breath. "Okay. I know you don't like me very much, but—"

Her face changed. "Very well," she said quickly. "I apologize for being...unfriendly this morning. I didn't feel unfriendly, I just felt—"

"Scared," he supplied.

She stared at him. The waitress returned with his coffee, flicked a glance from Cal to Leah and back again, shrugged, and walked back into the kitchen.

"Cal," Leah said after a long silence. "I have something to tell you."

His gut tightened. "Yeah?" he said, his voice wary. "What about?"

"About that money we found in Johnny's satchel. That thousand dollars."

He waited, idly swirling a spoon around and around in his cup.

"I deposited the money in the bank this morning. Seven hundred dollars of it is yours."

He jerked, and his coffee slopped over. "No, Leah."

She met his gaze with such anguish in her eyes for a moment he couldn't breathe. "Yes, Cal. Johnny owed you that money. I know you didn't cheat him. Sally swears you're an honest poker player, and I believe her. But I don't know about Johnny. I believe Johnny must have cheated you out of that money, and I am giving it back. I have opened an account at the bank in your name."

And that explains your unfriendly attitude this morning?"

"In a way, yes." But she didn't elaborate.

Cal couldn't think of one sensible thing to say. He watched her pour half the pitcher of cream into her coffee and stir it until it turned a muddy tan color.

"I thought you liked your coffee black," he said.

"I did while we were camping. We didn't have access to a cow."

His chuckle turned into a laugh, and to his relief she joined in.

"I would never lie to you, Cal," she said. "It's true, I do like cream in my coffee."

He reached for the sugar bowl. "I won't lie to you either, Leah. The truth is I like two spoons of sugar in *my* coffee."

"Then," she quipped, "it would seem we have been keeping secrets from each other!"

He bit the inside of his cheek. *God, yes, Leah Rydell. Big secrets.*

****

For the rest of that day, Leah watched a veritable stream of Maple Shade females flood into Nanetti's Mercantile and walk out with shiny new hair ribbons. *Hair ribbons?* When had all the women in town suddenly started wearing ribbons? It wasn't until Mrs. Crawley bustled in and purchased two yards of green satin ribbon that Leah discovered what was going on.

"Why, dearie," the woman confided, "it's the box supper social this Saturday. You know, all the men are bidding on our fancy-wrapped picnic suppers, and the boxes are tied with different colored ribbon so the gentlemen can identify the supper-maker. That is," she added, "if the gentleman wishes."

"Oh," Leah managed. "How quaint."

"'Course there's no earthly reason *why* a gentleman absolutely has to know who made which supper, but if a woman should *want* him to know, well…she can whisper to him what color ribbon she's wrapped up her box in."

Leah nodded. "I see." She watched the two young Crawley twins head for the candy jars on the counter and turned away to rescue the caramels.

"You goin' to the box social?" Mrs. Crawley inquired.

"Oh, I don't think—"

"It's for a good cause, dearie. New desks for the

schoolhouse."

"Oh. Of course. In that case, I will seriously consider it."

"You do that, Miss Leah. I bet there's plenty of young men who'd be pleased to eat supper with you."

Leah smiled, handed each twin a caramel, and measured out Mrs. Crawley's two yards of green ribbon. When the woman herded her two boys out the door, Leah set about straightening up the rolls of ribbon, then re-stacking the bolts of calico and dimity that had just arrived. She worked steadily until late afternoon, took a brief break to drink half a cup of cold black coffee, and worked on until it began to grow dark. When she could no longer see to check the stock, Mr. Nanetti closed the store and sent her home.

Just in time, she thought. Her back and shoulders ached from hefting heavy bolts of yardage, but all afternoon she had resisted her employer's entreaties to "get Mr. Cal to do lifting for you." For some reason she didn't want to be anywhere near Cal Zander.

That realization brought her up short. *Now, why is that, Leah? Why don't you want to be near Cal?* She shook the question out of her head. The less time she spent thinking about Cal Zander the better, and she resolved to start right this minute.

But when she dragged her tired body up the boardinghouse steps, an immaculately attired Belle Fontaine made avoiding the subject next to impossible.

"You look like someone has pulled you through a very small knothole, Leah. Sit down and have some lemonade." Belle gestured to the seat beside her on the swing. "Mrs. Swerdlow made cookies, too," Belle added. "Molasses. My favorite."

"Belle, have you ever baked cookies?" Leah asked in a tired voice.

"Me! Gracious, no. Whyever would I do that?"

Leah sighed. "Don't you suppose you might want to get married someday?"

"Well, of course! Right now getting married is my number one goal."

"Then has it not occurred to you that when you are a wife you might be expected to cook for your husband?"

Belle's peal of laughter set Leah's teeth on edge. "Of course not," she scoffed. "I expect I will have servants."

"Servants! Belle, this is Oregon, not New Orleans. Can you think of any woman in Lake County who has servants?"

"Well, Amanda Begley has a housekeeper."

"Mrs. Begley is seventy-eight years old! She lives alone eight miles outside town, and her housekeeper gets paid!"

Belle made no answer, just sipped her lemonade and nibbled another molasses cookie.

Leah's empty stomach rumbled just as Martha arrived, her school satchel bulging with what Leah assumed were student essays. "Oh, good, lemonade," the young schoolteacher said. "It was so hot in the schoolhouse today I thought I would melt before lunchtime." She plopped her satchel on the porch and sank onto a straight-backed chair. Leah poured a tall glass of lemonade and handed it to her.

Martha gulped down two big swallows. "Where is Sally?" she asked.

"At work," Belle said, her tone disapproving. "At the Shady Lady."

"Oh, that's right. Golly, sometimes I feel so sorry for Sally."

Belle glanced at her. "Why? She's lucky. Every single evening, she has Cal Zander to keep her company."

Martha sent her a tight-lipped smile. "Why is that lucky, Belle?"

Belle fluttered her eyelashes. "Because…well, because Cal Zander is extremely handsome, don't you think? And he's strong and brave and…"

"And handsome," Martha supplied dryly. "Honestly, Belle, your tongue is hanging out!"

"Pass the cookies, would you?" Leah said quickly. She hated to see her housemates quarrel, no matter the subject.

Belle pushed the swing into motion with one shiny leather slipper. "When will Sally be home?"

"Late, probably," Leah said. "After the saloon closes."

"Does the Shady Lady ever close?" Martha asked, her lips pursed in disapproval.

"Oh, Martha, don't be such a Goody Two Shoes!" Belle exclaimed.

Leah stood up and set her lemonade glass on the tray. "I'm going inside and help Mrs. Swerdlow with supper." After a beat she sent a sideways look at Belle. "That would be a good way to increase one's cooking skills, Belle."

Belle pretended not to hear. Leah glanced at her as she passed, but the pretty, pale face that had rarely if ever felt the sun's rays betrayed not one twitch of understanding. Belle, Leah thought with an inward laugh, would most likely set her cap for a husband who already had both a housekeeper *and* a cook.

Chapter Twenty

After a supper of chicken and dumplings and peach cobbler, Leah decided to sit out on the porch and wait for Sally to come home from the Shady Lady. She knew Sally loved peaches; she'd saved her a dish of peach cobbler.

She leaned back in the swing and closed her eyes. What really went on at the Shady Lady every night? Did Cal really play such a skilled game of poker that he took home some winnings each night? Ever since Johnny had confessed he'd learned the game in prison, she had been intensely curious about it. Maybe she would get Cal to explain it to her…Oh, no, she decided instantly. She would not.

The swing jolted suddenly as a body plopped down beside her. "Wake up, sleepyhead," Belle sang. "I want to ask you some things."

"What things?" Leah asked. "About learning how to bake cookies?"

"No, silly. About Cal Zander!"

Leah groaned inwardly. She didn't want to talk about Cal. She didn't want to see Cal, and she didn't want to think about him. And she didn't want to spend time wondering why.

"Leah, are you listening?"

"Yes, Belle, I'm listening. Ask your question."

"Well," her housemate began, a note of triumph in her voice, "first of all…"

Leah closed her eyes again and waited.

"What I want to know first is what you and Cal talked about all day while you were traveling to Idaho?"

"We didn't talk much, Belle. Traveling on horseback is tiring. Mostly we talked about stopping to water the horses and where might be a good place to camp for the night."

"That's all?"

Leah smiled. "That's all. Did you expect us to conduct deep literary discussions?"

"Well, what about at night?"

"Oh, at night we talked about whether to mix a can of corn with a can of tomatoes or a can of beans, and which one of us would wash up the plate after supper. Important things like that."

"Plate?" Belle said sharply. "One plate? You only had one plate?"

"Yes," Leah answered. "It was a tin plate, just like one of Mrs. Swerdlow's pie pans."

"How inelegant!"

Leah gritted her teeth. "When you're really hungry, 'elegant' doesn't seem important."

"What about…later?"

"Later?"

"You know, after supper. When you were…um…going to sleep."

Leah smiled. "Well, we discussed President Grant's latest edicts, and the political rebellion in Mexico, and…oh, I almost forgot. We talked about whether Byron's poems are superior to Shakespeare's sonnets."

Belle's eyes widened. "Did you *really*?"

"Oh, Belle," Leah said with a laugh. "Of course not. We were so tired at night we scarcely said a word to each other."

Which wasn't strictly true, she acknowledged. She and Cal had talked at night, sometimes until the campfire burned down to coals. They talked about how good the pine trees smelled and the twittering of the song sparrows over their heads and the river they had crossed earlier, and...oh, many things.

They hadn't seemed important, really, but she had to admit she liked talking with him. She liked hearing Cal's voice near her ear. She liked lying next to him, listening to his breathing. And she liked watching him open his eyes in the morning and look at her. His eyes were the most unnerving shade of gray-green, a cross between soft, wet moss and hard Chinese jade.

"Belle, why on earth do you want to know these things?"

"Because." She jostled the swing into motion. "I want to know what Cal Zander thinks is important. Does he like pretty girls, for instance. Does he like a girl to be quiet or does he prefer one who talks a lot?"

And you also want to know how you can entice him into kissing you again, Leah thought. Belle was being pitifully obvious. Martha was right. Belle wanted to lasso Cal and pull the rope tight.

At that moment, Sally stepped through the front gate and walked up the porch steps. "Aha, a reception committee! How nice."

"Have you had supper?" Leah asked.

"Oh, yes. Adam, the bartender at the Shady Lady, makes sure I have plenty to eat."

"And drink, no doubt," Belle murmured.

"No," Sally corrected. She sat down and smoothed the skirt of her red satin gown over her knees. "You know I don't touch liquor, and Adam limits himself to one shot of whiskey a night."

"Does Cal drink whiskey?" Belle asked.

"Yes, he does."

"Does he drink a *lot* of whiskey?"

"Sometimes. Lately he's been drinking more than usual."

Belle fluffed her long curls. "I imagine there's something on his mind. Or some *one*," she added.

"I wouldn't get my hopes up, *macushlah*. I think Cal Zander might be a one-woman man."

"Oh?" Belle's voice shot up an octave.

"Cal doesn't say much," Sally added. "But I've learned it's what a man *doesn't* say that's important."

"Oh, I know that," Belle said smugly. "But you'll listen real close, won't you, Sally? Pick up any little hints?"

"Jesus, Joseph, and Mary!" Sally blurted. "No, I won't. First of all, what Cal Zander and I talk about is nobody's business but ours. I told you before, Belle, I'm not going to spy for you, and I'm not going to betray Cal Zander's confidence. Ever."

Leah found herself smiling all the way to the kitchen.

Chapter Twenty-One

For Cal, the next week dragged by, and what made the days seem extra slow was the endless stream of tasks Florio Nanetti asked him to do, everything from scrubbing the storeroom floor to rearranging a dozen bushels of ripe peaches and half again as many bushels of green beans, ears of fresh corn, and ripe tomatoes. But every time he tramped back and forth from the back of the store to the boardwalk out front, loaded down with baskets of produce, Leah ducked into a handy aisle.

He didn't begrudge the mercantile owner's reliance on him, but he did wish Leah would at least *look* at him sometimes. After they'd shared coffee at the Lark and Peahen that morning, he thought she might be friendlier. But whenever she heard him coming, she still made herself scarce.

At night, he retired to the Shady Lady and joined a table of poker-playing ranch hands and a couple of sheriff's deputies. After he cleaned most of them out, he ended up at the bar, drank a shot or two or three of whiskey, and talked to Sally Flannigan when she wasn't singing Irish ballads to the patrons.

It was a relief to talk with Sally, and he talked to the attractive singer for hours. Sally Flannigan was a down-to-earth Irish woman who tolerated no nonsense from the Shady Lady patrons, and she was a good listener as well. She let him ramble on for hours without interrupting. He told her about growing up in Texas. About going to prison. About becoming a circuit preacher. Sally was no fool. She'd been around, which meant he didn't need to do too much explaining about the details.

In return, Sally shared her experiences as a girl in Ireland, her parents' death during the Potato Famine, how she came out West in a covered wagon, and the two husbands she'd married and buried before she became a saloon singer.

But one thing she wouldn't talk about was Leah Rydell. Every time he brought her up, Sally changed the subject, and tonight was no exception. Cal sat swirling his third shot of whiskey around and around in the glass while Sally nibbled on the bowl of beef stew bartender Adam Martindale had provided and evaded his questions.

"Aren't you hungry, Cal?" the singer inquired.

"Nah. I've got supper makings at my cabin. I'll eat later."

"Are you planning to attend the box social on Saturday night?"

He grinned. "Didn't know you could cook, Sally."

She batted at his arm with her spoon. "I didn't mean *I* was attending. Who'd buy *my* supper, anyway?"

"Somebody would, Sally. You're good company."

"In case you're interested, Cal, Belle always wraps up her supper box with a big pink bow."

"Uh-huh."

She sent him a grin. "Interested?"

"Huh-uh. I plan to be, um, writing my sermon for church Sunday morning."

"And you might *not*, right?" She tapped her spoon against his forearm again. "Your sermons are plenty good, Cal. I bet you could just stand up at the altar and talk off the top of your head and the congregation would think you're inspired by the Holy Spirit."

He laughed. "I might do that some Sunday. "The sermon might not make much sense, though."

"Leah Rydell usually wraps her supper box up in a blue ribbon," Sally said quietly. "And I know that because I usually use one of her blue hair ribbons, too. Last year, deputy Randy Sawyer bid twenty bucks for what he thought was Leah's box, only to end up eating supper with me instead! To this day, he hasn't forgiven me."

Cal chuckled. *Blue hair ribbon, huh?* Very interesting.

****

Saturday turned out to be a real scorcher, so hot that the Crawley twins stole an egg from under Nina Nanetti's prize hen and tried to fry it on the boardwalk in front of the mercantile while their mother was inside buying fresh tomatoes.

By four o'clock that afternoon, Leah was completely drained. Her camisole was stuck to her skin, and the thought of spending an hour in Mrs. Swerdlow's stifling kitchen frying chicken and making potato salad made her groan.

"I close shop early," Mr. Nanetti announced. "So can attend social box this evening, okay?" He beamed at her.

"Okay," she murmured.

"Is good cause, eh?" her employer pursued. "Desks for teaching?"

"Yes," Leah said languidly.

"My Nina, she make big supper for box, enough to

feed big family." He swept up and down the aisles, straightening the shovels and re-folding shirts and dungarees. "You go home now, Leah. Make social box for supper."

By the time she tramped up onto the boardinghouse porch, she felt as limp as one of Mrs. Swerdlow's dishrags. If it wasn't to support donations for new school desks, she would crawl into her bed upstairs and sleep until noon tomorrow. But if she skipped the box social, schoolteacher Martha Carmichael would never forgive her. She heaved a tired sigh and walked into the kitchen, feeling lifeless as an overcooked noodle.

Mrs. Swerdlow looked up from the sink where she was washing two big kettles and tipped her head toward the wooden counter. Four neat supper boxes sat waiting to be filled up.

"It's too hot for you girls to spend time slaving over a woodstove," the landlady announced. "So I fried up some chicken and made potato salad for all four of you."

"But, my goodness, Mrs. Swerdlow, I bet you're just as hot as we are, and *you* slaved over the stove!"

"Oh, pshaw, child. The minute you've all gone off to the social, I intend to have me a long, cool bath and sit in the parlor without my corset!"

Leah gave the portly woman a hug, then went upstairs to sponge off and put on a clean shirtwaist. When she returned, all the supper boxes were wrapped up with ribbon. Martha's was pale green; Belle's box sported a wide pink ribbon that was double-looped on top, and Sally's ribbon was pale blue. Leah's box was similarly wrapped, but the ribbon was a darker shade of blue.

"Mrs. Swerdlow, did you save some supper for

yourself?"

"Oh, land's sake, Leah, 'course I did. Kept the biggest chicken breast for my supper."

An hour later, all four housemates walked over to the schoolyard, where the auction would be held. Sheriff's deputy Clem Harkins motioned them over to the picnic table where the wrapped box suppers were piling up. "Put yer boxes right here, ladies! Bidding will start in just a few minutes."

Leah was the last one to set her box on the table, and after she nestled it among the bevy of other beribboned boxes, she drifted over to the baseball diamond where she settled down on the grass, propped her knees up, and wrapped her skirt around them. Then she lowered her head onto her knees. If she fell asleep, maybe she could avoid eating supper with anyone. Today the thought of talking to another human being made her head ache.

She tipped her head slightly and scanned the school grounds. There was no sign of Cal Zander, and that brought a sigh of relief. Even sharing another meal with deputy Clem Harkins, as she had at last year's box social, would be preferable to eating supper with Cal Zander.

But that is downright silly! She knew Cal didn't particularly like her, so why would he bid on her box?

Well, of course he would *not* bid on her box. Unless…She swallowed a laugh. Unless he didn't know it *was* her box. In that case, if he outbid every other male, he would be even more discombobulated than *she* would!

****

Cal positioned himself at the far side of the schoolhouse and stepped back into the shadows. From his vantage point he could see the entire baseball diamond and the grassy outfield where people were lounging and various-size children romped and shouted. The sun began turning the sky pink and orange.

He watched the Swerdlow boardinghouse ladies deposit their ribbon-wrapped supper boxes on the wooden picnic table in the center of the diamond. Schoolteacher Martha Carmichael's box was tied with pale green ribbon; Belle Fontaine had tied up her supper with an ostentatious double bow of wide pink ribbon. The last two boxes added to the pile belonged to his friend, Sally Flannigan, the singer at the Shady Lady, and Leah Rydell. A pale blue ribbon decorated Sally's supper; Leah's box was tied with ribbon in a darker shade.

Sheriff's deputy Clem Harkins stepped out of the crowd, ran his hand over the pile of supper boxes, and faced the crowd. "All right, folks, you all know how this here auction works. The gentlemen bid on the ladies' boxes." He cleared his throat. "The highest bid wins the right to eat supper with the lady who brought the box."

When the bidding started, Cal made sure he stayed back in the shadows. The first box Clem picked up was Nina Nanetti's oversized supper. "One dollar," someone bid. "Dollar and a half," another male voice called.

"Two dollar," Florio Nanetti yelled.

Back and forth it went until Florio won the auction with a final bid of four dollars, collected his wife and his supper, and retired to the blanket Nina had spread out near third base.

Not every husband ended up eating with his wife, which Cal privately thought was half the fun. A husband could have a perfectly innocent supper night out with another woman and suffer no consequences. Derrick

Crawley, for instance, ended up not with Mrs. Crawley's box but with Elvira Dalrymple's supper. However, the joke was on Derrick; gray-bunned Elvira was sixty years old if she was a day and known to be a poor cook.

Adam Martindale, bartender at the Shady Lady Saloon, ended up sharing prim, proper Martha Carmichael's supper, and Cal watched Sally Flanigan dissolve into a paroxysm of laughter because schoolteacher Martha was a teetotaler.

Cora Sue Holt ended up eating her picnic supper with Alma Meyberg's husband, who claimed he forgot what his wife's box looked like. And old Mrs. Bentinck giggled through a meal that was inadvertently purchased by twenty-three-year-old Arne Cowgill.

Clem methodically auctioned off all the boxes but the last three while Cal shifted his weight restlessly from foot to foot. Waiting to be claimed were Belle Fontaine's fancy pink-ribboned offering, Sally Flannigan's supper box. and Leah Rydell's, wrapped up in a dark blue ribbon. Sally's supper was won by Sheriff Morgan Mankewicz, who almost swallowed his cigar when he realized he'd won the company of the Shady Lady Saloon girl.

Finally, only two boxes remained. Auctioneer Clem Harkins paced around the table ostentatiously rubbing his palms together. "Now, gents, what am I bid for this pretty pink offering?" he called.

"Two bucks," someone yelled.

"And fifty cents," Lewis Christie countered. Cal swallowed a laugh. Lewis Christie was only fourteen years old, one of Martha's school students. The bidding escalated, but Cal resolutely kept his mouth shut. It wasn't Belle's supper he wanted to share.

Leah was surprised when Belle's supper box brought the sum of six dollars, and she was even more surprised when the winner turned out to be one of Martha's students. She choked back a giggle at the look of shock on Belle's face. No doubt Belle had planned to eat supper with Cal Zander.

Well, she thought to herself, the best laid plans…Cal wasn't even here, much less bidding on Belle's pink-ribbon-festooned supper. No doubt he was down at the Shady Lady, playing poker.

Her own box was the last one remaining on the table, and Clem made quite a fuss over it. "Last but not least is this handsome box." He leaned over and sniffed it theatrically. "My, my, I smell fried chicken! What am I bid, gents?"

"Two dollars," someone called out.

"Two-fifty."

"Three dollars!" Emer Janson's voice. Poor Emer had been out-bid on another supper and now he was in danger of going hungry.

"Five bucks!" someone yelled.

"Six!" Emer shouted.

"Eight dollars and a half," someone called. It was a voice Leah hadn't heard during any of the preceding bidding.

"Ten dollars!" Emer called.

An expectant hush fell over the crowd as they realized what was going on—a hot and heavy bidding war for the last box supper on the table.

"Twelve dollars," came the unidentified voice.

"Uh…fourteen dollars," Emer offered.

There was a long pause, during which it seemed the entire schoolyard full of people held their breath. Leah clenched her hands in her lap. *Who is that man?*

And then the stranger's voice came again. "Twenty silver dollars!"

A gasp traveled around the schoolyard.

"Twenty silver dollars!" Clem shouted. "Ya hear that, folks? I'm bid twenty silver dollars. Emer, you still in?"

Emer threw up his hands and stalked off toward first base, and people all over the schoolyard craned to see who had claimed the box tied with dark blue ribbon for the unheard of sum of 20 silver dollars. Leah, too, found herself holding her breath, and then a tall figure stepped out of the shadows next to the schoolhouse.

Cal! Oh, good heavens, he must realize he'd made a terrible mistake. She felt half-way sorry for him. Cal must be twice as disappointed as Emer Janson, who had stuffed his hands in his jeans pockets and walked off across the grass with his head down.

A shadow fell over her, and when she looked up Cal Zander stood before her with her supper box in his hand.

"You hungry?" he asked.

"Well…" She hesitated.

"I could build a campfire," he said, a smile in his voice.

"Oh, Cal, you didn't bargain for this."

"You're right, Leah. I didn't bargain for this. I *bid* for this. I won the auction, and I'm damned hungry, so…" He held out his hand. "Come on. An auction is an auction, and a bargain is a bargain."

"And," she murmured, "I never renege on a bargain."

"Damn right."

They walked across the baseball diamond and

spread a blanket on the grass far out in center field. "You know," Leah said as she settled down on it, "Belle is going to be livid that she's sharing her supper with one of Martha's students and I am sharing supper with you."

"We'll tell her you didn't have a choice, since a bargain is a—"

"Bargain," she finished with a laugh. "Still, I'm sorry you got stuck with—"

"Leah."

"I mean, you could be eating supper with—"

"Leah," he said quietly. "Shut up."

She stared at him, then opened her mouth to say once again that she was sorry he was stuck with her when she knew he didn't like her very much. But when he calmly began to untie the ribbon on her box, she snapped her jaw shut.

"Ah," he said, folding back the flap, "I see some fried chicken,"

"And potato salad. I didn't make it, Cal. Mrs. Swerdlow did."

"I don't care who made it, I'm starving."

Eating supper with Cal turned out to be more pleasant than Leah expected. She could almost forget they were sitting together on a warm, pine-scented evening in the middle of a schoolyard full of Maple Shade townspeople. But she couldn't forget her puzzlement about how the box social auction had worked out. Why on earth would Cal want to share *her* supper when he could be enjoying the evening with Belle Fontaine?

They didn't talk much. Then she remembered Cal never did talk much while he was eating supper, and now she realized it wasn't because he was weary from riding all day. That was just how Cal *was*. Quiet. When he wasn't preaching a sermon, Cal Zander was a soft-spoken man.

By the time they finished sharing a slab of Mrs. Swerdlow's fudge cake, it was growing dark. Deputy Clem Harkins tallied up the auction money and handed it over to Mayor Grimes. Couples folded up blankets and began sorting themselves out so that wives ended up going home with their respective husbands.

A silent Cal walked Leah back to her boardinghouse, thanked her for providing a fine supper, and left her at the front gate. All told, she estimated, they had spoken at most forty words, and almost all of them were "please" and "thank you."

She was still puzzled over how he had mistakenly ended up with *her* box. He didn't explain, and she didn't ask. When she commiserated with him about having to eat supper with her instead of Belle Fontaine, he had said nothing, and after a while she stopped talking about it.

But she was sure to hear about it from Belle! Even so, at the moment she was too tired to care.

Chapter Twenty-Two

Sunday turned out to be an extremely unpeaceful day. After her housemates and Mrs. Swerdlow had bustled off to church, Leah lay in bed for another hour, then rose, took a leisurely sponge bath, and sat in the porch swing reading *Ivanhoe*.

Thunderclouds gathered overhead. It was hot and muggy, and she knew the ladies would be thirsty when they returned from church, so she stirred up a pitcher of lemonade. She couldn't summon up energy enough to bake cookies.

The unpeaceful part came in the middle of Chapter Seventeen of *Ivanhoe*, when her housemates and Mrs. Swerdlow returned from church. Cal must have given a rousing sermon, because she could hear the women's excited voices from halfway down the block. Belle's voice rose above the others.

"It *is* true!"

"No, it isn't!" Sally challenged.

"Are you calling me a liar?"

Martha's calm voice sounded. "Oh, for pity's sake, calm down, both of you!"

"Girls! Girls!" Mrs. Swerdlow tried in vain to restore order, but Leah's housemates were pretty fired up.

"Calm down?" Belle screeched. "I am perfectly calm. I am merely outraged."

"Oh, Belle," Sally said in a bored tone, "you're always outraged about something or other."

"I am not!"

"You are, too," Martha replied.

"Well…" Belle hesitated. "This is *important*!"

Sally snorted. "Oh, pish-tush! What is so important about fried chicken and potato salad?"

"My *life* is important," Belle wailed. "My future! My happiness!"

When the women reached the front walk, Leah watched with dismay as Belle flung the gate open so hard it snapped off one of the hinges.

"Now look what you've done!" Martha shouted. Leah jolted upright. Calm, collected Martha *never* shouted.

"Oh, mind your own business, Miss Priss!"

"Belle!" Sally scolded. "Where are your manners?"

Belle stomped up the porch steps, then caught sight of Leah in the swing and stopped short.

Sally and Martha marched through the sagging gate; Mrs. Swerdlow followed them and disappeared into the house with a sniff. She appeared a moment later with a hammer, but after some desultory whacks at the broken hinge, she gave up.

Sally sank down on the top step, and Martha slipped into the swing beside Leah.

"How was church?" Leah asked. "I made some lemon—"

"Church was dreadful!" Belle interrupted.

"Church was just fine," Mrs. Swerdlow contradicted as she opened the screen door. "A fine sermon. Fine singing. Just…fine."

"Well, which was it?" Leah asked. "Dreadful or

fine?"

Sally fanned herself with a lace-edged handkerchief. "Belle is out of sorts."

"Belle," Martha said in a voice full of disdain, "is spitting mad!"

Leah watched tall, willowy Belle plop onto a chair, fluff out her blue dimity skirt, and reach for an empty glass.

"And why is that?" Leah asked, filling Belle's glass with lemonade.

"Well!" Belle said theatrically. "I'm surprised you have to ask, Leah, because after all, it is all *your* fault."

"*My* fault? Whatever have I done?"

"You haven't done a blessed thing," Sally said, holding out her glass for lemonade.

"Then why—?" Leah asked as she filled Sally's glass and one for Martha.

Martha smoothed one hand over her plain green poplin skirt. "Because our elegant housemate likes to make accusations."

"But it *is* Leah's fault!" Belle insisted.

Leah was beginning to wish she had stayed in bed. "Belle, for heaven's sake, if you don't tell me what I have done, how can I apologize?"

"Well, then, I'll tell you." Belle glared at her. "Yesterday at the picnic I had to eat supper with Lewis Christie of all people! *Lewis Christie!*"

"Lewis didn't like your fried chicken?" Leah asked blandly. "Excuse me, I mean *Mrs. Swerdlow's* fried chicken?"

"Lewis Christie," Belle's voice rose, "is only thirteen years old!"

Martha shook her head. "No, Belle. Lewis Christie

is fourteen years old."

"And he doesn't like fried chicken?" Leah couldn't resist asking.

"Of course he likes fried chicken," Belle moaned. "He *loves* fried chicken. He ate every last piece of fried chicken in my box while *you* shared your supper with Cal Zander!"

"Oh, Belle, Cal had no idea that supper box was mine."

Belle's green eyes widened. "How do you know that?"

"Because," Leah said calmly, "I would be the last person Cal Zander would want to eat supper with. Cal doesn't like me very much."

Sally choked on a swallow of lemonade.

Belle's eyebrows went up. "He doesn't?"

"No, he doesn't. At the mercantile, Cal scarcely speaks to me."

"What about when you were traveling to Idaho with him?"

"He didn't talk much then, either." But, Leah remembered, when Cal *did* speak, he was always kind, especially during those terrible days after Johnny's death. She would never forget how he had held her the night of Johnny's burial, when she crawled into bed with him and he wrapped his arms around her while she wept. And once, on the trail, he had even kissed her.

But that didn't mean anything, she reasoned. Men kissed girls for all sorts of reasons. Especially worldly men like Cal Zander.

Sally poked a finger at Belle. "Just why does this eating supper thing matter so much to you, Belle?"

"Why? *Why!* Because we-we're...practically

engaged, that's why."

Sally again choked on her lemonade. "Engaged?" she said when she could talk. "What makes you think that, Belle? Has Cal proposed?"

"Well, no. But he will. Of that I am quite sure."

"How come you're so sure?" Martha asked quietly.

"Because." Belle fluffed her skirt again. "Because I'm going to make sure he *wants* to marry me!"

"And just how are you going to convince him of that?" Sally asked.

"Oh, you know, Sally. A girl has ways."

Martha huffed out a laugh. "You mean you intend to trick him?"

"Oh, no," Belle said airily. "I intend to entice him."

Leah stared at her. *Entice him?* How did a girl *entice* a man into marrying her?

"You mean," Martha pursued, "you flatter him and cuddle up close every chance you get, is that it?"

Belle smiled. "Exactly."

Leah thunked her lemonade glass down on the tray. *Oh, poor Cal.*

"Girls," Mrs. Swerdlow called from the parlor. "I forgot to tell you I've invited a guest for supper tonight."

"Oh?" Martha said. "Who?"

"Callahan Zander."

Chapter Twenty-Three

Cal walked around the block twice before he turned in at Mrs. Swerdlow's gate. Which, he noted, was hanging by only one hinge. The elderly woman had praised his sermon Sunday morning, and she had followed it up by insisting that he join her and her boarders for supper.

He would much rather eat his solitary meal of beans and bacon cooked over the potbelly stove in his cabin than make conversation with four chattery females and try to keep his eyes off Leah. But, he reasoned, Mrs. Swerdlow and three of her boarders were steady church-goers, and he guessed a preacher should minister to his flock.

Leah was not part of his flock. Since that first Sunday, she hadn't set foot in his church. But it was Leah who answered his knock.

"Cal!" She sounded half-way surprised.

"Leah." The instant he stepped past the screen door, she disappeared into the kitchen. He set his hat on the side table in the parlor, then became aware of Belle Fontaine, sitting regally on the green velvet settee with a filmy-looking blue skirt draped artfully over her shoes.

Sally and schoolteacher Martha Carmichael were perched on side chairs. He grinned at Sally, and the singer rolled her eyes at him. Martha smiled primly, but when Belle dramatically held out a limp-wristed hand to him, he saw the schoolteacher shoot a look at Sally and roll *her* eyes as well.

He bit back a chuckle. "Something sure smells good," he managed. He started to take the chair next to Sally, but Belle swished her skirt aside and patted the space on the settee.

"Come sit here, Cal," she purred. "Next to me."

He didn't dare look at either Sally or Martha for fear he would roll his own eyes. He sat stiffly next to Belle and listened to her chatter on about his Sunday sermon. "So eloquent," Belle gushed. "So…inspiring."

Finally, Leah stepped into the parlor and announced that supper was served.

Oh, thank you, Lord.

In Mrs. Swerdlow's spacious dining room he tried to figure out which straight-backed dining chair would be Leah's so he could sit next to her, but Mrs. Swerdlow swooped in and pointed to the head of the table. "Sit there, Mr. Zander. So we can all see you," she quipped.

Belle made a bee-line for the chair on his right. Sally and Martha took seats across from her, which left the only empty chair for Leah next to Belle. Maybe that was preferable, he thought. That way if he looked at Belle he could still see Leah out of the corner of his eye.

"I hope you like chicken and dumplings, Mr. Zander," the landlady said as she set a brimming bowl of chicken stew at his place.

"I do, yes, Mrs. Swerdlow. Never figured out how to make dumplings. Maybe you could give me some instruction."

"Oh, Leah made the dumplings."

He shot at glance at Leah, who was studiously studying her silverware. "Dumplings are just biscuit dough dropped into the hot stew," she said.

"Better than baking them on a hot rock," he said lightly.

"Oh, yes. Even baked on a hot *greased* rock." He caught her eye, but she quickly focused on her bowl of chicken stew.

"Cal gave the most inspiring sermon Sunday morning," Belle announced. "Why, it almost brought me to tears."

"Oh?" Leah asked. "What was the topic?"

"Friendship," Sally volunteered.

"And the obligations friends have in the way of loyalty," Mrs. Swerdlow added.

"And…other things," Belle said.

Cal blinked. Other things? What "other things" was Belle referring to? Maybe his message to the congregation Sunday morning had been more meaningful than he thought.

"Have you always been a preacher?" schoolteacher Martha inquired politely.

Belle fluttered her eyelashes at him. "Oh, yes, Cal, tell us all about yourself."

"No, I haven't always been a preacher," he said quietly. "I…did other things before I started preaching."

"What other things?" Martha and Belle said together.

He hesitated. "I was a gambling man down in Texas," he confessed. "That's where I grew up, Texas."

"On a big cattle ranch?" Belle asked.

"Nah. In a one-room shack on the grubbiest street in town, eating tortillas and beans and not much else."

"That's how I grew up, too," Sally said, her voice soft. "Only the shack was in Ireland, and we ate potatoes.

That is until the potatoes all rotted. Then we ate nothing at all." She held Cal's eyes in a long look, and he nodded. He and Sally had shared many such stories.

Belle carefully rearranged her skirts. "I was raised in New Orleans," she announced. "My daddy was the mayor, the most important man in town."

Leah looked up. "I never knew that, Belle. Did you grow up in a big house?"

"Oh, my yes. We had scads of servants. My mother even had her own special dressmaker."

"How did you end up in Oregon?" Cal asked.

"Well, that was a pure mistake," Belle said with a simper. "Mama wanted to see the mountains out West, so Daddy sent us on a wagon train up through Texas and Oklahoma Territory. We got all the way to Oregon, but then Mama got sick. When she died, Papa wired me funds to pay my way home, but the stagecoach broke down in Maple Shade, and then Papa... Well, Papa remarried, and my new stepmother suggested that I stay up here in the north."

Leah frowned. That wasn't the story she'd heard Belle recount before. In that version, her mother had run off with another man, leaving Belle with the man's spinster sister who had abandoned her in Maple Shade. Truth could certainly be slippery!

They talked sporadically about the places they'd lived and the things they had seen until Mrs. Swerdlow and Leah cleared the plates and bowls and served up apple pie and coffee. Cal watched Leah pour a healthy dollop of cream into her cup, and when she saw that he noticed, he made a show of stirring two heaping spoonfuls of sugar into his own cup. He caught her eye and grinned. On the trail, he remembered, they had both

161

drunk their coffee black. He liked sharing secrets with Leah, even small, inconsequential ones like how they liked their coffee.

Halfway through his second cup, Mrs. Swerdlow suggested that he and Belle retire to the porch swing. She did not suggest that Sally or Martha or Leah join them, he noted. Just Belle. Looked to him like Belle had put a bug in the landlady's ear.

He swallowed a sigh. A man stood no chance against a scheming woman. Maybe he'd write his next sermon on that subject. He thought about that on his way out to the front porch.

Once settled in the swing, Belle curled up close beside him, and for the next hour she flattered and cajoled him so blatantly he wanted to laugh. Then, when she unexpectedly snuggled her head onto his shoulder, he no longer wanted to laugh. He wanted to escape.

She smelled good, he had to admit. And her body felt warm and soft and female. This time when she undid the buttons on his shirt cuff, he watched with considerable apprehension as she turned back the fabric with her smooth fingers. Then she slowly pressed her palm onto his bare forearm.

Was she trying to seduce him?

Hell, yes.

He stopped the swing and stood up. Suddenly he found Belle clinging to him, running her hand up and down his shirt front. She reached one hand behind his neck and pulled his head down to hers.

For a woman who'd been abandoned as a girl in a small Oregon town, she sure knew some big-city things! She undid the top button of his shirt and ran one finger back and forth across the base of his neck.

He pulled her hand away. "Belle, you don't want to be doing this."

"Oh, but I do, Cal. Don't you?"

Well, yes and no, he thought. Yes, because he was male and only human. And no, because Belle's hands weren't the ones he wanted on his body.

He lifted her hand away. "You're not listening, Belle." He re-buttoned his shirt and escaped into the house to thank Mrs. Swerdlow for supper.

Leah was in the kitchen, helping the landlady with the dishes. She took one look at his rolled-up shirt sleeve and sent him a questioning look. He wanted to explain, but not in front of Mrs. Swerdlow.

When he walked back out onto the porch Belle was gone, thank God, and in her place sat a cool-eyed Sally Flannigan.

"Have a nice evening?" she inquired.

"Some and some," he said.

"Oh, aye, boyo," she said with a broad smile. "I can just imagine which 'some' meant the most to you." Her voice was full of amusement. "And which 'some' you were missing."

Sally's laughter followed him all the way to the broken front gate.

Chapter Twenty-Four

The next morning, Leah rose early, gobbled a slice of toast and some of Mrs. Swerdlow's raspberry jam, and headed for the mercantile. Before she pushed the screen door open she caught sight of a figure bent over the front gate, and when she started across the porch, he straightened up.

"Cal! What are you doing here?"

"Fixing Mrs. Swerdlow's gate." He held up the hammer in his hand. "I told her last night I'd repair the broken hinge."

"That is good of you, Cal. No one in this house full of women can hammer a nail into the side of a barn."

"Barns don't need nailing," he said. "Gates do." He grinned and again bent over the gate, whacked something into the wood fence, and slipped a screwdriver out of his pocket.

"Tell Florio I'll be there in half an hour to move the heavy bags out of the storeroom."

"All right." She stepped past him and slipped out through the gap in the fence where the gate hung on a single hinge. As she moved on down the street, she could feel Cal's eyes on her.

Why is he watching me? Is my petticoat showing? She shrugged and moved on.

Mr. Nanetti couldn't stop talking about the box social on Saturday. "Mr. Cal, he bid twenty dollar for your supper! What you put in that box, Miss Leah?"

"Just plain old fried chicken and potato salad," she said.

"Why he pay so much?"

"Actually, Mr. Nanetti, it was a mistake. He thought it was someone else's supper. He bought mine in error."

Her employer's dark eyebrows drew into a frown. "You think?"

"Yes, Mr. Nanetti, I think." She smiled to herself. If she told the storekeeper how furious Belle had been about it, well…she wouldn't share that.

Cal arrived an hour later, and spent all morning lugging heavy bags of dried beans and peas and coffee beans from the storeroom. Leah decided to ignore him.

"Mr. Nanetti, shall I sort through the garden tools this morning?" she asked.

"Ah, sure, Miss Leah." He moved toward the back of the store, but she could hear his voice. "Twenty dollar," he muttered. "Much money, twenty silver dollar."

Poor Cal. And poor, frustrated Belle. She had wanted his company, and she was plainly upset about how things had worked out. He had acted unconcerned while sharing Leah's picnic supper, but both Belle and Cal would no doubt have wanted a different supper partner.

However, she wasn't a bit sorry. One single hour spent in Cal Zander's company made her oddly happy. Except, she admitted, here at Nanetti's Mercantile where she found it was difficult being around him. It was more than difficult, it was unsettling. It was apparent that Cal didn't care whether she was around him or not. And so, she decided as she made her way down the aisle of shovels and hoes and rakes, to avoid getting her feelings hurt, she resolved stay out of Cal Zander's way.

She propped up a shovel that had fallen into the rack of flower seeds and was just straightening two garden rakes when the bell over the door tinkled, and she heard Belle's voice.

"Leah, honey, would you help me?"

Leah, honey? Since when did Belle Fontaine consider her a bosom friend?

"What can I do for you, Belle?"

Belle leaned forward. "You can tell me where Cal is."

"I don't really know where he is. Maybe you should ask Mr. Nanetti, at the cash register."

Belle swept toward the back of the store, and Leah got a whiff of her scent, something sweet and lilac-y. She went back to the seed packets and heard Mr. Nanetti's voice.

"Sorry, Miss, I no see Mr. Cal today."

What? Cal had been hefting bags of flour and coffee beans out of the storeroom since nine o'clock this morning!

"Could he perhaps be in your storeroom?"

"Ah, no, Miss. Nobody in storeroom."

"Oh." Belle sounded so disappointed Leah almost laughed aloud. She had obviously launched her "lasso and hogtie" campaign, but the quarry was proving to be elusive. Still, Leah thought, a realistic assessment of feminine wiles pitted against an unsuspecting male would favor the female.

The bell over the door rang again as Belle swept out of the mercantile, and Leah sighed and went back to her flower seeds. To her surprise, the minute the front door closed, Cal stepped out of the storeroom.

"Thanks, Florio. I sure didn't feel up to coping with Miss Fontaine this morning."

"Maybe later, eh?" Mr. Nanetti queried. "Ver' pretty girl."

"Yeah," Cal said dryly. "Very pretty." And other things. Belle was very female and very seductive, the kind of seductive female he'd always stayed away from. Worse, Belle Fontaine was aggressive.

He caught sight of Leah at the front of the store, apparently absorbed by the rack of flower seeds. Then she was bustling up and down the aisles, straightening rakes, arranging bolts of fabric, polishing fingerprints off the glass candy jars on the counter, and generally being not only indispensable but cheerful. Florio was lucky to have her. Every time he looked at her he felt a catch in his chest.

The next time he looked up, Leah was gone.

"Florio, did you send Miss Leah on an errand?"

"No, I send her to restaurant to get coffee. She look ver' tired."

"Mind if I step out and join her?"

Mr. Nanetti gave him a long look and then shrugged. "Sure, Mister Cal. You look tired, too," he said with a grin.

Cal snagged a handful of ripe cherries from the bushel basket he'd just lugged to the boardwalk and strode down to the Lark and Peahen. Through the front window he spied Leah sitting at a table, slowly swirling a spoon around and around in her coffee cup. Her dark braid hung over one shoulder; he noted it was tied with the same dark blue ribbon she'd used to wrap up her box social supper.

He slid into the chair across from her. "Leah?"

She jerked and her coffee slopped over the edge of the cup. "Cal! What are you doing here?"

"Having coffee, like you are." He signaled the waitress, then unfolded his napkin, reached over, and mopped up her spill.

"Gee, Mr. Zander," the young waitress chirped, "you'd make a good waitress." She set a brimming cup before him.

"No thanks, Miss. I already have a job."

"Actually," Leah said, "he has three jobs."

"Really?" The girl's voice swooped upward.

"Oh, yes," Leah said. "Mr. Zander helps out at the mercantile. And he gives sermons at church every Sunday. And…" She hesitated. "He, um, plays poker at the Shady Lady."

"Golly," the girl breathed. "You must be rich!"

Cal choked on his coffee, and Leah laughed. When the girl retreated, he set his cup down on the china saucer with a sharp click. "Money talks, huh?"

She looked up at him with assessing blue eyes. "*Money* doesn't make a peep," she said. "It's actions that are the measure of a man."

"Well." He dumped two spoonfuls of sugar into his coffee. "I just happen to have seven hundred dollars in the bank, donated by the upstanding sister of a losing poker opponent."

"And I…" she said quietly, "still have three hundred dollars left over. I'm wondering what to do with it."

"Invest in your future," he suggested.

Her eyebrows rose and she sent him a startled look. "Whatever do you mean?"

He dumped the handful of cherries on the table

between them. "Well," he said with a grin, "what about buying a cherry orchard?"

She stared at him. "You can't be serious! I don't know the first thing about farming."

"You could hire someone to farm it. Me, for instance." He dangled a ripe cherry in front of her. "I've always wanted to own some land. Besides," he joked, "I could always use another job."

"You're not a farmer, either," she said. After a pause she added, "Are you?"

Cal laughed, offered her a cherry, and changed the subject. "Emer Janson is holding a square dance out at his barn on Saturday."

"I'm not going," she said flatly.

"I'm hoping you'll change your mind, Leah. I need your help."

She looked genuinely surprised. "My help? Doing what?"

"Uh…I plan to rent a buggy at the livery. I'd like to drive you and your housemates and Mrs. Swerdlow out to the Janson place."

Her eyes narrowed. "Why?"

"I…well, I think I might need the company. All of you together could, um, dilute an awkward situation."

A slow smile tugged at her mouth. "Ah," she breathed. "A *situation*." She slipped another cherry past her lips. "What are you prepared to pay?"

"Pay?"

Leah tried hard not to smile. Now it was his turn to be surprised. "Why, of course," she said as smoothly as she could manage. "You're offering me a bribe, are you not?"

He groaned and gulped down a swallow of coffee.

"Jehosephat, Leah, there's more of Johnny Rydell in you than I thought!"

"Oh, pooh, you don't need a dose of Johnny Rydell to see an opportunity to—"

"To put a man over a barrel," he said with a chuckle. He looked at her for so long she began to squirm.

"You know something, Miss Rydell?"

She studied the handful of cherries on the table between them. "At times I feel I know very little, Cal."

He threw back his head and laughed. "That's what Eve said to Adam with the apple still dangling in her hand."

She sent him a questioning glance. "What on earth am I tempting you with?"

"Cherries," he said quickly.

"But *you* brought the cherries, Cal."

He swallowed, deposited a cherry pit on his saucer, and sighed. "Let's get back to the bribe, all right? If you and your housemates agree to ride out to Janson's in my buggy, I will, um, buy you supper at the hotel."

"*Two* suppers," she said.

"Done!" Cal extended his hand, and she grasped it and squeezed hard. He resisted the impulse to lean across the table and kiss her.

"Thanks, Leah. Thanks a lot."

Chapter Twenty-Five

When Cal finally gave in to Belle's hints about the dance on Saturday night, he let her know he would be driving *all* the boardinghouse ladies out to Emer Janson's barn. Instantly she began to pout. "But why?" she wailed. "It would be so much more…intimate if it could just be the two of us."

Exactly, he thought. *There's safety in numbers.* But he couldn't say that. "I owe Mrs. Swerdlow a favor," he said. "For supper last Sunday."

"But that was just Mrs. Swerdlow," Belle whined. "You don't owe Sally or Martha or…" Her voice trailed off.

"It would be ungentlemanly to invite just you and Mrs. Swerdlow and not the others, don't you think?"

****

On Saturday evening Cal rented a large two-seated wagon at the livery stable, loaded all the ladies and their plates of cookies and tubs of coleslaw into the tufted leather seats, and drove out to Emer Janson's wheat ranch. Belle and Mrs. Swerdlow were both squeezed next to him, and he grew uncomfortably aware that Belle was pressing against him unnecessarily.

Leah, Martha, and Sally sat chattering in the rear seat. Or rather, Sally and Martha were chattering. Leah was noticeably silent.

It was a beautiful, still evening, the scent of farmers'

fields blending with the sweet smell of wild roses along the way. Evening sparrows sang in the maple trees. The gentle gray horse trotted along, and the wagon and its load of ladies rolled smoothly over the road.

Belle kept up a steady stream of comments about everything—the squeaky buggy seats, where she had learned to square dance, how dusty the road was, and couldn't they please hurry up? Mrs. Swerdlow um-hummed and oh-my'd; Sally hummed Irish ballads under her breath; and Martha disagreed with everything Belle said.

He wished Leah would say something.

By the time he pulled the wagon to a stop in front of Janson's big red barn, Cal hankered for a stiff shot of whiskey and a quiet corner to sip it in.

The ladies disembarked in a flurry of ruffles and shawls, and he drove the wagon on around to the side of the barn, parked it, and fed the gray mare an apple he'd filched from a bushel basket at the mercantile.

Inside it was noisy with animated talk and laughter and music played by two guitars, a fiddle, and a washtub bass thumped loudly by rancher Arne Cowgill. The square dance caller, Mayor Timothy Grimes, was shouting instructions at the top of his voice.

Cal drew in a deep breath and closed his eyes. The air smelled of cigar smoke, ladies perfume, and sweat. He liked this little community. Liked the mercantile where he worked, liked the little cabin where he lived. And he *really* liked his crowded church on Sunday mornings, where he could deliver the sermons he spent most of Saturday writing.

What he *didn't* like was the fact that he couldn't get Leah Rydell out of his mind, and that scared the bejeesus out of him. Leah was a good woman. A proper woman, from the right side of the railroad tracks. He didn't fit with a woman like Leah. It didn't matter how much he liked her; sooner or later she'd figure out he was nothing but a made-over gambler from the wrong side of town, and she'd dump him faster than a fox can raid a chicken house.

And the alternative? He clamped his jaws together. The alternative was sashaying across the floor toward him.

"Oh, Cal, I've been looking all over for you," Belle cried. "They're playing a waltz, can you hear it?" She cocked her head. "Don't you want to dance with me?" She posed theatrically in front of him and swished her ruffled skirt back and forth.

The fiddle player, Emer Janson, was sawing away on "Clementine," and Cal nodded. "It's a waltz, all right," he acknowledged.

"Well, then…" She stepped in so close he had no choice but to slide an arm around her waist and move his feet.

Belle was quiet for exactly 60 seconds. "Oh, isn't that just the prettiest song? I just love waltzing, don't you, Cal? It's so elegant! Why, when I was just a girl I recall an evening in New Orleans when the young men lined up three deep to partner me."

"I thought you left New Orleans when you were eight," Cal said, his voice bland. "Did your mother allow you to go to dances at that age?"

"Oh, well, n-no. I had dancing lessons for years before I was allowed to attend a ball." The waltz ended, and when the musicians began a square dance to "Turkey in the Straw," Belle laid a possessive hand on his arm.

"When I came out West I also became an expert square dancer."

Cal made a show of scanning the dance floor. "I don't see a square that's short a couple."

"Well, I do!" Belle tugged him across the floor to a half-formed set, and jockeyed him into position. Mayor Grimes, the caller, tipped his brown Stetson and sent him a welcoming grin.

One of the couples in the set was fourteen-year-old Lewis Christie; the girl he partnered looked no older than twelve or thirteen. When Christie's glance landed on Belle, the young man turned a ripe tomato color.

A ladies star formed in the center of their square. Belle raised one hand to join the figure, and with the other she swished her flounced skirt back and forth. In the obligatory "swing your partner" that followed, she clung to Cal as if she feared he would escape.

Which he would have, if he thought he could get away with it. He managed to keep his mind on the caller's instructions until the set mercifully ended. The minute the music stopped, Belle began pulling him toward the hay bale seats on the sidelines, but he managed to extricate his hand from her grip.

"You thirsty?" he asked hopefully.

"No. I haven't danced enough to work up a thirst."

"Well, I am." He sat her down on a hay bale. "I'll be at the bar."

Arne Cowgill was manning the array of liquor bottles displayed on a two-by-twelve plank propped between two sawhorses. "What'll you have, Cal?" the young man asked.

"A shot of good whiskey, Arne." He stifled the urge to look for Leah.

"I see you hooked up with Belle Fontaine," Arne said as he reached for a fancy-shaped glass bottle. "Mighty pretty woman. Pretty clingy, too, looks like."

"Yeah. Make it a double, all right?"

"Sure thing, Cal. Helps to maintain one's, ah, equilibrium."

Equilibrium be damned, he thought. Something told him he'd need more than "equilibrium" to escape Belle's clutches. What he needed was... His eye fell on one of the young Nanetti girls, Sonia or Sofia, he could never remember which twin was which. She was standing uncertainly at the edge of the floor full of swirling couples, looking hopeful and trying hard not to. Cal downed his whiskey, plunked the glass onto the bar, and headed across the room toward her.

"Would you care to dance, Miss Nanetti?"

Her brown eyes widened. "Oh, Mr. Zander, thank you!"

He whirled her away into a spirited polka, and as they circled the room he caught sight of Leah dancing with Florio. Cal managed to keep his mind on his feet, and Sonia, or maybe it was Sofia, proved to be an expert polka partner. When the music stopped, he felt a tug on his arm.

Belle elbowed Sonia out of the way and pulled Cal into a waltz.

"I just love to waltz, don't you, Cal?"

"Sure."

"Can you tell I've had years of dancing lessons?"

"Sure." He waltzed her to an empty spot on the floor and wished someone would cut in.

"All the women bring food for a midnight supper," Belle remarked. "That's nice, don't you think?"

"Yeah. Real nice." The last thing he wanted was to get cornered into eating supper with Belle. He scanned the room for the Nanetti family, hoping he could join them for supper. Or maybe Sally Flannigan would come to his rescue. Or even Mrs. Swerdlow. Anyone but Belle.

He sure wished Leah had been less tense on their return trip from Idaho. Ever since Johnny died, she hadn't been the same. After they buried her brother, Leah seemed to pull into herself. *Except for that one night after the burial when she crawled into bed with you.* But what she'd wanted was comfort, not love.

"Cal!" Belle's voice jolted him back to the present. "Cal, are you listening to me?"

"What? Oh sure. But I'm also trying to hear the music we're supposed to be waltzing to."

"We are not waltzing, Cal. This is a two-step."

"Right. Sorry." Waltz. Two-step. Whatever it was, it made no difference. What he really wanted to do was talk to Leah, not two-step around the barn with Belle.

So why don't you?

In the next minute he'd two-stepped Belle to a standstill. "I'm real sorry, Belle, but there's something I need to do." He walked her over to the sidelines, brought her a glass of lemonade, and escaped.

****

Leah had just refused a third offer of lemonade, this time from sawmill owner Willem Nordgren, when she saw Cal heading straight for the bench where she sat talking with Nina Nanetti.

Nina wasn't dancing because, as she put it, "baby too close," and Leah had decided to keep her company. The twins, Sonia and Sofia, were practicing waltz steps, and Sonia was still burbling about dancing with Cal.

Leah grudgingly acknowledged his kindness in doing so.

Or maybe he had wanted to escape Belle? That thought, she admitted with a dart of guilt, was uncharitable. Nevertheless, she would wager it was true.

When Cal got within several yards of her, young Sofia dropped her sister's hand and flew into his path. "Oh, Mr. Zander, I just knew you would come and ask me to dance! I've been practicing with Sonia!"

Cal sent Leah a stricken look.

"Well, go on," Sonia urged. "Ask her!"

Leah would wager that Cal had no such plan, but she watched him bow and extend his hand to the yet-undanced-with Nanetti twin. When Sonia beamed and made shooing motions with her hands, Sofia floated off toward the dance floor with Cal.

"It must be wonderful to have a sister to share things with," she murmured to Mrs. Nanetti.

"Not so wonderful," Mrs. Nanetti said, touching her arm. "My family in Italy very big. Four sisters I had. Not easy."

Leah nodded.

"But my Florio, he want only me," the blushing woman confided. "Older sisters more pretty, and younger ones more smart maybe, but is me he want." She leaned toward Leah and lowered her voice. "Maybe because I laugh at things with Florio. A man, he like to laugh."

Leah wondered suddenly if Johnny had ever laughed with a girl. She still thought of her brother as being ten years old, but of course he had grown up since she last saw him. Had he ever courted someone? She hoped so. She prayed that Johnny had some happiness in his life before he—

"Oh, Miss Leah," Nina cried. "What have I say that

177

make you look so sad?"

"N-nothing, Mrs. Nanetti. I was just thinking about…about families. I miss my brother. My father and mother died when we were young, and now I have no family at all."

"Ah. You will maybe make a new family, with babies, when you marry a young man."

"I will have to find one who makes me laugh, like Florio," Leah said quickly.

"That is not so easy," Nina said. "I know. I wait many years for Florio." She glanced at her daughter. "Sonia, bring your mama and Miss Leah some lemonade. We are have thirsty talk."

Sonia's return also brought Cal and her sister Sofia, who was out of breath. "We danced a Virginia Reel, me and Mister Zander," Sofia exclaimed. "It goes so fast!"

The two girls raced off to compare notes, and Cal stood before Leah, an expectant look on his tanned face.

"I don't want to dance right now, Cal. I just started drinking my lemonade."

"I don't want to dance, either," he said. "I want to talk." He lifted the glass out of her hand and set it on the bench.

"Talk? What about?"

He didn't answer, just held out his hand.

"And," Nina whispered when she hesitated, "maybe Mister Cal want to laugh! I will save your lemonade."

Reluctantly Leah rose. Before she knew it, Cal had walked her around the edge of the dance floor and out the barn door.

"Where are we going?"

"I don't care, just *away*."

It had grown so dark she could scarcely see. "Where

did you leave the wagon? We could sit in it."

"Good thought, Leah. It's parked behind the barn, but it's dark out there. Give me your hand."

He closed his fingers around hers, and they made their way around behind the barn and climbed up onto the wagon seat. "It's real warm out here," he remarked. "You should have brought your lemonade."

"It's a lot warmer inside, with everyone doing reels and waltzes. I thought you were dancing with Belle."

"I was."

She couldn't see his expression in the dark, but his voice told her things. "Cal, what did you want to talk about?"

"It doesn't seem important now. I just wanted to get out of there."

"I see."

"I don't think you do see, Leah. What is obvious to me is most likely not obvious to you."

She suppressed a ladylike snort. "I am quite intelligent, Cal. I can fire a revolver and bake biscuits on a rock. I'll wager I can tell what is obvious."

"Yeah?"

"Yeah," she echoed with a smile. "Try me."

When he said nothing, she leaned forward to peer into his face. "It's Belle, isn't it?"

Chapter Twenty-Six

"Yeah," Cal said, in a resigned tone. "It's Belle. She's...hungry."

"Oh."

He couldn't tell a thing from Leah's tone, so he didn't know whether she saw the obvious or not. Probably not, since Belle was one of Leah's housemates. Maybe they were even friends. But with her very next sentence, Leah blew that thought over the treetops.

"I would be wary of Belle," she said quietly. "She is, as you say, *hungry*. And I suspect it is you she is hungry for."

A chill settled in the pit of his stomach. It helped that Leah understood something he was only guessing at. It *didn't* help to learn he was on Belle's Wanted list. But it sure felt good that he could confide in Leah. He wanted more, but he figured now wasn't the time.

"Are you enjoying yourself at the dance?" he asked.

"Well, ye-es. And no. I like spending time with Nina Nanetti and her girls. Nina is clear-eyed and down-to-earth about a great many things."

"What's the *no* part?"

She was quiet for a long minute. "Cal, I arrived in Maple Shade when I was just fifteen, and right away I went to work for Mr. Nanetti to support myself. I feel...I feel unskilled socially. I never had time to learn any of the feminine arts."

180

Cal blinked. "Like what? What's a *feminine art?*"

"Oh, I never learned how to pour tea or make proper conversation. I've never walked out with a man. Before you, I'd never even been on a picnic with a man! And…as you may have noticed, I never really learned to dance."

"No, I hadn't noticed that, Leah. You looked like you knew what you were doing when you were dancing with Florio Nanetti."

She stared at him. "How would you know that?"

"Because I was watching you."

She laughed. "That's ridiculous, Cal. You were busy waltzing with Belle, not paying attention to me. And then you danced a polka with Sonia Nanetti. Heavens, after you asked her to dance the girl was floating on a cloud. And now Sofia is, as well. Really, Cal," she said with a smile, "for a preacher, you have a distinctly un-pulpit-like way with women!"

"You think a preacher should be a monk?"

"Well, no," she said quickly. "But he shouldn't be a…a ladies man, either. He should be upstanding and…and honorable."

He bit off a short laugh. "How do you know I'm not upstanding and honorable?"

"Well…" She searched for words. "You don't preach anything about leading an upstanding and honorable life."

"Are you sure about that? How many of my sermons have you heard lately?"

Leah didn't answer that, so he pressed the issue. "Come to church on Sunday and see," he challenged.

She caught her breath. Come to church? Even before Johnny died, she had avoided attending church. Hearing one of Cal's sermons, where she knew he would talk about things like family, would drive a jagged knife into her heart.

Instead of answering his challenge, she raised the issue that had brought them out here in the first place. Belle. "I trust you are behaving honorably when it comes to Belle Fontaine," she said, her voice quiet.

Cal sighed. "I'm sure trying, Leah. But it isn't easy."

"Ah. I can imagine."

"No, you can't," he growled. "In your wildest imagination, you could never understand your friend Belle's behavior. I have a hard time understanding it myself."

She could think of nothing to say to that, so after a minute of awkward silence, they walked back into Emer Janson's barn. Before he was inside the door, Belle pounced on him. "Cal! Where have you—?"

She broke off when she spied Leah. "Come on! They're starting another Virginia reel." She grabbed his arm and started to pull him across the floor.

"Hold on a minute, Belle." Cal lifted her hand off his arm. "I've danced one Virginia reel tonight with Sofia Nanetti. I don't feel like another one right now."

Belle's mouth turned down, and she refocused her attention on Leah. Before she could say anything, Leah touched his hand. "Cal, I promised to bring Mrs. Nanetti a supper plate. Please excuse me."

She turned away, and again, Belle latched onto his arm. Once again, Cal calmly removed her hand. "You know something, Miss Fontaine? Sometimes, a man likes a bit of breathing room. And right now is one of those times."

Leah couldn't hear what Cal said, but she distinctly

heard Belle's sudden indrawn breath and then her shoes tapping, or rather stomping, across the floor. She didn't dare look back at Cal, but apparently he had the good sense to walk off in the opposite direction. Good. A smart man does not wake a sleeping tiger.

When she reached Nina Nanetti on the sidelines, she sank onto the bench beside her and scanned the room. Belle had disappeared, but Cal stood at the bar, talking to Arne Cowgill. Then she caught sight of Belle, partnered with someone in the Virginia reel, but Leah couldn't see who it was until the couples advanced toward each other for the opening bow. My goodness, it was young Lewis Christie!

Nina was watching Belle, too. "Ah, pretty lady. She look hard for Mister Cal, but not find him, so she ask young boy to dance."

"She did find Cal, Nina. He...um...escaped. He's over at the bar."

Nina grabbed her belly. "Ah, don' make me laugh! Jiggle baby inside."

Both women shared a barely stifled giggle, and then Sonia launched herself at Leah, followed by Sofia. "Why are you and Mama laughing?"

"Ah," Nina said, wiping her eyes with a corner of her black bombazine skirt, "we laugh at anxious lady."

"What's she anxious about?" Sofia wondered.

"She is tall lady," their mother replied, "who finds short partner."

The twins gazed at the Virginia reel dancers. "Look!" Sofia blurted. "That's Lewis Christie. He's in my class at school."

"And he doesn't like girls," Sonia added. She narrowed her eyes and stared at the dancers. "But he's dancing with that tall lady Tommy saw kissing Mister Cal at the picnic."

Leah clapped her hand over her mouth to stop a burst of laughter and watched Belle and the Christie boy awkwardly join hands to form the bridge under which the other couples ducked. *Better Lewis Christie than Cal*, she thought. She moved her gaze back to the bar, where Cal still stood talking with Arne Cowgill.

As she watched, Arne upended a bottle of something and dribbled some liquid into a small glass, then reached out and patted Cal's slumped shoulder. The men apparently exchanged some words, and then Cal threw back his head and laughed. Arne joined in, and at a nod from Cal, he splashed more liquor into Cal's now-empty glass.

How fortunate men are, Leah thought. They can drink spirits to ease a difficulty or an awkward situation or even drown a trouble. All a woman had was a safe, sober cup of tea! And lemonade, which Nina was now offering her.

"Miss Leah, after you have talk with Mister Cal, now you look worry. You need lemonade."

True enough. Her talk with Cal had left an uneasy feeling in her midsection. Oh, my goodness, sometimes she did wish for something stronger than lemonade!

****

On Sunday morning, Leah heard her housemates rattle down the stairs, then heard the screen door whap shut as they went off to church. She wanted nothing more than to roll over and snuggle under her quilt for another hour. Even more, she wanted to ignore Cal's challenge about listening to his Sunday sermon.

But she had to admit she was curious. She decided

to ignore her curiosity and nestle under the quilt, but her eyelids popped open anyway. *Oh, all right, I'll get up and go listen to the man's sermon.*

She shook the wrinkles out of her red gingham dress, stopped in the kitchen long enough to grab a piece of cold toast, and marched up the hill to the Maple Shade Community Church. Strains of a fervently sung hymn floated from the open door. She waited until the singing was over, then slipped in the back entrance.

Cal was just stepping up to the altar. He looked none the worse for wear after downing a significant amount of alcohol last night with Arne Cargill. A quick glance at the congregation told her that Arne had slept in this morning, no doubt with a hangover. However, Arne's wife, Verna, and three blond stair-step-sized boys were sitting right up front in the second pew.

Cal looked just like he always did, not the least bit tired and with a welcoming Sunday-morning smile on his tanned face. His eyes scanned the congregation, rested briefly on Dora Swerdlow, Martha, and Belle sitting in the front pew, and then came to rest on Leah standing at the back of the church. Even from here, she could see those gray-green eyes of his widen. His smile broadened.

She leaned back against the far wall as a hush fell over the worshippers. *All right, Mr. Upstanding, preach away!*

Cal cleared his throat. "This morning I'm going to talk to you about what kind of lives we're trying to live. Honorable lives, I hope. Believe me, I know that's not easy. I confess that I spent a large part of my life behaving in ways that were less than honorable."

At least he's honest. But Leah did wonder how honorable it was to make his living playing poker. Even worse, teaching her brother to gamble. Maybe even teaching Johnny to cheat!

"An honorable man, or woman," Cal continued, "tells the truth, even when speaking the truth is hard to do. An honorable person does not lie, even when it's tempting to do so."

Hah! You lied to me about Johnny. Well, she amended, Cal hadn't exactly told her a lie; he just didn't tell her the whole truth. He lied by omission.

"Folks, I know from my own experience that telling the truth isn't as easy as it sounds. When I was a boy in Texas, I was mighty ashamed of where I lived, so I usually walked home from school heading in the opposite direction from my cabin, and I did that because, to be honest, the place where I lived was downright shabby."

Leah felt a dart of sympathy at his admission. She remembered feeling the same way after her parents died, when she and Johnny had next to no money to live on. Their tiny house began to look more and more run down.

Cal cleared his throat again. "But the hardest part of living honorably is not what you say or don't say. It's what you *do.* The hard part is doing what is right."

Leah straightened.

"Now," Cal went on, "you're probably wondering what that really means, doing what's right. Well, it means dealing honestly with people. Not taking advantage of them."

She clenched her jaw so hard her teeth ached. *You are a hypocrite, Callahan Zander. You took advantage of my brother Johnny in prison. He was young and inexperienced, and you taught him to play poker. And even now, you play poker every night at the Shady Lady*

Saloon, and you win money! You take advantage of players who aren't as skilled as you, and surely that is not an honorable way to make a living. That is definitely not "doing what is right."

She'd heard all she could stomach from Cal Zander this morning. She didn't want to listen to him one more minute, but then suddenly he said something that pinned her in place.

"An honorable person does not purposely mislead a fellow human being. I confess that sometimes a person *wants* to be misled. Such a person can be duped. Talked into things. And blind-sided."

Leah gritted her teeth, but for some reason she couldn't move.

"I have a confession to make, folks," Cal continued in a barely audible voice. "I have persuaded people to do, or not do, certain things. Sometimes I told myself it was for their own good, but I was arrogant in deciding what was, in *my* opinion, good for someone else. Sometimes I withheld information. To be honest about it, I persuaded someone in this very congregation to reach out to an estranged family member, and it ended badly."

That did it. Leah whirled around and stomped out the rear door. She took care to slam it extra-hard.

At the sound, Cal looked up and halted in mid-sentence. Oh, Lord, his confessed-sin sermon had backfired. Leah wanted to believe he had led her brother astray. Apparently she saw things only in black and white. He gritted his teeth. Only a child looked at things in such stark terms. The real world was more complicated than that.

He could scarcely remember what he said during the rest of his sermon, and when the service mercifully drew to a close with a prayer and a benediction, Cal marched out of the church and went for a long, long walk by the river.

Chapter Twenty-Seven

That Sunday afternoon was stiflingly hot. At four o'clock, the residents of Dora Swerdlow's boardinghouse drooped onto the front porch but couldn't face a pot of hot tea. Instead, Leah helped her landlady squeeze seven plump lemons and mix up a pitcher of cool lemonade.

She was still steaming over Cal's sermon that morning, but she drew in a deep breath, pushed through the screen door, and set the pitcher and a tray of glasses down on the side table. She doubted the lemonade would ease her headache, but maybe it would bring some measure of calm. Mrs. Swerdlow followed with a plate of sugar cookies.

"Mercy!" Belle sighed. "I am about to die in this heat."

"It was a lot hotter in the kitchen," Mrs. Swerdlow observed tartly, "where I was baking these cookies."

Belle ignored her and reached for a tall glass. "Quick, Leah, fill this up for me! I am about to expire."

"Oh, hold your horses," Sally said. "Leah and Mrs. Swerdlow are a lot hotter than you are."

"And probably a lot thirstier, too," Martha inserted.

Leah splashed all four glasses full of lemonade, and Mrs. Swerdlow took the empty pitcher and disappeared into the house.

"That woman is a saint," Sally breathed. "Baking

189

cookies on a sweltering day like today."

"Pooh," Belle shot. She reached for a cookie, stuffed one into her mouth, and grabbed two more. "Baking cookies doesn't take that long."

Martha snorted at that. "How on earth would *you* know, Belle? Have you ever in your life baked a single cookie?"

"Ladies," Leah said in a weary voice. "It is far too hot this afternoon to waste our energy arguing."

Sally leaned forward and lifted her red hair off the back of her neck. "Besides, you have a headache, don't you, Leah?"

Leah nodded. "Is it that obvious?"

"Oh, *macushlah*, you're frowning like the world's about to end. You never frown like that unless you're hurting."

Leah stared at her. Sally was far more astute than she'd ever realized. Schoolmarm Martha was usually too tired and distracted after a day of teaching to notice how anyone was feeling, and Belle…Belle was so focused on herself she rarely noticed anything beyond the ruffles on her skirt.

Gracious, she felt positively waspish this afternoon. She'd had headaches all her life, but never had they made her feel so uncharitable toward someone else. She downed a gulp of lemonade and tried to get her emotions under control, but every time she looked at Belle she felt her stomach tighten.

What is wrong with me? She sipped her lemonade and tried to think clearly. When she heard Cal's name come up, she jerked.

"Wasn't he wonderful this morning?" Belle gushed. "So eloquent. So wise and…and heartfelt."

Heartfelt? Hah! Cal Zander was a calculating, sneaky ne'er do well.

Oh, no he isn't, Leah. Be fair.

She didn't feel like being fair. Cal had shamelessly played on her emotions this morning. She swallowed another mouthful of lemonade. *Well, hadn't he?*

"Leah?" Sally touched her arm. "Leah, what is the matter? You haven't heard a word I've said for the last five minutes."

Slowly Sally's concerned face swam into focus. "Oh, I am sorry, Sally. What were you saying?"

"My goodness, honey, you're acting like you're on the moon!"

"Maybe she's tired," Belle said sharply. "You know, from all that dancing she did last night."

Martha choked on a cookie. "That's a laugh! Last night Leah spent more time talking with Mrs. Nanetti than dancing."

"She did not," Belle cried. "I was watching her."

Leah stared at her. Belle was watching her? Why on earth would Belle…

Because of Cal Zander? Did Belle think she posed an obstacle to her snagging Cal's attention? Leah, of all people? Ever since they'd returned from Idaho, Cal had seemed different. And then this morning he'd preached on and on about honesty and other things she knew he didn't believe in.

Her temples began to pound with renewed intensity, as if someone was driving iron spikes into her brain. *I am no threat to Belle. None whatsoever. Cal is polite around me, but I truly believe that underneath he really doesn't like me very much.* Not for one second did she think Cal had *wanted* to travel to Idaho with her. The only reason he did was to recover the $700 her brother owed him.

True, he had been very kind during those awful days when Johnny was dying. *And what about that night when he kissed me?* She closed her eyes and tried to calm her heartbeat. *Well, what about it?* No doubt men like Cal Zander kissed girls at the drop of a handkerchief. It meant nothing.

But now…well, now she didn't know. Now she was certain of only one thing, that Cal had no great fondness for Belle Fontaine.

The hot, muggy afternoon dragged on. Martha described every single student in her classroom and then launched into the lessons she planned on spelling and geography and science and arithmetic the coming week. Even deportment. *Deportment?* That made Leah smile. Strait-laced Martha was the acknowledged authority on proper behavior.

Sally relayed amusing stories about poker games at the Shady Lady and arguments she'd overheard at the bar between shopkeepers and ranch owners about the price of wheat and alfalfa seed and whether a new railroad line from Portland to Idaho was a good idea. And Belle…Belle boasted again about the fancy life she'd enjoyed as a girl in New Orleans, and then she mooned over how handsome and manly Cal Zander was until Leah thought she would scream.

All conversation came to a halt when Cal himself walked through the front gate. He looked hot and tired, and when he spied them all on the porch, he hesitated. For a moment, Leah thought he'd changed his mind, but then Belle fluffed her pink dimity ruffles and pounced.

"Why, Cal honey, I didn't expect you to come calling this afternoon!"

His mouth went from a half-smile to a straight line. "Actually, Belle, I came to see Mrs. Swerdlow." He wiped his hand across his forehead. "Sure is hot today, isn't it?"

Leah quickly filled her lemonade glass and handed it to him. He might not be her favorite person, but he didn't deserve to suffer in this heat.

He sent her a grateful look and downed three big gulps. "Thanks, Leah. Thought I'd melt before I got five feet from the church."

Leah stood up and motioned him to take her chair. "Sit down, Cal. I was just going inside to get some more cookies."

She moved toward the front door and heard him speak to the other women on the porch. "Miss Martha. Sally." His voice sounded scratchy. Then he finished off her lemonade and sank onto the straight-backed chair Leah had vacated. "Is Mrs. Swerdlow around?"

The landlady had apparently retreated upstairs to her bedroom. Leah debated whether to climb the stairs and tap on her door, then decided instead to make another pitcher of lemonade. Cal looked drained and tired. Mrs. Swerdlow could wait.

She had just squeezed six more lemons when she heard a scream from the front porch, followed by a cry of distress and the sound of a chair thunking onto the porch floor. Mrs. Swerdlow flew down the stairs, her silk wrapper untied and her hair unpinned. "What on earth is going on out there?"

When another cry came from the porch, Leah dropped the lemon in her hand and sped out through the screen door.

Belle was standing on one of the chairs, shaking out

her skirt, while Cal knelt before her, fumbling under her ruffles.

"Bee," he said tersely.

"It flew right up under my hem!" Belle cried. "Quick, Cal, find it!"

"A bee?" Mrs. Swerdlow shouted. "Oh, come now, Belle. There haven't been any bees around here for thirty years!"

Belle lifted her skirt another six inches. "Oooh, Cal, it's crawling up my leg! Catch it!"

Out of the corner of her eye Leah caught a glimpse of Martha's face. The schoolteacher looked as if she was trying hard not to smile! Sally had her back turned, and suddenly Leah understood everything.

There was no bee. Belle's cries of distress were simply a ploy to focus Cal's attention on her.

Belle teetered on the chair, screaming "I'm stung! I'm stung!" Cal stood up suddenly, one fist raised over his head. "Got it!" he announced. He walked over to edge of the porch and opened his hand. "It's gone. Flown off."

He exchanged a significant look with Mrs. Swerdlow, then turned and caught Leah's gaze. She could swear he was laughing.

"Why didn't you kill it?" Belle demanded. "It could fly right back here and land on me again!"

"A bee never stings twice in the same place," Cal said blandly. "I didn't kill it because it's one of God's creatures."

"But it attacked me!"

Sally snorted. Martha rolled her eyes. Cal just shrugged. "Can you feel where it stung you?"

"No. I mean Yes," she amended quickly. "On my knee." She started to lift her skirt, but Mrs. Swerdlow intervened.

"What you need is some baking soda," she announced. "I have some in the kitchen. Come on." She opened the screen door and stood waiting for Belle.

Belle hesitated. "Oh, I don't think—"

"Yes, you do," Sally interrupted. "Go on in and get your bee sting doctored. And while you're in there, maybe you could make us some more lemonade!"

Belle sent her a venomous look and flounced through the screen door into the house.

"She won't make any lemonade," Martha muttered. "She couldn't squeeze a lemon if her life depended on it."

Leah grinned. "She doesn't have to squeeze them. I just squeezed six of them, so the juice is all ready to mix up."

"Want to bet she can't pour in the water?" Martha shot.

No one said a word. Cal set the overturned chair back on its legs, and then the screen door flapped open and a very quiet Belle emerged with the pitcher of lemonade in her hand. Right behind her came Mrs. Swerdlow with another plate of cookies.

"Wasn't such a big sting," the landlady said evenly. "Fact is, a body could hardly see it."

Belle plopped back in the swing and smoothed her skirt down. "Well, it *felt* like a big sting."

"I'm sure it did," Sally said. "And you were so brave, Belle. You didn't shed a single tear."

Mrs. Swerdlow beckoned to Cal. "Are you ready to talk about that matter we spoke of earlier?"

Instantly Belle went completely still and cocked her head. "What matter is that?"

"Just a *matter*," Cal said smoothly. "Between Mrs. Swerdlow and me."

Sally sent him a grin. Martha pressed one hand over her mouth to hide a smile, and again Cal caught Leah's eye. This time he winked, and Leah suddenly found that her headache was completely gone.

Chapter Twenty-Eight

Mrs. Swerdlow opened the screen door and beckoned Cal inside. Not a moment too soon, he acknowledged. One more minute of Belle's battle with an imaginary bee and he'd give up accepting the landlady's offer of the bookcase she was discarding.

"Step inside, Cal," the older woman invited. "My old bookcase is in the parlor."

He moved through the screen door, and she pointed to a scarred dark-wood bookcase with two shelves. Ten minutes later he shouldered the front door screen open and set Mrs. Swerdlow's donated item of furniture on the porch.

"A bookcase!" Belle exclaimed. Dramatically she clapped both hands to her cheeks. "Whatever do you want a bookcase for?"

Cal sent her a long-suffering look. "For books, of course. A whole crate of them is waiting for me at the railroad station, but I have no place to keep them."

"Cal," Sally interjected. "Would you like a book of Irish poetry?"

"And," Martha added, "perhaps one of my students could borrow some of your books now and then? I have a dearth of appropriate reading material for my advanced students."

"Yes to you both," he said. He lifted the small bookcase onto one shoulder and stepped off the porch.

"Thank you, ladies. Martha, maybe you'd like to come by sometime and take a look at my library, such as it is."

"Yes, I most certainly would," the schoolteacher said with a grin. "Thank you, Mr. Zander."

"I'll bring my poetry book to the Shady Lady tomorrow night," Sally called as he went down the steps.

Belle remained uncharacteristically silent. Cal heaved a sigh of relief, opened the front gate, and strode off down the street.

****

When Leah arrived at the mercantile the next morning, she noticed a large wooden shipping crate sitting in front of the store between two bushel baskets of ripe apricots. She bent to inspect the address label. *Calahan Zander c/o Nanetti's Mercantile, Maple Shade, Oregon.*

Cal's books, she guessed. She itched to peek inside. What did he like to read? The Bible, of course. Maybe a hymn book? A book of sermons? No, Cal's sermons were too uniquely personal to come from a book. Not that she agreed with any of his sentiments, especially the ones about honesty and family loyalty.

Oh, pooh! What did the contents matter? Cal Zander could read whatever he wished. She swept past the wooden crate and ran into Mr. Nanetti just inside the front door.

"Ah, Miss Leah," the proprietor said, "is good you are here. Mister Cal, he goes down to hotel for coffee."

"Coffee! He left a big crate of books out in front of the store and went off down the street? Shouldn't he have unloaded it first?"

"Coffee is for me, Miss Leah. I stay up all night with Nina."

Leah sucked in a breath. "Is she all right? She's not—"

"Ah, no, not yet baby. But she not sleep, and so I not sleep, either."

The bell over the mercantile door jangled, and Cal stepped inside, a Mason jar of black liquid in his hand. "Here's your coffee, Florio. It was hot when I left the restaurant, but…"

"Is all right, Mister Cal." The mercantile owner reached for the jar. "I drink cold coffee all the time."

Leah frowned. "Mr. Nanetti, you probably need more than coffee. Why don't you go home and rest for a while? I can manage the store."

"Thank you, Miss Leah, I will do. You send Cal if you need help."

When the proprietor left, Leah stationed herself behind the counter while Cal dragged his crate inside and pried it open with a screwdriver. Then he began carting armloads of books out the back door to his cabin. She tried to read the titles as he marched past, but he was moving too quickly. However, she did notice the embossed gold lettering on some of the spines. What impoverished young Texan could afford valuable, leather-bound books? Was he really being honest about his impoverished background? Or had he stolen them?

The next time he started past her counter with his arms full of volumes, she stepped into his path. "Those are very handsome books, Cal. Expensive-looking. I thought you said you were a poor boy from Texas."

"I was when I was young. Up until my thirteenth birthday, the only books I ever saw were the ones the teacher kept on her desk at school. I never owned one."

"What changed after you were thirteen?"

199

He shifted his load from one arm to the other. "I got a job sweeping out the livery stable. Every time I could save up enough money, I sent away for a book."

"Leather-bound volumes with gold lettering? Not penny-dreadfuls?"

"I admit I read my share of dime novels, but I borrowed them from ranch hands at the saloon. But they weren't *real* books"

"That was the saloon where you learned to play poker," she said dryly.

He gave her a long look. "You have some objection to card-playing? Or are you still mad because I taught your brother to play poker?"

Leah bit her lip. She was honest enough to admit she did hold Cal responsible for Johnny's card-playing.

"Leah, I bought these books because I wanted to read more than dime novels. And when I started to win playing poker, I bought a lot more books. Okay?"

"Oh," she said in a small voice. She clenched her teeth and watched him tramp out the back door. Why did this man make her so mad? When he returned, he stopped at the counter where she stood polishing the fingerprint-smudged candy jars.

"Don't you want to know what books I'm unloading into my new bookcase?"

She had no answer to that. The truth was, she *did* want to know. She just didn't want Cal to know that she wanted to know. She was full of curiosity, but she wasn't about to ask him. All his books were probably religious works. Along with Sally's volume of Irish poetry, of course.

For the rest of the day, Cal alternately unloaded books from the wooden crate at the front of the mercantile and wrestled heavy sacks of flour and cornmeal and coffee beans into customers' wagons. Leah kept herself busy straightening shelves and trying not to pay much attention to him.

Late in the afternoon Mr. Nanetti returned, looking somewhat rested. He regaled her with the antics of his children and the difficulties of his very pregnant wife. When it grew dark, Cal retired to his cabin and his books, but just as Leah was about to lock the front door, Belle Fontaine of all people rushed in. She was out of breath, and she had a book clutched in her hand.

"I'm not too late, am I?" she panted.

Leah stared at her. "Too late for what?"

"For Cal. I, um, brought a book for his bookcase. Is he in his cabin?"

All at once Leah noticed Sheriff Morgan Mankewicz pacing up and down in front of the mercantile. She tapped on the window. "We're closed," she mouthed.

He nodded, spun on his boot heel, and sauntered off down the block. Leah thought no more about the sheriff and directed Belle to the mercantile's rear entrance. "Cal's cabin is just outside our back door."

She watched Belle glide through the store and quietly open the rear door. Before she stepped outside, Belle waved at Morgan Mankewicz, who was still pacing back and forth on the boardwalk.

How very strange. Belle was always such a stickler for "proper behavior," and it struck Leah odd that she had come alone to visit Cal. Visiting a man's living quarters, alone, and at night was highly unusual.

A niggle of unease crept up the back of Leah's neck. She shook off the feeling, folded up her apron, and laid it on the counter. Giving a final look around the deepening interior gloom, she briefly wondered if Belle would like to walk back to the boardinghouse with her.

In the next instant she dismissed that thought. The last person Belle would want to walk home with would be Leah. Sheriff Mankewicz, maybe. Anyone but Leah. With a shrug she slipped out the back door, kept her eyes carefully averted as she moved past the cabin's softly lit window, and headed home.

Chapter Twenty-Nine

Cal had just slipped the last volume of Shakespeare into his new bookcase when someone tapped on the cabin door. Probably Florio. "It's open," he called. "Come on in."

He was bent over the bookcase, his back to the door, when a familiar feminine voice spoke his name. He jerked upright.

"Belle! What are you doing here?"

Smiling, she moved toward him. "I brought a book for you." She held out a slim leather-bound volume.

"Yeah? What is it?"

"Poems. You do like poetry, don't you? These are poems by Byron and Wordsworth."

He straightened. "Well, sure I like poetry, Belle. Thanks." He reached for the book. "But you shouldn't have come all the way over here to—"

She stepped in closer. "Would you like to hear my very favorite poem?"

Something in her voice was different, and he felt a warning chill in his belly. He sent her a quick glance. "Uh…sure. Then you'd better go."

"Cal, could we sit down?"

He gestured to one of the straight-backed wooden chairs at his kitchen table and watched her sink down and fluff out her skirt.

"Why don't you come sit beside me, Cal?"

He frowned, then hitched the other chair over near hers.

She opened the book and began riffling through the pages. "Oh, here it is. It's by Wordsworth. 'She walks in beauty, like the night...' she read in a soft voice. She looked over at him and gave a long, drawn-out sigh. "Isn't that description of a woman just beautiful?"

"Yes, it is, Belle. But it wasn't written by Wordsworth. Byron wrote that poem."

Her eyes widened. "Really? Are you sure?"

"I'm sure. I didn't learn much in school, so I read a lot on my own. That poem is by Lord Byron."

She closed the book. "Why don't you tell me about when you were young, Cal. I've always wondered."

"Uh, Belle, maybe we could talk about that some other time? You really shouldn't be here."

"Whyever not?" She fluttered her eyelashes.

"Well, for one thing it's late. And you're a single woman. A respectable woman."

She reached out to touch his shirt sleeve. "Why, I feel perfectly safe with you, Cal. You're a real gentleman." She unbuttoned his shirt cuff and started to turn it back, the same way she had that day in the town park. Before she could fold his sleeve back, he caught her hand.

"Belle, stop this."

"Why? Don't you like it?"

Cal gritted his teeth. "Look, Belle, any man would like it, but—"

She lifted his hand away and turned back another fold of his sleeve. "But?" she breathed.

He stood up. "Thanks for the book and the poem,

Belle. I'm going to walk you back to Mrs. Swerdlow's."

"Oh, Cal, do you have to?" She pouted, then closed the volume of poetry, laid it on the kitchen table, and rose. She was standing way too close to him, but before he could move away she took another step toward him and lifted her face. When her hand crept up to rest on his shoulder, he got the message. She wanted him to kiss her.

Hell, no. He was hot and tired and he didn't feel like kissing anyone, least of all her. "Belle—"

Quickly she undid the top two buttons of her dress and pulled his head down to hers, and at that instant the door burst open and there stood Sheriff Mankewicz.

"Oh, Sheriff," she cried, you've come just in time! This man has accosted me."

Cal stared at her. What in God's name was going on? He hadn't accosted her. He hadn't even touched her! Why was she making up this tale?

The sheriff's dark eyebrows went up. "That true, Zander?"

"No, it's not true!"

"Then how come she's alone with you here in your cabin? I find this respectable lady in a man's living quarters, at night, what am I s'posed to think?"

Cal opened his mouth to reply, but Belle laid her hand on his arm. "Oh, don't try to protect me, Cal. I know you will do the honorable thing."

"What? What are you talking about?"

"Why, now that you have compromised my virtue, you'll have to marry me, of course. To save my reputation from being ruined," she added. "There is no alternative."

"She's right, Zander," Sheriff Mankewicz said. "You'll have to do the honorable thing and marry the lady."

"The hell I will. Belle, explain to the sheriff how you brought a book—"

Belle fluttered her lashes at him. "Oh, Cal, you know there was more to it than that. You made improper advances. You know you did. You took advantage of me."

"I did no such thing, and you know it."

"It's your word against mine," she purred. "Isn't that right, Sheriff? He took advantage of me, and…" She dabbed at her eyes with a lace handkerchief. "and now he has to do right by me. Tell him, Sheriff."

Sheriff Mankewicz looked like a cornered rabbit.

"I don't believe this," Cal muttered.

"Oh, Cal honey, now that you have, well, forced my hand so to speak, I just know you will do the honorable thing and marry me."

The sheriff looked from Cal to Belle and patted his sidearm. "Glad to hear it, folks. Always best to resolve things peaceable-like." He backed out the cabin door and disappeared into the night.

This was like a bad dream. A nightmare.

In stony silence he escorted Belle back to the boardinghouse, while she twittered and giggled and kept trying to capture his hand. Finally, he managed to get her up onto the porch, pushed her through the screen door into the parlor, and escaped.

His head pounded as if someone had scrubbed his brain up and down across a tin washboard. What the heck had happened? He hadn't *accosted* Belle Fontaine, and she knew it. He'd felt decidedly uneasy about even letting her inside his cabin, much less listen to her read a poem to him.

It was obvious she had planned this whole thing. She set him up, got the sheriff to wait outside so she could trap him into marrying her. He could hardly believe a respectable woman would go to such lengths.

Suddenly he stopped walking. *Belle Fontaine is not a respectable woman.*

Oh, Lord, he felt as if he'd just woken up from a bizarre nightmare. He reversed direction and stumbled off to the Shady Lady Saloon for a stiff shot of whiskey.

Chapter Thirty

Leah rose early the next morning and left the boardinghouse before breakfast, anxious to get to the mercantile. Mrs. Swerdlow insisted she have at least a piece of toast and some strawberry jam, which Leah ate as she walked down the street.

She found Mr. Nanetti carting bushel baskets of ripe tomatoes and sweet corn out to the front of the store. "Why not let Cal do all that lifting, Mr. Nanetti?"

"Ah, Mister Cal, he go talk to sheriff this morning."

"The sheriff! Why? Have we had a robbery?"

"No, not robbery. Mister Cal not say why he go see sheriff, but he look very bad this morning. Very worry."

Worried? Now that Cal had Johnny's $700, what did he have to be worried about? Still, she couldn't help but be concerned, and to keep her mind off it she kept herself extra-busy all morning straightening shelves and polishing the Crawley twins' fingerprints off the candy jars.

By noon Cal still had not returned, and now both she and Mr. Nanetti were worried. It wasn't like Cal to fail to appear and help out at the mercantile. He'd done so every day since he'd arrived in Maple Shade.

"Did he say anything at all before he went to see the sheriff?" Leah asked.

Mr. Nanetti shook his head. "Only thing I notice was his shirt."

"His shirt? What about his shirt?"

"Was same shirt he wear yesterday, but all rumpled. Look like he sleep in it. That not like him."

Leah caught her breath. Even on their trip to Idaho, Cal had worn the same shirt day after day, but it had never looked rumpled. Something was wrong.

But what?

By late afternoon Cal still had not shown up, and Leah left the mercantile and walked quickly across the street to Sheriff Mankewicz's office. When she stepped through the doorway, the short, paunchy man removed his boots from his paper-strewn desk and jerked to attention.

"Why, Miss Leah, it isn't often you come to see the sheriff. What's on your mind?"

"Callahan Zander is on my mind," she said evenly. "I understand he paid you a visit this morning."

"He did at that, Miss Leah. He surely did."

"Cal did not show up at the mercantile today to help out as he always does. Mr. Nanetti and I are wondering if anything is wrong."

The sheriff cleared his throat. "Nuthin' *wrong* exactly. Just…" He cleared his throat again. "…difficult."

Leah's breath caught. "*What* is difficult?"

"Well, maybe not difficult so much, I guess, as embarrassing." He scratched his chin. "Yeah, that's it, embarrassing."

"Yes?" Leah waited. Morgan Mankewicz was an honest man and a good sheriff, but he wasn't too bright. She watched his gaze move from the coffee cup on his desk to the wall of Wanted posters and then to the front window.

"Well, lookee there. Miz Crawley and them rambunctious twins of hers are peekin' in the window of the mercantile."

"Morgan?" she reminded. "About Cal Zander?"

"Oh. Well, seems he's got himself into a little pickle, and he stopped in to talk it over."

Leah folded her arms across her body and tried to keep her voice even. "What sort of little pickle?"

"Uh, well, I guess it's a *big* pickle, now you mention it. Yessir, our preacher's got himself into a great big pickle."

"Cal's been cheating at poker, is that it? I knew it. I just knew—"

"Hold on a minute, Miss Leah. Cal hasn't done anything wrong. Well, not exactly. I mean, nothin', uh, criminal."

Leah's temples began to pound. "Is he here in your jail?"

The sheriff blinked. "In jail? Now why would I clap a man in jail just for bein' in a pickle?"

Leah gritted her teeth so hard her jaw hurt. "For heaven's sake, Morgan, what pickle has Cal gotten into?"

Again, the sheriff cleared his throat, then slurped down a gulp from the coffee mug on his desk. "Well, now, I don't feel right tellin' you 'bout it, Miss Leah. It's kinda private-like. You better ask Cal."

"I would do that, Morgan, but I don't know where Cal is. He's not at his cabin, and he hasn't shown up at the mercantile all day."

"Might try the church," Mankewicz said. "Could be he's up there sayin' some prayers."

Leah stared at him. *Prayers!* Something must be

dreadfully wrong if Morgan wouldn't talk about it and Cal was praying. All right, she would look for Cal at the church.

But first she would go back to the boardinghouse and lie down with a cool cloth on her forehead. "Thank you, Sheriff."

"Sure thing, Miss Leah. Tell Cal I'm prayin' for him, too."

She reached Mrs. Swerdlow's just as the landlady was serving supper. It smelled so enticing she decided to forego the cool cloth for a bowl of thick potato soup and some coleslaw.

"I'd about given you up, Leah," Mrs. Swerdlow said. "It isn't often you miss supper, but I figured something came up at the mercantile."

"Yes," she murmured. "Something did come up." She slid gratefully into her place at the table and nodded at Martha and Sally. Belle was missing. That wasn't like Belle, Leah thought. In all the years Leah had lived at the boardinghouse, Belle had never missed a meal or afternoon tea or anything that had to do with eating. It was a wonder she didn't weigh two-hundred pounds.

"Where is Belle?" she asked.

"Up in her bedroom," Martha volunteered. "She said she wanted to make an entrance."

"Belle always makes an entrance," Sally said pointedly. "Even at church on Sunday."

Mrs. Swerdlow ladled soup into Leah's china bowl. "Well, if she doesn't hurry up with her *entrance,* she's going to miss supper. Soup's getting cold."

"And I'm due at the Shady Lady in an hour," Sally added. "I don't sing well on an empty stomach."

Mrs. Swerdlow took her place at the head of the

table, and just as she lifted her spoon, Belle floated across the parlor and into the dining room.

"Ladies," she announced dramatically, "You will never guess what?" Belle seated herself and fluffed out her skirt.

"What?" Martha and Sally said together.

"I'm guessing you have a new dress of some kind," the landlady remarked blandly.

"How very perceptive of you, Mrs. Swerdlow," Belle trilled. "You are not far off the mark because I most definitely *will* be getting a new dress, one that will be specially made just for me."

"I thought all your dresses were specially made just for you," Sally observed. "You keep the dressmaker working late most nights."

"Oh," Belle said, "this dress will be really and truly extraordinary."

"Why?" Sally asked in a dry tone.

Belle sent her a beaming smile. "Because," she said dramatically, "it will be a wedding dress! I am engaged to be married!"

Four spoons clunked into four bowls of potato soup. All at once Leah put two and two together. Oh, no, surely not. It wasn't possible. It was just not possible. Was it?

Was it?

Suddenly she felt sick inside. She listened to Belle prattle on and on, drawing out the suspense, reveling in being the center of attention, and all at once she wanted to scream.

"Well, tell us who you're engaged to," Sally said.

Belle waited, and then, just when Sally opened her mouth again, Belle dropped a name into the expectant silence.

"I am engaged to Cal Zander."

Now Leah thought she really *would* scream.

It was the longest supper hour she had ever endured at the boardinghouse, and only Mrs. Swerdlow's excellent potato soup and a dessert of apple pie warm from the oven kept her from bolting for the front door to find Cal. Maybe he'd left town. But upon reflection she knew he wouldn't do that. Cal Zander might be a lot of things, things Leah tried hard to dislike, but he was not a coward.

Finally, she excused herself from the table and made a beeline for the front porch. She stumbled down the walkway to the street, then gathered up her skirt and began to run.

Out of breath, she reached the church where she instinctively knew she would find Cal Zander.

Chapter Thirty-One

Cal saw her coming, moving purposefully with her dark head down, her hands clenched at her sides. He moved to meet her, and when she saw him, she stopped short. Her face looked pale and determined.

"Leah." He reached her in two strides.

"Cal, what have you done? Whatever are you thinking?"

"I'm trying *not* to think," he said heavily.

She shook her head. "You don't care for Belle Fontaine. You don't even like her."

He sighed. "And I don't want to marry her!"

"Then why—? Belle made a big blathery fuss about it at supper. By tomorrow the whole town will know."

He couldn't help the groan that escaped. Leah sent him a long, assessing look and then waited patiently while he explained how Belle had trapped him. When he finished, she said nothing for a very long time, and then she touched his arm.

"You cannot marry her, Cal."

"I don't see how I can avoid it," he said heavily. "She set it up so she could claim I ruined her, that I had compromised her. And a man doesn't walk away from a woman who's been ruined."

"Even if it's all a lie?"

"Belle's going to make damn sure the whole town thinks it's not a lie, that I really have ruined her. I figure

I don't have a choice."

"But it's still a lie, Cal. It's not honest."

"I know it, and you know it. But Leah, it's her word against mine."

She spun away from him, then quickly turned back. "You preach about honesty. How can you even think about doing this and live with yourself?"

"I don't know, Leah. I honestly don't know."

She propped both hands on her hips and her eyes narrowed. "But you *must* think about it, and think about it before it's too late." Her voice was hard. Accusing. He shut his eyes. Guess he deserved that.

"Leah—"

"Oh, don't say anything, Cal. It will just make me cry." She gave a little half-laugh. "I don't know which of you I want to kill more, you or Belle."

"Belle," he grated. "And I'll help you."

****

That night at the Shady Lady, Cal found himself unable to concentrate long enough to win even a single hand of five-card stud. Finally, he caught Sally Flannigan's eye and joined her at the bar where she sat sipping her usual mug of apple cider. Cal ordered a double shot of whiskey from the bartender and sat in silence, turning the glass around and around on the polished bar top.

Sally peered at him. "Cal, I just watched you lose four hands of poker in a row, and that's not like you. I can't help asking what's wrong."

He downed a big swallow of his whiskey, then another, and told her. When he finished talking, she signaled the bartender, pointed at his empty glass, and bent her head close to his.

"I already guessed it was about Belle," she said. "The Irish have a saying, Cal. 'Don't look under a rock if you're afraid of spiders.' "

He barked out a laugh. "I've seen what's under the rock, Sally. I just don't know what to do about it."

She reached out a manicured hand to pat his arm. "You're a smart man, Cal. You'll figure it out."

He had just opened his mouth to reply when the saloon doors banged open and Florio Nanetti stumbled in. After a frantic look around, he spied Cal at the bar and tramped across the floor, a gaggle of children clinging to each hand.

Something was wrong. Cal stood up. "Florio! What are you doing here?"

The man was gasping for breath. "Ah, Mister Cal, you help, please. My Nina, she makes labor all day with new baby, but…something not right and doctor not home. Wife say he go to Portland. Cal, what I do?"

Sally began detaching the children's hands from their father's and moving them toward the door. "Please," Florio called after her, "take children to Miss Leah."

Cal stopped her. "Sally, is there a doctor in Gillette Springs?"

"Yes. Doc Polonsky. Ask at the Riverfront Hotel."

Cal turned toward Florio. "I'll ride for the doctor in Gillette Springs. You stay with Nina. I'm going over to the livery for my horse."

"A-all right."

"Sally, ask Mrs. Swerdlow if she could go over to the Nanetti's and help." He clapped Florio's thin shoulder and bolted for the door.

Leah and Mrs. Swerdlow heard the commotion on

the front porch at the same instant and stared at each other across a bowl of peeled apples. "Now what?" the landlady muttered. She followed Leah through the screen door.

"Sally!" Leah exclaimed. "And…Sonia and Sofia and the twins. Whatever are you all doing here at this hour?"

"I'm delivering the Nanetti children here," Sally said. "Their mother is home delivering another one. Cal's gone for the doctor in Gillette Springs, but Mrs. Nanetti could use your help, Mrs. Swerdlow. Men are no help at a time like this."

Without a word, the older woman untied her apron and started off down the walkway. "Leah, make those young'uns some hot cocoa," she called. "And bed them down in the parlor."

Leah herded the five Nanetti children into the kitchen while Sally raced upstairs for blankets and quilts.

"Is Mama sick?" Sonia asked, her voice clogged with tears.

"No," her sister answered. "Mama's making a new baby."

"How come we can't watch?" the oldest boy, Tommy, wondered.

"Aw, you wouldn't like it," Sofia, replied loftily. "It gets all messy."

Leah stirred up the fire in the stove and set a saucepan of cocoa over the flames. "Sally, see if Belle is awake. Maybe she could help."

Sally snorted. "Are you crazy? Help with what? Belle's too squeamish to be any help to Mrs. Nanetti, and she's too addlepated to be trusted around children. She could warm the cocoa, but I've never seen her come within five feet of the stove."

"You're right," Leah murmured. She sent Sally a quick look. "You know, don't you Sally? About Cal and Belle?"

"Yes. He told me all about it. I could kill her."

Little Joseph cocked his head. "Who're ya gonna kill, Miss?"

"Never you mind, *macushlah*."

"What's *macushlah* mean?"

Sally bent down to his level. "*Macushlah* means 'dear one.' "

"Yuck," he spluttered. "I don't want to be anybody's 'dear one.' Just my mama's," he added as an afterthought.

Leah filled five china mugs and sat all the children down at the dining table. While they slurped their cocoa, she helped Sally make up bedrolls on the soft carpet in the parlor. When they finished, they stood together in the kitchen and watched the Nanetti children grow droopy-eyed and quiet and finally curl up in their blankets and go to sleep.

"Amazing, isn't it?" Leah murmured.

Sally pressed her arm. "All life is amazing," she said. "Sometimes it's just more amazing than others."

****

Leah chased Sally's words around and around in her head until early morning, when she finally climbed the stairs to her bedroom and crawled under her quilt. Life was certainly unexpected. And difficult, so much more difficult than she had ever imagined when she left Ohio. Lately she had begun to feel downright uneasy about her life here in Maple Shade.

She had been content until Cal Zander had dropped

into her life, bringing news about her brother, about knowing him in prison. The suspicion still lingered that it was the $700 Johnny owed him that brought Cal to her aid, but now she had to admit she felt sorry for him because Belle had snared him into a marriage he didn't want.

A loud thumping and the sound of children's laughter brought her fully awake. Mrs. Swerdlow must be back! If the landlady had returned, surely there would be some news about Nina? The landlady must be dead tired, but someone had to make breakfast for the five Nanetti children. She tossed back the quilt and hurriedly splashed water onto her face, combed her hair and twisted it into a single thick braid, then donned her blue denim work skirt and a blue shirtwaist.

Halfway down the stairs she met Mrs. Swerdlow. The woman's face was gray with fatigue, and her shoulders drooped in a way Leah had never seen before.

"Mrs. Swerdlow, is everything all right?"

The older woman gave her a weak smile. "Oh, everything is fine if you don't count an exhausted mother and seven children."

"*Seven?* I thought there were only—"

"Seven," Mrs. Swerdlow said decisively. "Mrs. Nanetti has produced another set of twins. I've been up all night, and now I'm going to get some sleep." She plodded on past her and up the stairs.

Twins! Seven children and three sets of twins. Oh, poor Nina. And poor Mr. Nanetti, having to provide for such a large brood. She flew on down the stairs to the dining room where all five children sat meekly waiting to be fed. From the kitchen came the spit and fizzle of frying bacon and the smell of fresh coffee.

"Oh, Sally, you should have woke me up so I could help you make—" She broke off as Cal Zander turned from the stove, an oversized fork in his hand.

"Cal! Whatever are you doing here? Where's Sally?"

"Asleep upstairs, I guess. I'm making biscuits and bacon. Want some?"

He looked as exhausted as Mrs. Swerdlow, his eyes dull and his uncombed dark hair flopping into his eyes. "Cal, have you been up all night?"

"Well, yeah. I brought Doc Polonsky from Gillette Springs, but he, uh, when he got here he needed some help, and Florio was so unstrung he wasn't very coherent, so I…" He turned back to the stove and forked over a slice of bacon. "You could pull the biscuits out of the oven, Leah. Dump them into that bowl." He tipped his chin toward a blue ceramic bowl on the table.

"How is Nina?"

"Nina is just fine. Florio, on the other hand, is another story."

"And how are *you*, Cal?"

He chuckled. "You mean after getting engaged against my will and helping to deliver twins? Also, against my will," he added. "I'm in better shape than Florio," he said with a laugh, "but I'm dead tired."

Leah moved toward him and lifted the fork out of his hand. "Go home, Cal. Get some sleep. I will finish breakfast."

He nodded and started for the parlor.

"Where ya goin', Cal?" one of the twins asked.

"Home."

Sonia looked up from the butter dish. "Is Mama better?"

"Yeah," Tommy said. "Do we got a brother?"

"Yep." Cal ruffled the boy's dark hair.

"Aw fudge," Sofia said. "I asked God for a sister!"

Cal gave her a tired smile. "Well, God must have heard you, because that's what you've got, a sister."

The girl's big brown eyes widened. "But you said—"

Sonia bounced out of her chair. "*I* know! It's twins! We got a sister *and* a brother!"

Leah filled a platter with crisp bacon slices and set it on the table. "Eat your breakfast, now. Then you can go home and see the new twins. Cal, you should eat something, too."

"Thanks, Leah, but I'm too played out to eat anything. I'll get some coffee later."

She watched him push through the screen door and move onto the front porch. It seemed to her he wasn't too steady on his feet.

She went back to stirring the eggs she'd cracked in the skillet and tried to ignore the queer little dart of something warm and unsettling in her chest.

Chapter Thirty-Two

Leah had the mercantile all to herself that day, with no sign of either Mr. Nanetti or Cal. She spent the morning sweeping the boardwalk in front of the store, then wrestled baskets of ripe tomatoes and green beans and apricots to the front, straightened the aisle displays of skillets and kettles, measured out lengths of percale and cotton gingham, and manned the cash register.

Customers had to load their own heavy sacks of flour and sugar, and when the Crawley twins descended on the candy counter, Leah doled out lemon drops and caramels and then wiped the fingerprints off the glass jars while Ellen Crawley relayed the latest town gossip. Which, she thought with relief, was *not* about Belle and Cal. Late in the afternoon Mr. Nanetti staggered in, looking bleary-eyed but beaming with pride.

"Is twins!" he exulted. "Boy and girl together."

"Congratulations, Mr. Nanetti. And give Nina a hug for me."

"Ah, I can do. Should give hug to Mr. Cal, too. Without him, doctor not manage two babies."

She certainly would *not* give Cal a hug. Shaking his hand was as close as she would allow herself to get. But she *had* felt like giving him a hug this morning when she discovered him frying bacon in Mrs. Swerdlow's kitchen.

By closing time she was tired, but just when Mr.

222

Nanetti stepped forward to lock the front door, the bell jangled and an out-of-breath Belle burst in.

"Is Leah here?" she panted.

"Yah, back in store room."

"No," Leah countered from the ladies hat aisle. "I'm finished in there. What can I do for you, Belle?"

"I need your advice."

Leah blinked. "*My* advice?" Belle Fontaine had never asked the advice of anyone, much less her. "Advice about what?"

"About my wedding dress, of course," Belle huffed. "I'm on my way to the dressmaker, and I...well, I thought two heads would be better than one."

Again Leah blinked. *Two heads?* Since when had Belle consulted with anyone about her wardrobe, or anything else? "Isn't the dressmaker's shop closed at this hour?"

"Oh, no," Belle said with obvious relish. "This afternoon Mrs. Stanek is staying open late just for me."

"Go on, Miss Leah," Mr. Nanetti urged. "You go help your friend. I can lock up."

"Please, Leah," Belle pleaded. "I need your advice."

Leah studied her for a long moment, and suddenly the light dawned. Belle wanted her advice like she wanted a pair of rubber galoshes. What Belle *really* wanted was to needle her about Cal, to brag because Cal wanted Belle and not her. She wasn't fooled for one second. And then a wicked imp wriggled into her brain. Very well. If Belle could manipulate her, she could manipulate right back.

"What time does Mrs. Stanek close her shop?"

Now it was Belle's turn to blink. "Why, in just a few minutes, I think."

Leah smiled. "Then we'd better hurry, hadn't we?" She lifted her shawl from the shelf behind the cash register.

Belle suddenly came to life. "Um...well, yes!"

The minute the mercantile door closed behind them, Belle began to chatter. "I've always wanted an elegant white wedding gown, one with a long train."

Leah shot her an incredulous look. "But nobody in Maple Shade gets married wearing such a—"

"And I want to wear a long veil, all the way to the floor."

Leah reached out, caught Belle's arm, and pulled her to a halt. "Belle, Maple Shade is a small town, and it's not a very prosperous town. No girl in the entire county can afford a fancy dress with a long veil!"

"Of course I know that! What is your point, Leah?"

She looked straight into Belle's green eyes. "My point is that such a...a sumptuous wedding dress would be really unusual here in Maple—"

"Exactly!" Belle clapped her hands. "I want every other girl in town to be pea-green with envy."

"But Belle—"

"Oh, look, there's Mrs. Stanek just getting ready to lock up her shop. Yoo-hoo, Mrs. Stanek!"

The slim, stylish dressmaker looked up. "Oh, Miss Fontaine. I was just closing up."

"Stop!" Belle ordered. "I'm getting married, and I want—"

Leah laid a restraining hand on her arm. "Belle..."

Mrs. Stanek sighed. "Miss Fontaine, you are not the only young woman in town who is planning a wedding."

"But...but I am far more—"

"Belle!" Leah cut her off with a firm squeeze on her

arm. "You should really take your time in selecting an appropriate dress pattern, not make such an important decision in a hurry."

The dressmaker sent her a grateful look. "Leah is right. I will be open at ten o'clock tomorrow morning, and I'm sure—"

Belle frowned. "Oh, but I—"

"Ten o'clock," Mrs. Stanek repeated.

"Belle," Leah interjected. "Haste makes waste."

"Oh, pooh, Leah. You're no—"

"Fun?" Leah supplied. "So you have often reminded me. But really, Belle, now is not a convenient time for either Mrs. Stanek or for me."

"Well, why not?" Belle's voice was almost a whine.

"Because," Leah said quietly, "both Mrs. Stanek and I have been working all day long, and we are tired. Too tired to be much help to you in making a decision about the pattern for your wedding dress."

Mrs. Stanek sent her another grateful look, finished locking the door to her shop, and dropped the key into her reticule. "Tomorrow," she repeated firmly. "Ten o'clock."

Leah resisted an impulse to applaud the woman and pulled Belle around to face in the opposite direction. "Mrs. Swerdlow will be serving supper soon. We shouldn't be late."

To Leah's amusement, Belle stamped her foot. Nevertheless, she allowed herself to be propelled down the street to the boardinghouse, which they reached just in time for supper.

****

"Mister Cal," Florio Nanetti said the next morning. "Why you look so…like world is ending?"

Cal plunked a ten-pound sack of brown sugar for Mrs. Dalrymple down on the counter and stared at it without raising his eyes.

"I will guess, okay?" Florio said. "You see babies born and is frighten you, is right?"

"Wrong, Florio," Cal said heavily. "It takes more than a screaming woman to frighten me."

"What it take?" his employer pursued. "Run-off horse? Robber at bank? What?"

Cal would give anything if it was a bank robber or a runaway horse. Anything other than Belle Fontaine. He sent a surreptitious glance down the nearest aisle, looking for Leah, then stepped closer to the mercantile owner.

Before he could say a word, Florio grabbed his shirt front. "Ah, is a woman!" the proprietor whispered. "I can tell by tired look."

"Yeah," Cal said heavily.

"Ah," Florio said again. "I know all about women."

Cal laughed. "That's a pretty tall tale coming from a man who's fathered seven children with the same wife."

"Ah, well. Is true, but my Nina, she tells me much about women."

He tried to suppress a groan, but the thought of Belle Fontaine brought one anyway. "Florio, when you married Nina, did you feel…well, trapped?"

Florio glanced up sharply. "Trapped? No, when I marry my Nina I feel lucky. Ver' lucky."

Cal groaned again. "Lucky," he murmured. At the moment, he felt more like he was cursed.

Florio studied him. "For you, wrong woman, maybe. That make you frown, eh?"

Cal nodded. *Wrong woman* was an understatement.

All at once he couldn't think about it one more minute. "I'll load this sugar into Mrs. Dalrymple's wagon out front." He hefted the sack onto his shoulder and strode out the front door just as Leah was coming in.

"Cal," she said. "Good morning."

"Morning," he mumbled. He twisted sideways so the bag of sugar wouldn't hit her and edged past.

"Would you have time for—?" she called.

"Later," he called. "But yes to whatever it is." He loaded the sugar into Mrs. Dalrymple's splintery farm wagon, helped her up onto the driver's bench, and watched her pick up the reins. When she rattled off down the street he stood looking after her, wishing with every fiber of his being he was any place on earth but within the sound of Belle Fontaine's voice.

He sensed someone at his elbow and tensed without turning around. Couldn't be Belle, he thought. Some instinct told him Belle Fontaine wouldn't be up and about this early. He turned to find Leah beside him, and relief made him suck in a breath.

"I'm going down to the Lark and Peahen to get coffee for Mr. Nanetti," she said quietly. "Would you like to join me?"

He didn't answer, just took her elbow and turned her toward the restaurant. Then he surreptitiously studied the face of the young woman walking at his side. When he'd first ridden into town, he remembered Leah had been sitting on the front porch of Mrs. Swerdlow's boardinghouse, and he recalled how struck he'd been by the calm expression in her penetrating blue eyes.

He was still struck by Leah Rydell. He'd seen her exhausted after a long day's ride through the mountains and elated when her rock-baked biscuits turned out halfway edible. He'd watched her help old Mrs. Bentinck try on new hats at the mercantile and polish the candy jars after the Crawley twins got their sticky paw prints all over the glass. And he'd seen her white-faced and tear-ravaged when Johnny died.

But he had never seen Leah as studiedly calm as she looked this morning. He'd give twenty silver dollars to know what was going on in that steady, sensible mind of hers.

Leah was a good friend, he acknowledged. Maybe she really didn't like him very much, but she still treated him with forthright honesty, and she always said exactly what she thought. Leah didn't put on airs, and she didn't play games. He sighed and tightened his hand on her arm.

At the restaurant he guided her to a table by the front window, but he was surprised when she pointed to a table near the back.

"Why?" he murmured.

"Belle is visiting the dressmaker this morning," she explained. "I don't want her to see me because I don't want to talk to her."

"Me neither," he said with a chuckle.

The next minute Leah surprised him again. She leaned across the table and asked, "How are you bearing up?"

"I'm not," he answered shortly.

"Me neither," she said.

That surprised him for the third time in the last four minutes. Then he remembered Leah was often surprising.

The waitress, who looked scarcely older than Nina Nanetti's oldest girl, danced up with her pad and pencil.

"What can I get you, Mr. Zander?"

"Coffee, please." He looked across the table. "Leah?"

"Coffee for me. And a mason jar refill for Mr. Nanetti at the mercantile." The girl slapped her pad into an apron pocket and glided away.

"Cal, let's talk about *bearing up*."

Cal groaned. "I'm not sure I am bearing up, Leah. Part of me wants to climb on my horse and ride straight back to Texas."

The waitress returned and set two cups of coffee before them, gave Cal a lingering look, and retreated. Leah stirred lots of cream into her cup, then looked up at him with that unperturbable expression she often wore when waiting for something.

"And the other part?" she asked, her voice quiet.

"Oh, God, Leah, I can't just run off. That's a coward's way out."

"So the other alternative is to stay in Maple Shade and—"

"Face the consequences."

She sipped her coffee. "It's too bad the consequences include marrying Belle Fontaine."

He groaned. "Yeah."

"Look, Cal. You have seven hundred dollars in the Maple Shade Bank. What were you planning to do with it?"

"Don't laugh, but I'd thought about buying a farm. A cherry orchard, in fact. You know, maybe farm cherries!"

She gave him a steady, clear-eyed look, poured more cream in her coffee, and then smiled. "Actually, I think that is an excellent idea."

He choked on a swallow of coffee. "You do?"

"Yes, I do. Seven hundred dollars will buy a lot of land."

"A cherry orchard, in fact," he said with a laugh. "There's an orchard for sale out on—"

"Holohan Road," she supplied. "Yes, I know."

He stared at her, unable to think of a single thing to say.

She sent him a smile. "I have only one question, Cal."

"Yeah? What's that?"

She smiled and picked up her coffee cup. "What are you waiting for?"

"Hot damn, Leah, are you serious?"

She plunked her cup down on the saucer with a sharp click. "Of course I'm serious. Cherries are…important," she said with a soft laugh.

Cal shot out of his chair, leaned over, and planted a kiss on her cheek.

"Oh!" When she jerked, he couldn't resist kissing her other cheek.

"Come on, Leah. Florio must be desperate for his coffee."

Out of the corner of his eye he noticed the young waitress watching them and smiling.

Chapter Thirty-Three

On Sunday evening a week later, Mrs. Swerdlow stepped out onto the porch and announced that she had again invited Cal to supper at the boardinghouse. "Mr. Zander gave such an inspiring sermon at church this morning," the landlady said, "and he looked so exhausted I decided he deserved a good home-cooked meal."

Belle, sipping tea in the porch swing, sat up straighter and brightened. "Why, that's wonderful news, Mrs. Swerdlow. Cal's been so busy of late I've scarcely had a minute alone with him."

Mrs. Swerdlow sniffed. "Well, my girl, he's not coming to supper just to see *you*. There are three more ladies who take meals at my table." She turned on her heel and yanked open the screen door. "Sally and Leah are busy helping me in the kitchen," she said pointedly.

"What about Martha?"

"Martha is at the schoolhouse," Mrs. Swerdlow returned, "preparing her lessons for tomorrow. And..." She paused significantly. "My blue-flowered Sunday plates and silverware need to be set out on the dining table."

"Oh, very well," Belle said with a sigh. She fluffed out the ruffles on her skirt and reluctantly got to her feet.

In the kitchen, Leah gave a final stir to the gravy and watched Belle clatter plates onto the lace-covered table, then slap down knives and forks in haphazard fashion.

Sally slid a pan of biscuits into the hot oven and untied her gingham apron. "I hear Martha on the porch," she murmured. "Wonder where Cal is? I know he cooks for himself in that little cabin in back of the mercantile, so he's not likely to be late for a good meal."

At six o'clock, when Cal still hadn't shown up, Mrs. Swerdlow sighed, called everyone to supper, and set a platter of fried chicken on the table. Sally dumped the biscuits into a ceramic bowl, and Leah set out a bowl of mashed potatoes and the gravy boat.

Martha dropped an armload of books and papers onto the settee in the parlor and flew into the dining room. "I'm not late, am I? I was drawing a map of Africa for my geography lesson tomorrow and lost track of time."

"You're just in time," Mrs. Swerdlow assured her. "Come. Sit."

Sally and Leah slid onto chairs across from Martha, and Mrs. Swerdlow took her place at the head of the table. At the last minute Belle sauntered in to join them, patting her springy blonde curls. "Why, where's Cal?" she exclaimed.

"Maybe he forgot," Maratha said primly.

"Oh, he wouldn't forget," Belle replied. "Especially not now that we're engaged."

Martha rolled her eyes and picked up her fork. Just as the landlady finished passing the gravy boat, heavy footsteps sounded on the porch and Cal called a hello through the screen door. Belle flew to let him in.

"Sorry I'm late, Mrs. Swerdlow. I…had to finish up some business in town."

"Sit yourself down," the landlady invited, pointing

to the opposite end of the table. "I was just passing the biscuits."

Cal nodded at Martha and Sally, sent Leah the ghost of a smile, and sat down in the only empty chair.

Belle sat on his left. "What sort of business?" she inquired.

He spent what seemed to Leah like an unusually long time unfolding his napkin. "I was, uh, buying some property."

"Oooh!" Belle trilled. "A house? Where is it? Is it big and—?"

"No, not a house. Well, there *is* a house, but mostly it's, um, land."

Belle frowned. "Land? What do you mean, *land*?"

"I mean…" He shot a quick look at Leah. "I've bought a farm."

Belle gasped. "A farm!"

Leah resisted an impulse to applaud.

"Actually," Cal continued, helping himself to a biscuit, "it's an orchard. A cherry orchard. And there's an old farmhouse on the property."

Belle stared at him. "A farmhouse? You mean it's outside town? On a…" She shuddered. "…a *farm*?"

"That's usually where a farmhouse is," Martha said in a crisp voice. Sally caught Leah's eye and sent her a grin.

"How big a farmhouse, Cal?" Sally asked.

"Uh, well, it's got two bedrooms downstairs and four, no five, upstairs. Hasn't been lived in since old Mr. Strader died, so it's pretty rundown."

"Rundown," Belle echoed.

"Naturally," Mrs. Swerdlow said, handing the platter of chicken to Cal. "A farmhouse that's been left unoccupied would need a real thorough cleaning."

"And," Sally interjected, "all the windows will need washing, and the floors—"

"Will certainly need to be thoroughly scrubbed," the landlady added. "With hot water and lots of strong lye soap."

"But…" Belle faltered. "But it's outside of town!"

"Of course," Martha snapped. "It's a *farmhouse*. On a *farm*."

Sally gave Belle a long look. "Don't worry, Belle, we'll all help you do the cleaning. Won't we, ladies?"

"After it's all spiffed up," Mrs. Swerdlow said, "it's just a matter of maintaining it. You know, mopping once a week and—"

"Mopping! Once a—"

The landlady tightened her lips. "Well, of course, my girl. You don't think a house keeps itself clean, do you? You have no idea how many hours I spend on my hands and knees every single week."

Belle's usually rosy cheeks paled. "How far out of town is this house, Cal?"

"Oh, I'd say a couple of miles. Not more than five, probably."

"Oh."

Leah noted that Belle's voice had grown very small in the last few minutes. Part of her was amused. But another part couldn't help feeling sorry for her. Sally, on the other hand, was having a hard time looking serious.

Cal sent Belle a steady look. "The orchard is beautiful, Belle. The cherry trees are in fine shape, and the neighboring farmers assured me that the harvest increases every year. This year's cherries should bring in a good income."

"You...you mean you expect me to live there? So far from town? What about all my friends, and my dressmaker, and...?" Her voice trailed off.

"Oh, I'm sure your friends will come out to visit," Martha said. "And you can serve tea and cookies every afternoon, just like we do here at Mrs. Swerdlow's."

"Of course," Mrs. Swerdlow said evenly. "As the hostess, of course, you'll have to brew the tea and bake the cookies. Do have another piece of chicken, Cal." She pushed the platter toward him.

"Cal," Sally said slowly, "I think you have made an extremely wise investment. Of course it will mean very hard work every summer when the cherries come on."

"I thought I might buy a few cows, too," Cal said quietly. "I could sell butter and cream at the mercantile. Maybe even get a few chickens and sell eggs, too."

"Chickens!" Belle exclaimed.

"Oh, chickens are no problem," Mrs. Swerdlow said, ladling gravy over her mashed potatoes. "You just toss out a handful of chicken scratch at dawn every morning and mind the rooster doesn't peck you when you gather the eggs."

"Just think of the angel food cakes you can bake with all those egg whites," Sally said. "And the yolks are excellent added to sauces. My mam used to swear by hollandaise sauce made with extra egg yolks."

Leah choked on a bite of biscuit. She knew for a fact that Sally's mother had lived during the potato famine in Ireland. Fat chance she would have come within ten miles of a hollandaise sauce when her family was starving.

Cal grew more and more animated about his cherry orchard, while Belle grew quieter and quieter. Through the remainder of the meal, Leah resolved she would say nothing more, and she tried hard not to meet Cal's eyes.

Later, as she stood in the kitchen washing up the dishes with Sally, she thought only Shakespeare could come up with a fitting end to the scene at supper. "Sally, could you possibly imagine that Mrs. Swerdlow's dessert tonight would turn out to be fresh-baked cherry pie! Mrs. Swerdlow couldn't possibly have known about Cal's cherry orchard, could she?"

Sally, who stood drying a platter, rolled her eyes. "Not unless you believe in leprechauns with a wicked sense of humor," she said with a giggle.

The two women didn't stop laughing until the last plate was dried and put away in the china cabinet.

****

"Miss Leah, you come see babies tonight," Mr. Nanetti urged the next morning. "My Nina, she make special supper, lots of sauce with ripe tomatoes from garden. You come, please?"

Leah looked into the eager brown eyes of her employer and smiled. She would rather be *anywhere* than the boardinghouse for supper tonight, listening to another of Belle's tirades about Cal and his cherry orchard. It was all she could do to keep from slapping the petulant look off Belle's face, and if she had to listen to one more of her rapturous descriptions of her "elegant lace wedding gown," Leah thought she might dump the bowl of potato salad in her lap.

"Thank you, Mr. Nanetti. I will come early to help Nina in the kitchen."

He grasped her hand and pumped it up and down. "Good! But need not help in kitchen. Mister Cal will be there."

"But surely not in the kitchen. So I will come and—"

Mr. Nanetti beamed. "Yes, in kitchen! He come every night."

"But Sofia and Sonia are there to help out, aren't they?"

Her employer nodded. "Ah, yes, my girls very helping. But Mister Cal, he is learn to cook, and my Nina teach him."

Leah gaped at him. "Cal is learning to cook? But *why?*"

"For survival, he say. New wife will not learn fast enough."

"His new wife will not learn at all," she murmured. Oh, poor Cal. He has certainly gotten the short end of the stick. She turned away and busied herself straightening the shelf of boys' shirts and socks which were awry after young Lewis Christie and his three brothers had pawed through them. She also didn't want Mr. Nanetti to see the unexpected tears that stung into her eyes. Cal might be a great many things she disapproved of, but he didn't deserve to be saddled with Belle Fontaine for the rest of his life.

Mr. Nanetti shooed her out of the store early, insisting he would sweep up and lock the door, so she drew her blue crocheted shawl over her shoulders and headed over to the Nanetti's big two-story house on Spruce Street.

The house always looked so friendly and inviting, with two porch swings on the wraparound veranda and two trellises of pink climbing roses scenting the air. Halfway up the walkway, a tumble of Nanetti children spilled down the porch steps.

Sonia reached her first. "Oh, Miss Leah, come and see our new baby sister!"

"And brother," five-year-old Matteo added.

"Yeah," his twin brother added. "He's lots cuter than any old *sister*."

"He is not," Sonia retorted. "They both look exactly the same."

"Don't neither," dark-haired Matteo insisted.

"Oh, for heaven's sake," Sonia retorted, trying hard to sound superior. "It's only when they grow up that a boy baby looks different than a girl baby! Isn't that so, Miss Leah?"

Leah tried hard not to laugh. Short of giving both youngsters an anatomy lesson, she decided to keep her opinion to herself. "I would love to see both the new babies," she said. Whereupon Matteo and Sonia each grabbed one of her hands and tugged her up onto the porch and through the open screen door into the house.

"My, something smells simply delicious!" she exclaimed.

Matteo's twin brother, Tommy, met them in the parlor. "Oh, yeah, that's Cal cookin' something."

"Miss Leah wants to see the babies," Sonia reminded. She led Leah through the parlor into a second parlor, a sort of sitting room, with rose-flowered wallpaper and two burgundy velvet settees flanked by dark wood end tables. Nina Nanetti sat in a handsome wooden rocking chair, each of her outstretched hands pushing the cradle on either side of her. Sofia sat at her feet.

"Oh, Leah," Nina cried, "come see my new little ones!"

Sonia and the two boys conducted her on tiptoe to

first one cradle and then the other, where two tiny identical infants slumbered under two small knitted quilts. "That's Frank," Matteo pointed out, tipping his head toward one blanket-swathed baby. "And that other one is Francine."

"Our new baby sister," Sonia said with a poke at Matteo's shoulder.

"Oh," Leah breathed. A fringe of dark hair framed each little pink-and-white face, and it seemed to her that both babies were breathing in and out in unison. A long-ago picture floated into her memory, and Leah's heart squeezed unexpectedly. Her own brother, Johnny, had once looked as tiny and defenseless as these new little ones. She remembered her first sight of him, lying bundled up in just such a cradle with Mama rocking away beside him. She would never forget that.

"Oh, Nina, they are both just beautiful. You must be so proud!"

Mrs. Nanetti laughed. "Is Florio who is proud. I am only tired!"

"Yeah," Tommy cried. "Our little brother cries all night and Mama has to get up and feed him, and just when everybody goes back to sleep, then our sister starts in."

"Francine cries louder than Frank," Sonia announced.

"Well," Leah said, "maybe that's because girls are stronger than boys, so they make more noise."

Nina's laughter drowned out the boys' objections, and Leah had to smile. Johnny had quite a lusty yell, she remembered. A dart of pain stabbed into her chest.

"Leah, please come sit beside me for a minute. Sonia, Sofia, you go help Mister Cal in the kitchen.

Tommy and Matteo, go find your brother Joseph and wash up for supper."

The children scampered off, and Leah sat herself down on the cushioned chair beside Nina. "Florio comes late," the Italian woman said. "Is true that the babies cry and keep us awake at night. But Florio most of all. He sits with me while they nurse, and then he not go back to sleep. Is good he have you to help out at the mercantile."

Leah nodded. Every single morning since the twins had been born, Mr. Nanetti had looked exhausted. "I am glad to help, Nina. I care about you and Florio."

"And Mister Cal," Nina added. "He grow very tired, too. Now he owns big orchard and tries also to help Florio at the mercantile."

"Yes, I have noticed that Cal has been tired lately. I care about him, too."

"Ah." Nina brought her rocking chair to a halt. "You care *about* Cal? Does that mean you care *for* him? As a man?"

Leah stared at her. "Well, no. Caring *about* someone is not the same as caring *for* someone."

Nina laughed softly. "Dear Leah, you are right. I was wondering only if you knew the difference."

"Why, yes, I—" She broke off and gave Nina's face a closer look. Of course, she knew the difference between caring *about* a man and caring *for* him. And Nina knew it! She watched Mrs. Nanetti's smile slowly spread across her round face and resisted the impulse to protest.

She caught her breath. Yes, she *did* care about Cal. And yes, she had to reluctantly admit, she also cared *for* Cal. Nina Nanetti had seen it long before she herself had become aware of her feelings.

But now what? Now Belle Fontaine had hooked her sharp claws into Cal Zander. Leah had learned too late what she really felt for him. Or…she met Nina's sharp black eyes and sat up straighter.

Or *was* it too late?

The screen door flapped shut, and a chorus of voices greeted Florio Nanetti's return. "Papa, we're having fettuccini for supper," Matteo announced. "And Cal's making it!"

Sofia threw her arms around her father's solid form and nuzzled her cheek against his shirt. "Papa, Cal helped me slice up the cucumbers from our garden. And—"

Sonia interrupted her. "She kept eating all the cucumbers!"

"Shhhhh." Sofia put a finger to her lips. "You'll wake the babies."

Mr. Nanetti appeared in the sitting room, gazed down at the infant twins in their cradles, and bent to kiss his wife. A twinge of something niggled under Leah's breastbone. But this time it wasn't because Florio Nanetti's children obviously loved him, and Nina loved Florio. This time it was because…because…

Suddenly she realized *she* wanted to be loved, too.

At that moment Cal stepped into the room, an oversized wooden spoon in one hand. "Supper's ready." He caught Leah's eye and grinned.

All at once she couldn't breathe.

Chapter Thirty-Four

Cal Zander looked so wonderfully out of character standing there in that checked gingham apron with a smudge of flour smeared across one cheek, Leah knew she would never again see him as a Sunday-morning preacher. Or as the man who had taught her to fire a revolver and how to bake biscuits on a hot rock. From this moment forward, Cal Zander would always be the tall, lean man wearing Nina Nanetti's red gingham apron.

She wanted to laugh. And then suddenly she wanted to throw her arms around him. Life was full of such strange ironies! First it was finding her long-absent brother only to lose him in death. And then, in a cruel twist of fate, watching Cal become engaged to Belle Fontaine, only to unexpectedly discover how she herself really felt about him. Her throat began to ache.

Nina stepped past her and pointed into the kitchen. "Cal, now I show you how to dress salad. You slice up cucumbers?"

"Sonia sliced them," he said. He turned back to the kitchen, and Leah found herself following him. She watched in surprise as he paused at the stove to stir a large kettle of something that smelled so delicious her stomach rumbled, then moved to the sideboard where a wooden bowl of lettuce and tomatoes and cucumbers sat.

"To make dressing," Nina instructed, "you need

good olive oil from Italy and some of my special wine vinegar."

Cal scanned the shelf above the sink and selected a tin container of olive oil and a tall, slender bottle of something red and splashy.

"Now," Nina added, "you mix in some sprigs of parsley and fresh chives from the garden and then beat together fast, like whipping cream."

"I've never whipped cream," Cal said with a chuckle.

"Use fork," Nina advised. "And try not to splatter."

Fascinated, Leah watched Callahan Zander bite his lower lip and flail a fork through the oil and vinegar in a small ceramic bowl. He was doing a creditable job when he suddenly stopped and bent to slide a cherry pie out of the oven.

Well! Cal was certainly proving to be a man of hidden talents. Unusual talents that even included baking a pie. What next? A laugh bubbled out of her mouth.

He stopped stirring the salad dressing and glanced up. "What's so funny?"

"You are. Next thing we know you'll be heading off to be a chef at Delmonico's in New York."

"Nah," he growled. "I never liked big cities. I think I'll stay here in Nina's kitchen and learn how to make ravioli. And then spaghetti with meatballs."

"Keep stirring," Nina called. "Then pour dressing over lettuce and cucumbers and mix up. Girls, did you set extra plate for Miss Leah?"

"Yes, Mama," Sonia and Sofia said together.

"Then go call your papa and the boys to supper. Leah, you help Cal serve the supper, please? I am sit down now and rest. Teaching to cook is harder than tending to new babies!"

Mr. Nanetti and the three boys tramped into the dining room, and there was a general scramble for chairs around the long table. "I wanna sit next to Miss Leah," Sonia announced.

"No," Sofia yelled, "I get to sit next to her."

"Hold it!" Cal called. "That place is reserved for me." He dumped the contents of the kettle onto a large china platter and set it on the table, and Sofia placed the wooden salad bowl beside it. Then Cal pulled a loaf of fragrant-smelling bread from the oven and wrapped it in a clean dishtowel.

Leah stared at him. "My goodness, Cal, you can bake bread, too?"

He sent her an enigmatic smile and motioned for her to take one of the two remaining empty chairs. When everyone was seated, Cal untied his red gingham apron, hung it up on the hook by the stove, and slid into place beside Leah.

"Well done," she murmured. "It smells simply wonderful."

"You haven't tasted it yet," he replied. "Might be you won't like fettuccini."

"Of course I will like it, Cal," she whispered. "It's heartening to know you're not going to starve out there on your cherry farm."

"Yeah, maybe I'm not going to starve. It was good advice you gave me, Leah, about buying that orchard."

"Yes," she said quietly. "I thought it might be."

Cal gave her a long look, then bent his head to listen as Florio recited grace. While the Italian man mentioned the numerous blessings of the Nanetti household, Cal mentally reviewed his own. First was the cabin Florio

Nanetti had offered him when he first rode into Maple Shade, plus his job helping out at the mercantile. Then there was the $700 he'd used to purchase his cherry orchard, the same $700 he'd won playing poker with Johnny Rydell.

Another blessing was his growing congregation at the Maple Shade community church, and the good feeling he got every Sunday after speaking to them about some of the truths he'd figured out over the years. It felt good to reach out to people, good to share the things he'd learned.

But, Lord, right up at the top of the blessing list is Leah Rydell. From the moment he laid eyes on her, sitting on the boardinghouse porch that first afternoon when he'd ridden into town, he'd half-way regretted his decision to search her out and wait for her brother Johnny to find her. He knew the boy would eventually learn of Leah's whereabouts. In prison, Johnny Rydell had talked constantly about how he had resolved to come out West and find her when he was released.

Cal had finally located Leah living in Maple Shade, and now he had to admit he was sorry he'd used her as bait. But only half-way sorry. When they had ridden to Idaho to see Johnny, Cal had gotten to know Leah Rydell. He liked her. A lot. In fact, he liked Leah Rydell so much it scared him. Leah had changed him. He'd gone from living his life as a confirmed bachelor, a wanderer who never wanted to settle down with any woman, to…what?

Now Leah was sitting next to him at the Nanetti's supper table. She was so close he could reach out and touch her, and she was speaking to him in her usual calm, forthright way.

He groaned inwardly. Now he was hogtied to Belle Fontaine, and that would keep him away from Leah for the rest of his life. Over the last few weeks, he'd felt himself slowly ripping apart inside.

Then, in the middle of her second helping of his fettuccini, Leah unwittingly tossed him a lifeline. When she looked at him, as she was now, her eyes seemed to be telling him things she would never say out loud.

Florio was going on and on about the sermon Cal had given in church last Sunday. The subject had been forgiveness, something that apparently touched the older man's heart.

"Is hard when people do bad things," Florio was saying. "But all the time, every day, people make mistakes. Big mistakes. Little mistakes. Is hard to say it doesn't matter. Is hard to forgive."

Cal felt Leah stiffen, her body going rigid, her back straightening as if a poker was glued to her spine. She was never going to forgive him for getting tangled up with Belle Fontaine. No doubt she thought he was being hypocritical for choosing forgiveness as the topic for his Sunday morning sermon.

He risked a quick look at her face. She was studying the plate of fettuccini before her, her mouth set in an unsmiling line. Cal's heart sank. He'd mucked up his life for sure. This was worse than being sent to prison years ago.

"Papa?" Sonia asked. "Does what you say mean you're gonna forgive me?"

"Forgive you for what?" her father asked.

"For…" The girl hesitated. "For fighting with Sofia."

Florio's dark eyebrows went up. "Fighting? About

246

what, fighting?"

Sonia studied her father's face. "About, uh, about which one of us was gonna get to help Cal slice up the cucumbers."

"Well," their father asked with a chuckle, "who won this fight?"

"I did," Sonia admitted. "I got to slice up all the cucumbers."

"Then don't you think maybe is Sofia, not me, who must forgive you?"

A thick silence fell. At last Florio cleared his throat. "What was it you say on Sunday, Mister Cal? About being sorry?"

Cal tried not to look at Leah. "I, uh, I said that someone who asks for forgiveness should be genuinely sorry for whatever they had done."

Leah suddenly put her fork down, laid her napkin on the table, and stood up. "I'm sorry Nina, Mr. Nanetti, I…I find I have developed a terrible headache. I'm afraid I must go home."

"What, now?" Nina asked. "You leave in middle of Cal's supper?"

Cal jolted to his feet. "I'll walk you over to the boardinghouse."

"But you haven't finished your supper," Leah protested. "Besides, it's only a few blocks."

He folded his napkin and took Leah's arm. "Nina, thank you for the cooking lesson. And kids…" He looked over at the Nanetti children. "Thanks for your help in the kitchen. Florio, I'll see you in the morning. Gotta get ready for all those apricots coming in from Alma Meyberg tomorrow."

"All right, Mister Cal. I be there early in morning."

Nina and Cal both laughed at that. "Nah, you won't, Florio," Cal joked. "You'll be up half the night and you'll be exhausted come morning. Leah and I will manage."

He turned toward Leah. "Come on, Leah. Get your shawl."

It was only a short walk from the Nanetti's house to her boardinghouse, and she started out at a fairly fast clip. After half a block, Cal reached out and stopped her. "Slow down," he said with a tug on her arm. "You don't really have a headache, do you?"

"No, I—"

"You just don't want to think about forgiveness, do you?"

She just looked at him.

"You can't forgive me for finding you out here in Oregon and then waiting for your brother to contact you," he said. "With my seven hundred dollars," he added.

She said nothing, just looked up at him, her mouth twisting.

"Or maybe you can't forgive me for making you ride for hours and feeding you dry biscuits and bad coffee."

At that, she gave a soft laugh. "Your biscuits weren't dry, Cal. *My* biscuits were dry."

"Yeah," he murmured. "Come on, Leah, you gonna tell me what's put a burr under your saddle?"

"No, I—Oh, Cal, it's not you I can't forgive. It's Belle."

He stopped in his tracks. "What?"

"I said I can't for—"

He pulled her around to face him. "You mean you're not angry about—"

"About Belle? Well, yes I am. Actually, I am seething. I'm so upset about it I can't sleep at night."

"Yeah," he said heavily. "Me, too. To be honest, Leah, I don't know what I'm going to do."

"In that case, I have a suggestion, Cal. Why don't you move out to your farm and harvest your cherries?"

"What's that going to accomplish besides flooding Florio's mercantile with bushels of ripe cherries?"

Leah released an exasperated sigh. "It will give you something to do besides kick yourself for getting into the fix you're in. And," she added, "Mr. Nanetti needs ripe cherries."

"Oh, God, Leah, I always thought you were a sensible woman. Surely you don't think this idiotic situation with Belle can be solved with…with cherries?"

"Yes," she said, her voice calm. "I do. When your boat feels like it might sink…" They moved past a rambling white house with pale pink roses growing along the front fence.

Cal reached out and plucked one. "Yeah? What do you do when your boat really *is* sinking?"

"What do you do?" She gave him a long look. "What you do is pray to God and row toward shore."

He laughed and presented her with the rose. "I'm rowing, Leah. God knows I've never rowed so hard in my life."

"And I'm praying," she replied with a catch in her voice.

He stopped dead. "For me? You're praying for me?"

"Yes. Every night."

"Oh, dear God, Leah, why? What do you care if I marry Belle Fontaine or not?"

She was quiet for a long minute, and he pulled her

249

to a stop. "Leah?"

She looked everywhere but at him. Finally, he placed his forefinger under her chin and tipped her face up. "Leah?"

When she met his gaze her eyes looked shiny. "Oh, don't ask me, Cal. I just want you to know that I'm on your side."

He stared at her. "Really? You're on my side? Hell's bells, Leah, I thought you didn't like me!"

She swallowed and drew in a long breath of the warm, honeysuckle-scanted air. "I thought so, too."

"What changed?"

She hesitated. "You do a lot of things I don't like, Cal. Your Sunday sermons, for instance. For a long time, I thought you were being, well, hypocritical. But…but when Johnny died, something happened. You were s-so kind, and it h-helped me get through the awful parts when I felt I was coming unraveled at the seams. That's why I—"

Without thinking, he folded her into his arms. "Crawled into my bed that night," he finished. "That really raised Jason Halliday's eyebrows."

"Oh, my, I don't know what you must have thought of me," she said against his chest. "I was just so awfully glad you were there because m-my heart was breaking."

He let out a long, uneven breath. "And now it's *my* heart that's breaking. Man, that's ironic, isn't it?"

Unexpectedly, she laughed softly. "It's not just *your* heart, Cal."

He set her apart from him and looked into her eyes. "What did you say?"

"I-I said it's not just *your* heart that is breaking. And—"

He stopped her words with his lips, and when he felt her body begin to tremble, he pulled her closer and deepened his kiss. He felt like the top of his head was exploding, and a sweet, hot yearning flowed through him. He'd known all along how he felt about Leah, ever since the first time he'd laid eyes on her, sitting on Mrs. Swerdlow's front porch that stifling hot afternoon, looking at him with that calm, challenging expression.

And now, with her face buried against his shoulder, he knew that he cared deeply for Leah Rydell. Even worse, she cared for him.

He set her apart from him and wrenched his thoughts back to reality. "Leah…"

"I know, Cal. We have no right to be doing this."

"Maybe you're right," he breathed. "Now it's worse than before, isn't it? Now I'm in hell, and I don't know how to escape."

"Don't talk about it, Cal," she said quietly. "Just kiss me again."

He did so, gently settling his mouth over hers and holding her close for a long moment. When he felt her tears wash against his chin he forced himself to pull away.

"Dammit, Leah, don't cry. For God's sake, don't cry."

"All-all right." She swiped one hand across her cheek, sniffled, and gently kissed his cheek.

At that moment he thought his heart was going to split in two.

Chapter Thirty-Five

After the first unbroken night's sleep she'd had in weeks, Leah woke to the sound of sparrows twittering outside her open bedroom window and realized with a start she was late for work at the mercantile. She jerked upright and was about to set her feet on the rag rug beside her bed when she heard Belle's voice outside her bedroom door.

"Leah? Leah, are you awake?"

Leah groaned. What could her housemate possibly want at this hour? She stumbled to the door and cracked it open. "Yes, Belle, what is it?"

"I want you to go to the dressmaker's shop with me this morning."

Leah blinked. "This morning? Belle, you know I can't do that. I have to work at the mercantile. Mr. Nanetti expects me."

"Well, yes, I know that. But I need you to help me choose the pattern for my wedding dr—"

Leah swung her bedroom door partway open. "Belle, you're not listening. Why not ask Sally to help you. She doesn't go to work until evening."

Belle's lower lip came out in a much-practiced pout. "Sally refused to come with me."

"She did? Why?"

Belle swallowed. "Oh. Well, she said she was, um, too busy."

Ah. Leah suspected it wasn't so much that Sally was "too busy." It was more that Sally simply wasn't interested in Belle's wedding. If she was honest, *she* wasn't interested, either. If she were *really* being honest, Belle's wedding with Cal Zander was the very last thing she would ever be interested in.

She took a long look at her housemate's smug face. "Belle, you don't really want to marry Cal, do you?"

"Oh, but I do, Leah. Really, I do."

"And move out to his cherry farm?"

Belle's smile faltered. Well, actually, I plan to talk him out of moving to that farm of his."

Leah gritted her teeth. "Why on earth would you do that? Cal had his heart set on owning that farm."

"Well, I don't want him to own it. That farm is outside of town, and I'll be all alone out there, and—"

"But you wouldn't be alone, Belle. Cal would be there."

Belle's face fell. "Oh, well, yes, I suppose that's true."

That did it. Leah leveled a long look at her housemate. "You *suppose* so?" She yanked her bedroom door open wider, noting with satisfaction the sudden expression of alarm that crossed Belle's face.

"*You suppose so*? Belle, you don't marry a man you only *suppose* you want to make a life with. You marry a man because you care about him! Because you would do anything to spend your life with him!"

Belle looked taken aback, but it lasted all of 60 seconds before she twitched her ruffled skirt and smiled. "Very well, I will ask Martha to help me choose a wedding dress pattern. I want it to be simply *sumptuous!*"

Leah found she was shaking with rage. Belle didn't care a fig about Cal Zander's happiness. But *she* did! She cared very much about Cal's happiness. She couldn't stand Belle's prattling on about her wedding dress for one more minute.

"I'm sorry, Belle, I must get dressed and go to work." She shut the door in her housemate's startled face and heard her footsteps stomp down the staircase. Poor Martha. The minute she came home from school, Belle would pounce on her.

She skipped breakfast and sped down the street to the mercantile where she found Cal wrestling a bushel basket of ripe peaches out in front of the store. He gave her a long look. "Overslept, huh?"

She felt her face grow warm. "Well, yes, I did. I must have been more tired than I realized."

"Me, too. Best night's sleep I've had in weeks. I got here just when Florio arrived, and he's kept me busy ever since." He tipped his head toward the array of fruit baskets.

Leah stepped past him and entered the store to find Mr. Nanetti wiping fingerprints off the candy jars. "Missus Crawley here early," he explained. "Every time that lady come in, I want to hide candy jars."

Leah laughed. "I'm sorry I'm late and that you had to polish the candy jars, Mr. Nanetti. I overslept."

"Mercantile open late this morning," her employer said. "Mister Cal not even wake up until I knock on his door."

She caught her breath. Cal said he had overslept, too. Could it have been because…because of last night?

"Is all right," her employer said. "You bring me big cup of coffee from Lark and Peahen. And take Mister Cal with you. He not have breakfast this morning." He made shooing motions with his hands. "Go! Bring coffee!"

Cal stepped up and took her arm. "You heard the boss, Leah. Let's do what he says."

Neither of them uttered a word on the short walk to the restaurant, but over coffee and two orders of cinnamon toast, Leah told him about her confrontation with Belle that morning.

"I've got a bigger problem," Cal said.

"Oh? What about?"

"About my cherry orchard. Yesterday I hired young Lewis Christie and two of his friends to pick my cherries. It's a bumper crop this year, and they're dead ripe, so if they don't get harvested, they'll just rot on the trees. I'm pretty desperate because I promised nine bushels to old Mr. Petrini in Gillette Springs."

"What does Mr. Petrini want with nine bushels of cherries?"

"Florio says he makes some kind of spirits with them. Cordial, I think he called it."

Leah brushed a toast crumb off her shirtwaist. "I could help you pick cherries."

His dark eyebrows rose. "You? No, Leah. Picking cherries is back-breaking work. Besides, what about Florio and the mercantile?"

"I think Mr. Nanetti would let me leave early to help you out." She started to pick up her coffee cup, but he reached across the table to stay her hand. "Leah…Leah, I can't let you do that."

"Oh, yes you can, Cal. Just swallow your male pride and accept my help."

For a moment Cal's throat was so tight he couldn't speak.

"However," she added with a soft laugh, "I am *not* volunteering to get your farmhouse ready for you and Belle to move into."

"Oh, God." He sighed. "I'd forgotten about the farmhouse. Do you think Belle knows anything about housekeeping?"

A laugh burbled out of her throat. "She knows as much about housekeeping as I know about picking cherries."

They finished their toast and started back to the mercantile with Florio's jar of hot coffee. Just as they reached the store, Belle Fontaine flew out the front door.

"Well!" Belle's green eyes blazed as she advanced on Leah. "So you were too busy this morning to come to the dressmaker with me? And now I find you dallying with my fiancé!"

Cal stepped in front of her. "Now hold on a minute, Belle. We—"

Belle glared at him. "Oh, hush up, Cal!"

Cal blinked. "What?"

Belle ignored him and turned accusing eyes on Leah. "My wedding gown is very important, Leah. Right now, it's the most important thing in my life."

Leah sucked in her breath. "It seems to me your wedding gown is more important than the man you want to marry."

"Well," Belle huffed, "it *is* important! My wedding day is the most significant day of my entire existence."

Leah laid her hand on Belle's arm. "Just listen to yourself, Belle. It isn't just *your* wedding day. It's Cal's wedding day, too."

"I know that," Belle said. "And I know Cal wants me to look beauti—"

Cal grabbed Belle's shoulders and gave her a little shake. "Hush up, Belle! I don't give a damn about a fancy dress. In fact, I don't give a damn about this wedding at all."

"Oh, Cal, honey, you're just havin' pre-wedding jitters."

He stared at her for a full minute, then tightened his grasp on her shoulders and set her aside. "Come on, Leah. Florio's coffee is getting cold." He stepped past Belle, then reached for Leah's arm and gave it a little tug.

"Belle, I'll see you tonight after work," he said over his shoulder. "And it's not going to be pretty."

Belle gasped. The last thing Leah heard as she and Cal moved past her was a barely suppressed theatrical sniffle.

"Oh, Cal," Leah whispered as they walked into the mercantile. "She will never forgive you for that."

"You think so?" he asked, his voice hard.

"Yes, I do. You need to think about what you're doing. Belle can be…unforgiving."

"Yeah," he muttered. "I'm counting on it."

****

The afternoon dragged by slower than honey dripping out of a beehive on a day in December. Cal organized the storeroom and then reorganized it. Leah kept busy rearranging the bolts of fabric and ribbons and ladies hats on all seven shelves on three aisles. Finally, *finally*, Mr. Nanetti locked the front door, and Leah sped back to Mrs. Swerdlow's boardinghouse to wait for whatever was going to happen that night between Cal and Belle.

She could scarcely sit still during the landlady's excellent chicken soup and blackberry cobbler. Belle, however, leisurely sipped her soup and ate a goodly portion of cobbler with no apparent anxiety at all.

Leah's nerves were strung up tight as a telegraph wire. Sally, Martha, and Mrs. Swerdlow lingered over their coffee for so long she thought she would scream.

At last, supper was over. She and Sally rattled through the dishes while Martha spread out her school papers on the dining table, and Mrs. Swerdlow settled in the parlor and took up her needlepoint. Belle drifted out to the front porch to wait for Cal; Leah could hear the creak of the swing as she rocked back and forth.

She scrubbed through the last of the soup bowls until Sally leaned over and flapped her dishtowel. "What's the rush?" she intoned.

"Cal's coming over," she whispered.

"How do you know that?" the Irishwoman murmured. "Did Belle invite him?"

"Not exactly."

Sally stopped Leah's scrubbing arm. "Leah, what's going on?"

"I don't really know. There's some difficulty between Cal and Belle, and I can't wait for him to show up."

Sally gave her a long look and then smiled. "Well, then slow down, *macushlah*. From here we can hear everything that happens on the front porch, so we don't want to finish the dishes too soon, do we?"

Leah swallowed a chuckle. "Mercy, no." She glanced at Martha in the dining room, her head bent over her papers.

"I can hear you two," the schoolteacher called. "This evening is beginning to sound *very* interesting."

Suddenly Sally froze. "Hush! I hear the front gate."

She snatched the dishrag out of Leah's hand and slapped it down on the sideboard. "We're finished," she whispered.

Martha's head jerked up. "Quick!" She slipped out of her chair and tiptoed into the parlor, followed by Sally and Leah. Mrs. Swerdlow glanced up at them and frowned.

"What—?"

"Shhh!" Sally put her finger to her lips, then pointed to the front porch, where footsteps sounded on the steps. "Cal," she mouthed.

Instantly Martha dropped to the floor, and on hands and knees crept to the front door and silently propped it wide open with her geography book. Then she settled back on the carpet and wrapped her arms around her knees.

Sally tiptoed over to the settee, followed by Leah. Mrs. Swerdlow sent them a conspiratorial look, bent toward the front door, and turned her good ear toward the porch.

Scarcely daring to breathe, the four women leaned forward to listen.

Chapter Thirty-Six

Cal took a deep breath of the warm evening air and tramped up the porch steps of Mrs. Swerdlow's boardinghouse. Belle was waiting for him in the porch swing, and she carefully swept her ruffly skirt to one side and sent him a smile.

"Why, good evening, Cal," she murmured.

Cal cleared his throat. "Hello, Belle."

"I was hoping you would drop by tonight. It's such a lovely evening, isn't it?"

His response was a brief grunt.

"I have the most wonderful surprise for you, Cal. Something I found just this afternoon."

"Yeah?" he said warily. "What's that?"

She pushed the swing into motion with the toe of her shoe. "Why don't you sit down here beside me..." She patted the seat. "...and I'll tell you all about it."

The swing creaked as he sat down, and all at once he noticed there were no other chairs on the porch, just the swing, with Belle perched invitingly on the seat. "Okay, what's this surprise?"

She edged closer to him, but he shifted away. "The surprise?" he reminded dryly.

"Oh. Well, I found it this afternoon, on my way home from visiting the dressmaker. It's the cutest little house over on Poplar Lane. You know, old Mrs. Cowgill's house, that white one she used to live in."

"What about it?"

"Weell…" She drew out the word and paused significantly.

"Yeah? What about Mrs. Cowgill's house?"

"Mrs. Cowgill has moved to Idaho to be with her son, so her house is for sale. Isn't that wonderful?"

Cal tightened his lips, and there was a long pause. "No," he said quietly. "It's not wonderful."

Belle clutched his arm. "But don't you see? That means I-I mean we—don't have to move out to your farm. We could live here in town."

"I don't want to live in town, Belle. I own a farm now, and a big cherry orchard. There's a farmhouse on the property, and I plan to live there."

There was a long silence. And then Belle breathed a very subdued "Oh."

Cal went on, his voice deliberate. "I expect my wife to be a partner, to cook and keep house and maybe help with the cherry harvest if we're short-handed."

Another almost inaudible "Oh" from Belle.

All at once Cal became aware of another sound, a quick intake of breath, but it was not from Belle. He listened intently for a long minute, but all he heard was the twittering of an evening sparrow and the creak of the porch swing.

Then he heard it again. It was the sound of an indrawn breath and a softly whispered word, and it came from inside the house.

What the—?

Belle scooted closer. "But Cal, honey…what if I, um, don't know anything about keeping house or washing clothes or cooking?"

He reached over and patted her hand. "You're a

smart woman, Belle. I'm sure you can learn."

This time the sucked-in breath definitely came from inside the house, most likely from the parlor just inside the screen door. Someone was listening.

Suddenly he saw the humor of the situation, the bride-to-be wheedling to get her way and the groom who was avoiding being wheedled. Then Belle let her head drift onto his shoulder, and she began to unbutton his shirt sleeve. "Cal, honey, don't let's argue about things. After all, they're not really important, don't you see?"

Cal cleared his throat. "What *is* important to you, Belle? Living in town? Being taken care of? Having your meals cooked and your sheets washed and your petticoats ironed by someone else?"

Her busy fingers kept turning back his cuff and smoothing the exposed skin of his forearm. "Well," she said, her voice silky, "there are other important things in a marriage, don't you think? More…intimate things between a man and a woman."

"Look, Belle, let's be honest with each other. You tricked me into agreeing to marry you. I bet you never thought there'd be a price to pay."

"Price?" The smoothing stopped. "Whatever do you mean?"

He brushed her hand off his arm. "Think about it, Belle. I want a wife who is more than a bedmate."

"Oh, Cal, I could make it very pleasant for you. Very…" She reached for his arm. "…exciting. Don't you want that, Cal?"

Again he lifted her hand away and began rolling down his shirtsleeve. "Any man would want it. But there's more to a marriage than that. This isn't New Orleans, Belle. This is Maple Shade, Oregon. And I own a cherry orchard outside town. Seems to me you might have some thinking to do about that."

"Well!" Belle huffed. "I can see you are in an extremely negative mood tonight. Perhaps we should continue this conversation tomorrow evening, when you're feeling more approachable." She jolted out of the swing and stalked toward the front door. Just before she yanked the screen open, Cal heard a hurried scrambling from the dark interior of the parlor.

When the screen flapped shut, Cal closed his eyes and shoved the swing into motion. He'd laid it out as plainly as he could, but Belle wasn't having it. She'd roped and hogtied him, and to loosen her grip it would take more than his cherry orchard and his farmhouse and his expectations of a wife. He closed his eyes and groaned.

After a few minutes he heard the swish of the screen door, but he kept his eyes shut, hoping whoever it was would go away and leave him alone.

A full minute passed, then two, but no one said anything. Curious, he peeked through one eye-lid to see Mrs. Swerdlow set a tray down on the seat next to him. On the tray sat a bowl of blackberry cobbler, a mug of coffee, and a shot glass full of what he guessed was whiskey.

Without a word the landlady tiptoed back into the house.

He downed the whiskey in one gulp, closed his eyes again, and leaned his head back against the cushion. God bless Mrs. Swerdlow. *And Lord, if You're not too busy, please help me figure out how to get out of marrying Belle Fontaine.*

Chapter Thirty-Seven

The next morning, just as Cal was planning how best to use Lewis Christie and his two chums for the day's cherry picking, Verna Christie flew into the mercantile, wringing her hands. Cal dropped the sack of flour he was carrying onto the counter.

"Mrs. Christie, what can I do for you today?"

"You can forgive me for something," the gaunt woman puffed.

"Forgive you for what?"

"For letting my son Lewis go gallivanting off with those two rapscallions he calls friends. I know they was s'posed to pick cherries for you today, Mr. Zander, but Lewis ain't up to it. He's home in bed with a bellyache from eatin' too many green apples off Tad Dalrymple's tree."

Cal bit back a groan. "Guess you need some stomach powder for your son," he said heavily.

"Oh my, no. I got plenty of that at home. I'm just real sorry my boy's left you in the lurch." She bustled out the door just as Leah and Florio walked in. Leah quickly disappeared down the garden tool aisle.

Florio raised his bushy dark eyebrows. "What Missus Christie want so early?"

"She came to tell me that her son and his two chums aren't gonna help me pick cherries today."

"Ah. Mister Petrini, he not get his cherries for to

make his cordial, eh?"

"I dunno, Florio. The cherries are dead ripe, and I told Petrini he'd have nine bushels first thing tomorrow morning. A bargain's a bargain, so I guess I'll have to pick those cherries myself."

Florio's thick eyebrows waggled. "By yourself? You gonna fill nine bushel baskets with cherries all by yourself?"

"Yes, I am. Might take me until midnight, but Mr. Petrini's gonna get his cherries."

"Maybe my boys Matteo and Tommy can help?"

"Thanks, Florio, but they're too little to climb up and down those tall ladders. Guess I'd better get out there and get busy."

Leah stepped out from behind a display of flower seeds. "I'll help you, Cal."

"No, Leah. Thanks, but—"

"Why not? And don't you dare tell me I'm too little to climb up a ladder!"

Cal stared into Leah's calm, steady blue eyes for a long minute. Did nothing seem insurmountable to this woman? She hadn't been intimidated by that robber they'd run into on the trail, so he guessed a ten-foot ladder wasn't going to intimidate her, either. She was already pulling one of Florio's denim aprons over her head and tying the narrow straps around her waist.

"Leah, you have a job here, helping Florio at the mercantile. You don't want—"

"Oh, yes, I do want."

"Oh, yes, she does want," Florio said at the same time. "And Matteo and Tommy will help also. They could not climb up on ladder maybe, but could fill bushel baskets on ground. Cal, you go get wagon while I find

Miss Leah some overshoes."

"Overshoes!" Leah exclaimed. "What do I want with overshoes? It isn't muddy in your orchard, is it, Cal?"

Before he could answer, Florio held up a cautionary finger. "Miss Leah, you will need to cover up those funny shoes you wear, all wobbly with poked-up heels."

Cal laughed all the way to the livery stable to get the wagon. When he pulled the horse to a stop in front of the mercantile, Leah was waiting, wearing jeans and a boy's plaid shirt, with a pair of rubber overshoes in her hand. A stack of empty bushel baskets sat beside her.

On the way out of town they stopped at the Nanetti's house to pick up his two young sons, then rattled the five miles out of town to Cal's farm. The two boys giggled and chattered, but Leah didn't say a word until he pulled the wagon into the cherry orchard.

She stared up into the nearest fruit-laden tree. "Oh, how beautiful they are! And they're just loaded with cherries!" She scrambled down from the driver's bench and bent to pull on the overshoes.

The two boys tumbled out of the wagon bed and raced off into the orchard. Leah looked after them, then straightened and propped her hands on her hips. "All right, Cal. Show me how to pick cherries."

****

By two o'clock that afternoon Leah was more exhausted than she'd ever been in her life, and there were still dozens of unpicked cherry trees. Cal had Matteo and Tommy drag the filled bushel baskets into the shade under the newly stripped trees, which allowed Cal and Leah to stop and catch their breath until they started filling another container.

At six that evening they stopped to gobble down the sandwiches Nina Nanetti had sent. Leah didn't know whether she was alive or dead, but she forced herself to eat. Then she stretched out flat on the bare ground and let her eyelids drift closed. Her back ached. Her arms and shoulders ached. And her hands, stained crimson from ripe cherry juice, felt hot and throbbed all the way to the ends of her pinkie fingers.

When they finished the sandwiches, the ordeal began again. Cal worked steadily, climbing the tall ladder, twisting the ripe cherries off the leafy branches, then moving to another location. He steadfastly refused to let Leah climb the ladder, insisting that her overshoes made her too clumsy-footed to be safe.

They ended up picking in tandem, Cal working high over her head, dropping handfuls of ripe cherries into the sack tied around his waist, then climbing down and dumping them into the waiting basket. Leah worked at ground level, ignoring the sifting of dust and bits of leaf from Cal's activity over her head. When he moved the ladder to an unpicked tree, she moved with him. Matteo and Tommy dragged every basket they filled into the shade.

By eight o'clock, it was growing too dark to see. The two Nanetti boys had stopped talking altogether, and Leah struggled to keep going. Finally, it was so dark she couldn't tell if the cluster of cherries in her hand was ripe or not, and Cal climbed down off his ladder for the last time.

"That's enough, Leah. We've filled nine bushels for Mr. Petrini. We can quit now."

Numb with fatigue, she nodded and watched as he hefted the overflowing baskets into the wagon bed, then lifted the two boys in as well. He helped a shaky Leah up onto the driver's bench, climbed up beside her, and picked up the reins.

"Mrs. Swerdlow always saves some supper for me when I work late at the mercantile," she said. "She won't mind if you stay for something to eat at the boardinghouse."

"Thanks, Leah. I'm so bushed I don't think I could even light the stove in my cabin to make coffee."

When they reached town, he carried the two drowsy boys into Florio's house, then drove to the mercantile and parked the loaded wagon where Mr. Petrini had arranged to pick up his cherries in the morning. Then he and Leah stumbled off to the boardinghouse.

They were so exhausted and hungry when they walked through the gate they scarcely paid any attention to what was happening on the front porch.

"Sally!" Belle was screaming. "You take that back!"

Cal shut the gate and started up the walk with Leah behind him. At the sight of them, Belle gasped and leaped to her feet.

"My heaven's sake, Cal, whatever has happened to you? You're covered in…is that blood?"

"It's not blood, Belle," he said wearily. "It's cherry juice."

Sally stood up slowly. "And Leah, you are absolutely filthy!"

"I'm not surprised," Leah said tiredly. "I've been picking cherries."

"Picking cherries!" Sally gasped. "Whatever for?"

"To help me out, Sally," Cal said quietly. "For Mr. Petrini and his cherry cordial."

Sally pulled the screen door open so they could enter

the house, and as Leah passed, Belle yanked her skirt aside. In the parlor, Martha looked up from the papers spread over the dining room table, and Mrs. Swerdlow dropped her needlepoint into her lap.

"My gracious sakes, you two must be famished! I've been waiting for you ever since Florio Nanetti came by to say you'd be late. And hungry," she added. The landlady bustled into the kitchen and Martha gathered up her school papers.

Cal and Leah sank onto dining chairs and stared at each other.

The screen door swished open, and Sally stepped in to retrieve plates from the china cabinet and set them on the table. Then she moved into the kitchen to help Mrs. Swerdlow.

Belle tiptoed in and sat down beside Cal. "Cal, honey, surely you don't expect to work on your farm at night, do you?"

"Sometimes," he said tersely. "When it's necessary."

"But why was it necessary tonight? I expected you to come calling."

Sally plunked a platter of cold fried chicken onto the table, followed by Mrs. Swerdlow with a ceramic bowl of potato salad. "You two want some coffee? Or maybe some whiskey?"

Cal huffed out a laugh and opened his mouth to reply when he heard Leah's quiet voice. "Whiskey."

Sally hooted. Belle sucked in her breath. "Really," she drawled. "How very unladylike of you, Leah."

Leah lifted a chicken breast onto her plate, then pushed the platter over to Cal. " 'Ladylike' has nothing to do with it," she said. "You have never been so tired you couldn't feel your knees, have you, Belle?"

"Heaven forbid—I should hope not!"

"Then don't you dare tell me that drinking whiskey is unladylike."

Two half-tumblers of whiskey appeared at Cal's elbow. He slid one over to Leah, then took a healthy swallow of the other. When Leah lifted her glass, he intoned, "Sip it, remember?"

Remembering how she'd choked on the shot of whiskey she'd downed after Johnny had died, she nodded and tried to smile. Still, her first sip made her cough.

"Told ya," Cal said with a tired chuckle.

Belle looked from Leah to Cal and back again. "Cal, honey, after the wedding I assume you will have hired help on your farm."

He sent her a long look. "I sure will, Belle. For one thing, you'll be there."

A snort of laughter came from the kitchen.

"What? Me! Well, I didn't mean—"

Leah plunked her whiskey glass down and leaned forward. "Shut up, Belle."

At that, Cal choked on his whiskey. When he finished coughing, he reached for a drumstick.

"Have some potato salad, Cal," Sally murmured.

"And there's apple pie for dessert," Mrs. Swerdlow called from the kitchen.

Leah nibbled on her chicken breast, then reached for a drumstick. All at once she was ravenously hungry! Between bites she downed dainty sips of whiskey, and then her eyes met Cal's.

Suddenly everything seemed riotously funny, the whiskey, Belle, eating supper at ten o'clock at night,

Mrs. Swerdlow's chuckles from the kitchen. Cal, too, seemed amused. His lips twitched and his eyes, which a moment earlier had looked dull with exhaustion, now twinkled with laughter. She dropped her gaze before she burst into giggles.

It didn't help. Bubbles of hilarity floated into her throat and she closed her eyes and clenched her teeth to contain them.

"Leah," Belle demanded, "whatever is the matter with you?"

"N-nothing," she managed. Even the look on Belle's face seemed funny.

"Then why, may I ask, are you acting so strange tonight?"

Cal answered for her. "You can ask, Belle. Not sure you're gonna like the answer. It's a combination of exhaustion and—"

"Exasperation," Leah interrupted.

"And frustration," Sally added.

"And impatience," Martha and Mrs. Swerdlow said together.

"Oh, I think you're just tired, Leah," Belle ventured. "Perhaps you'll feel better in the morning."

"I don't think so," Leah said. "In the morning, I have to go to work at the mercantile."

"Oh, honey," Belle said, "when I feel tired, I sleep late."

Sally slammed her palm down on the table top. "What if you *can't* sleep late, Belle? What if the eggs need to be gathered from the henhouse? What if the cow needs to be milked?"

"Well, what if it does? I'm sure I will have hired help."

For a long minute no one said a word. Then Cal swallowed the last of his whiskey, set the glass on the table with a thump, and stood up.

"Folks, I'm so tired I can't think straight. I'm going home to bed. Leah, I can't thank you enough for your help today. And Belle…don't you say another damn word!"

Leah caught his eye. "Maybe Mr. Petrini will share some of his cherry cordial with us sometime."

Cal gave her a tired grin. "I'll see you tomorrow morning at the mercantile, Leah. Ought to feel like a holiday after the last twelve hours."

Belle sent him a smile. "Cal, honey, do say you'll come calling tomorrow evening."

He didn't answer, just opened the screen door and walked out.

Leah felt like cheering.

Chapter Thirty-Eight

Lewis Christie draped his lanky fourteen-year-old frame over the mercantile counter and sent Cal a soulful look. "Gee, Mr. Zander, I'm sure sorry we couldn't help out yesterday. Maybe we could pick cherries for you today?"

Leah, folding lengths of calico at the back of the store, groaned loud enough for Cal to hear. And when Mr. Nanetti rolled his eyes as he lifted the heavy bolt of calico onto the topmost shelf, Leah laughed out loud.

This morning the mercantile owner said both Matteo and Tommy were so tired they had slept through breakfast. But," her employer added, "both my boys say they want to have cherry orchard when they grow up."

"Your sons want to be farmers?" Cal said with a disbelieving look.

"And Sonia and Sophia, too!" Mr. Nanetti said. "They want big cherry orchard like yours and also big bed of strawberries."

"Well, why not?" Leah offered.

"Because," Cal said with a tired sigh, "farming is backbreaking work."

"Ah," the mercantile owner said. "And your lady, Miss Belle, she want to do this? Grow cherries and break back?"

Cal sighed. "Well, no she doesn't, Florio."

"But," Leah said, "this lady wants *Cal*. And she gets

the farm along with him."

Mr. Nanetti lowered his voice. "I remember my Nina, she doesn't want to come to America. But she want *me*, so she come anyway. Maybe Mister Cal's lady change her mind?"

Cal and Leah looked at each other and shook their heads, and their employer frowned. "Then why you want this lady, Mister Cal?"

"He didn't have much choice," Leah said quickly. "She wanted *him*."

Mr. Nanetti blinked. "Is how is done in America?"

"Not usually, no," Cal said heavily. "I was sort of—"

"Cornered," Leah supplied.

"Compromised," Cal corrected. "Like she claimed *she* was."

To hide her grin, Leah reached for the jar of caramels on the counter. "Have Mrs. Crawley and the twins been in this morning?" she said quickly. "I should wipe off the fingerprints in case anyone else wants some candy, shouldn't I, Mr. Nanetti?"

"What? Oh, sure, Miss Leah, you wipe off. And do quick, before social this afternoon."

Cal grabbed a twenty-pound sack of sugar and just as quickly plunked it back down on the counter. "Social? What social?"

"Pie social at schoolhouse. My Nina, she bake Italian peach pie like her mama teach her."

All at once something puzzling about this morning made sense to Leah. Long before breakfast, the smell of bacon and coffee had drifted up to her bedroom, along with another scent wafting through the boarding house. Something sweet and spicy. It must have been an apple pie!"

"When is the pie social, Mr. Nanetti?"

"Three o'clock, after students go home from school."

"Not for me," Cal grumbled. "I'm going out to my farm for some peace and quiet. Maybe I'll...uh...pick a few cherries," he said with a chuckle.

"Maybe your lady will bring to this social a pie?" Mr. Nanetti said.

Cal snorted. "I don't think so, Florio. I don't think Belle Fontaine has been within ten feet of a stove her entire life."

"Eh? Then how she cook for you after wedding?"

"God only knows," he muttered, re-balancing the sack of sugar on his shoulder. "Maybe my sermon this Sunday should be about—"

"Marriage," Leah interrupted. "And its obligations."

"You want to write my sermon?" he quipped. When she didn't answer he strode out the front door with the sack of sugar.

Mr. Nanetti stared at his receding back. "Miss Leah, is good idea, Mister Cal wedding with this lady?

"Is *not* a good idea, Mr. Nanetti. "But," she amended quickly, "I am far too opinionated about Mister Cal's marriage."

And, she thought with a catch in her breath, *I am certainly too opinionated about Cal's "lady."*

****

Late that afternoon, Leah and Sally strolled across the schoolyard to the long table set up next to the baseball diamond. Dozens of pies covered the crisp gingham tablecloth.

"Belle left the boardinghouse early," Sally said

slowly. "She said she wanted to snag Cal before he went out to his farm."

"I hope she was too late," Leah replied. "After picking cherries all day yesterday, Cal deserves a peaceful evening."

Sally touched her arm. "Watch out, *macushlah*. Here she comes."

Leah bit her lip as Belle approached. Oh, lordy," she moaned. "I don't have energy enough to deal with Belle today."

"Why, Leah," Belle trilled. "Did Cal leave the mercantile early today, too?"

"Yes, he did."

"Well, where is he? I've looked all over and I can't find him."

"He…" Sally bumped her shoulder and shook her head. "…went for a long walk," Leah lied.

"Oh. Did he say anything about me at the store today?"

Surreptitiously, Leah put her hands behind her back and crossed her fingers. "No," she lied again.

The hopeful look on Belle's face faded. "Oh, fiddlesticks." She sighed. "Well, Cal is such a gentleman. He keeps things that happen between us very private."

Sally succumbed to a fit of coughing, and it was all Leah could do to keep her mouth firmly closed. *How is it Belle can be so…so false?* Pride, she guessed. And self-absorption.

"Well, here we are," Belle announced. "Let me get a plate of pie and join you, shall I?"

"Sorry, Belle," Sally muttered. "I'm…um…joining Arne and Verna Cowgill, over by that tree."

"Oh, good," Belle chirped. "Actually, I've been wanting to talk to Leah."

Leah's heart dropped into the pit of her stomach. She watched Belle load a plate up with a wide slab of blueberry pie and a slightly narrower slice with apricots spilling out the sides. Leah cut a modest slice of Mrs. Swerdlow's French apple pie, wrapped it in a napkin, and looked for a shady spot.

"Tell me honestly, Leah," Belle said as she settled next to her under a leafy maple tree. "What things should I know in order to be a good wife to Cal?"

Is she joking? The list is so long I hardly know where to begin.

Belle waved her fork at Leah. "Well?" she prompted.

Leah nibbled at the edge of her pie. Should she be honest? Should she give Belle a good shake and tell her to grow up? She cleared her throat.

"Let me speak frankly, Belle. You don't really want to be a *wife* to Cal, do you?"

Belle's green eyes widened. "I don't?"

"No, you don't. You want to *marry* Cal, but you don't really want to be a wife. To put any effort into making him happy. For you, it's more the thrill of the capture than the day-to-day effort of being a partner to a man."

Belle pressed her lips together for a long moment, then opened them to take a bite of blueberry pie. "What things does Cal especially like?"

Leah sighed. *She hasn't heard one word I said. I suppose that's not so surprising. Belle never wants to hear anyone's opinions but Belle's.*

Leah sighed. "I am no expert on what a man prefers

in a woman."

"But you have traveled with Cal! You spent time with him at that ranch in Idaho, so you must have learned things about him, things no one else would know."

Oh, yes, Leah acknowledged. She had learned things about Cal. She'd learned more about Cal Zander than she could ever share with Belle Fontaine.

"Um…well, Cal likes his bacon crisp and his coffee black and very strong. And he sleeps with his revolver under his bedroll."

And when he kissed me his mouth tasted of cherries.

Belle devoured another bite of her pie. "I don't know how to make coffee or fry bacon. Do you think Cal will care about those things if I am very…well, loving and…um…well, you know."

Leah pressed her lips together. "Yes, Belle, he will care. A wife is expected to be more than just loving. A wife is expected to be a partner, to be willing to help. Cal will value a wife's skills inside the house as well as in bed."

Belle said nothing, just stabbed her fork into her pie in silence.

"Mrs. Swerdlow could teach you some things, Belle. How to scrub clothes on a washboard, for instance. How to heat up a sadiron. How to plant a veg—"

"Scrub clothes on a washboard? Plant things? In the *dirt?* Oh, I would so much rather live in town," she moaned.

Leah clenched her teeth. "But Cal will not be living in town, Belle. If you want to be Cal's wife, you must move out to his farm."

"But…but I don't *want* to move!"

Leah swallowed hard. "Then don't marry him."

"Well! My word, Leah, you are certainly no help!"

Leah shook her head in frustration. "Tell me, Belle, what would you like to hear me say?"

"Oh, that's easy," Belle said, tossing her blonde ringlets. "I'd like to hear about how much Cal wants to marry me and—"

Leah set her uneaten slice of apple pie down beside her. "Belle, never once have I heard you say that you care about Cal. That you love him."

"Oh, pooh, that's just understood!"

"Understood by whom?"

"Well, by Cal, of course."

Leah snapped her jaw shut and drew in a deep breath. "You know something, Belle? You are a very pretty, self-absorbed woman who understands nothing at all about a man except how to seduce him. You have done that, and now you're going to have to pay the price for your success."

Belle's eyes rounded. "Are you quite finished?" she asked, her tone frosty.

"No, I am not," Leah said quietly. "But I think I have told you what you wanted to know."

Belle rose to her feet in a flurry of dimity ruffles. "You certainly have. But let me remind you of something, Leah Rydell. I am younger than you are, and I am prettier than you are, too. I am also smarter than you are." She paused and reached over to poke her forefinger into Leah's breastbone.

"And I am going to marry Cal Zander!"

Chapter Thirty-Nine

Two hours after Leah stumbled home from the pie social she was still shaking with fury, even after two cups of strong tea, the last one laced with a dollop of Mrs. Swerdlow's diminishing supply of whiskey. Now she sat in the landlady's rose garden in the backyard with her arms wrapped around her knees.

She was not sorry for what she'd said to Belle. She had been direct, and she had been honest. She was only sorry that what she'd said had only solidified Belle's single-minded conviction that she was superior to everyone else and knew better than anyone else what she should do in life. And who she should do it with.

Cal had begged off work early that afternoon and managed to evade Florio's invitation to supper. Instead, he walked down to the livery stable, saddled his horse, and rode out to his cherry orchard.

The two workmen he'd hired, Willem Nordgren and his gangly young nephew Joren, had left five bushel-baskets of fresh-picked cherries sitting in the shade next to his tall ladder, and he smiled at the sight. Tomorrow he'd load them up in the mercantile delivery wagon and haul them to the mercantile in Gillette Springs.

But right now he was content to just visit his orchard. He dismounted, looped the reins around a drooping branch, and tramped out among his cherry trees. Sure smelled good out here, the air scented with the clean aroma of growing things. Nothing in Texas ever smelled as sweet. Texas had smelled…like the rotting potatoes he'd sometimes eaten for supper. Tainted.

He stared up into the branches of the nearest cherry tree. Never in his wildest dream did he think he would own his own land. And a farmhouse, with a well and a smokehouse out back and a fireplace in all six bedrooms. Sometimes he had to pinch himself to make sure this was real.

He closed his eyes and drew in an uneven breath. God was generous to allow him this. And then he opened his lids and looked around him. Actually, it was Johnny Rydell, Leah's brother, who had made it possible for him to own this small piece of God's green earth. For all Johnny's devious activities in prison, he'd done an honest thing by paying Cal the $700 he owed him. That $700 had bought him this cherry orchard.

Rest in peace, Johnny Rydell. I'll name my first child after—

He sucked in a gulp of warm, cherry-scented air and felt his heart hammer. No, he wouldn't. Couldn't. The thought of Belle Fontaine as the mother of his child sent a choking pain into his chest. Even worse, the thought of Belle living in his beautiful farmhouse, rocking away on his front porch, lying close to him at night…

No. *No, no, no!* The day he rode into this pretty little town he'd found a place where he felt needed. Where he felt whole and worthwhile and no longer lost. Even as a circuit preacher, moving from town to town, he'd never felt like he really belonged anywhere. Guess that's why he'd moved around so much. That and looking for Johnny Rydell. Sure was funny how life worked out sometimes. He'd wanted to find Johnny's sister, Leah, but he sure hadn't counted on her coming to mean so much to him.

And he sure as hell hadn't counted on Belle Fontaine.

This was all wrong. He'd let Belle trick him into marrying her, but the whole thing had been dishonest. It was scarcely even believable! And now, standing out here among his cherry trees, he realized that he couldn't do it. He'd known it all along, but he hadn't had the guts to acknowledge it and do something about it.

Cal Zander, you are a hypocrite.

He clenched his jaw. *You preach about honesty on Sunday, and then you take a detour into cowardice. You preach about courage, about being true to yourself, and what do you do? You don't listen to what you really feel or acknowledge who you really are.*

He didn't care for Belle Fontaine, not the way a husband should care about his wife. He didn't even like her! He drove his fist into the trunk of the nearest tree. Then, instead of holding his bruised and torn flesh to his chest, he reached for the reins of his horse and, using only his left hand, managed to climb into the saddle and head back to town.

Chapter Forty

Sally handed the plate of butterscotch cookies to Belle, who was lazily rocking back and forth in the porch swing.

"Oooh, cookies!" she exclaimed. "Mrs. Swerdlow makes the best cookies!"

Sally choked on her glass of cold tea. "Huh! Leah made these cookies."

"Oh." Belle instantly set the cookie she'd been about to pop into her mouth back on the plate.

Leah, sitting across from her on a straight-backed oak chair, pressed her lips together and caught Sally's eye. "They're not poisoned, Belle."

Martha closed the geography book in her lap and reached for the cookie plate. "Maybe they should be," she murmured under her breath.

Sally suppressed a spurt of laughter. "Belle, I've been puzzling over something for days. Tell me why, exactly, you want to marry Cal Zander?"

"Oh, my," Belle exclaimed. "I am so glad you asked. I just love talking about him. Well, I want to marry Cal because…well, because he is the most deliciously handsome man I've ever laid eyes on."

Martha snorted. "So he's handsome. So what?"

"And…well, if *I* didn't marry him, someone else would!"

"So what?" Sally shot. "What do you care if Cal

marries someone else?"

For a split-second Belle looked blank. "Um…well, I care because I, um, I want him to be happy, of course."

"Why couldn't he be happy with someone else?" Sally pursued.

"Yes," Martha added. "Why couldn't he be happy with someone else?"

A flustered Belle reached for her discarded cookie. "Because," she announced, "Cal is not in love with anyone else. Cal is in love with me."

"How do you know?" Sally asked.

"Oh, really, Sally," Belle exclaimed, "a woman can just tell."

"Then maybe you could enlighten us poor spinsters," Martha remarked, an edge in her voice.

Sally huffed out a half-laugh, half-snort and choked on her cookie.

"Weeell…" Belle drew the word out dramatically, enjoying the fact that she had an audience. "Cal has scarcely looked at another woman since he first came to town."

"Really," Martha said in a tone of disbelief. "How do you know that?"

"Oh, I've watched him," Belle answered. "Very, very closely."

Martha reached for another cookie. "And what did you see?"

"Well…" Belle spread her skirt out and twitched the ruffles in place. "When we're together, Cal doesn't even *look* at anyone else."

"Are you sure?" Sally said.

"Oh, yes. I watch him like a hawk."

"A hungry hawk," Martha muttered.

Sally again choked on her tea. "And that's why you want to marry Cal Zander? Because he's handsome and he doesn't look at other women?"

Belle stared at her. "Well, Cal *is* handsome. Don't you agree, Leah?"

Leah opened her mouth to reply, then thought better of it and pressed her lips together. Then she changed her mind. "Cal is much more than just a handsome man, Belle."

"Why, of course he is! He's…well, he's…he's a real gentleman."

"Would you care to give us an example of that?" Sally asked.

"Oh. Well, yes. When Cal compromised me, he did the gentlemanly thing and agreed to marry me."

That did it. Leah plunked her glass of tea onto the small table and rose to her feet. "I can't listen to this any longer. I'm going inside and help Mrs. Swerdlow with supper."

"Me, too," Martha said. She jumped up and yanked the screen door open.

Sally exchanged a long look with Belle. "You know, honey, I don't think you know a thing about Cal Zander *inside*. You just see the outside of the man."

"Why, Sally, that's not true at all. Not at all."

"And, Sally added, "I think you glommed onto him just to make sure he didn't marry anyone else!"

Belle's cheeks turned pink. "But—"

"I'm not finished," the Irish woman continued. "You threw your lasso around Cal Zander and pulled it tight just to beat your competition. Real love doesn't work that way, Belle."

Belle turned hard green eyes on her. "So?"

"So, turn him loose."

At that moment Leah poked her head out the screen door. "Supper is ready," she announced.

"Just in time, too," Sally breathed. "One more minute and they'd have to hang me for murder."

Chapter Forty-One

Cal showed up at the boardinghouse after supper to find Belle rocking in the porch swing. "Cal, honey! I was hoping you would come calling this evening, and here you are!"

She sent him a dazzling smile but, Cal noticed, it didn't touch her eyes. "Good evening, Belle."

She extended her hand. "Come on up here and sit beside me, Cal. My goodness, how I have missed you!"

"I ate supper here just the other night," he reminded as he sat down. "Maybe that slipped your mind."

"Oh, no, Cal. You never slip my mind. I think about you all the time."

He was silent.

"Don't you think of me?"

"No," he said in a low voice. "I don't."

Belle fluffed her skirt so the ruffles spilled across his lap. "I have a new dress. Do you like it?"

"What? Oh, sure. Real pretty."

"I can't wait for you to see my wedding dress, Cal. It's so elegant. It has simply yards and yards of Valenciennes lace. I can hardly wait for our wedding day."

Cal carefully brushed the ruffles off his lap and turned to face her. "Belle, I have something to tell you."

She snuggled her head onto his shoulder. "Oh, I do hope it's about the wedding."

He sat up straighter. "Yes, as a matter of fact, it is about the wedding."

"Oh, good. I've been dying to ask you—"

"Belle…"

"—about the ceremony and—"

"Belle…"

"—afterward, when we—"

"Belle! Will you hush up and listen?"

She snapped her jaw shut. Cal half-turned his body toward her and drew in a slow breath. "Belle, I am not going to marry you."

"What? But you promised!"

"No, I did not. The truth is you lied to the sheriff, claimed something happened that was untrue, and bamboozled me into agreeing to marry you."

"B-but, Cal, it's all planned. My wedding dress and everything!"

He twisted to look her full in the face. "I'm sorry, Belle. I am not going to marry you."

She jumped up and propped her hands on her hips. "You can't do that, Cal. That's breach of pr—"

"Maybe," he said evenly. "You tricked me. That isn't exactly a promise. I'm only sorry I let it go on for so long."

"But…but what will people say?"

He sighed and stood up. "Seems to me that's not what's important here, Belle. You don't love me, and I don't love you. That's what a marriage is built on, and we don't have that. I can't do it."

All the fight seemed to go out of her, and she sank back onto the swing. "Oh, this is just awful! I will be the laughingstock of the whole town."

He reached out and patted her hand. "Just tell

everybody the truth, that I backed out."

For a long moment she said nothing. Then she sent a furtive look toward the screen door and with one foot prodded the swing into motion. She rocked furiously back and forth for a full minute, then looked up at him.

Cal half-expected her to cry and carry on. Instead, she sat and combed the fingers of one hand through her tight blonde ringlets.

"Belle—"

"Oh, hush up, Cal, I'm thinking."

He blinked. *Thinking?* That seemed like an odd occupation for a suddenly un-engaged young woman. *Thinking about what?*

She brought the swing to an abrupt stop and looked at him. "Cal, you remember Clem Harkins? The deputy sheriff?"

A niggle of unease crawled up his spine. "Yeah. What about him?"

She smiled slowly. "Do you know if he's married?"

****

Summertime in the small town of Maple Shade was hot and lazy-feeling as usual. Kids were let out of school, and they could be found laughing and shouting at swimming holes and trekking along creeks with fishing poles over their shoulders and cans of wriggling worms clutched in their hands. Schoolteacher Martha Carmichael heaved a sigh of relief and stacked her geography books in the Schoolbooks section of the bookcase in her bedroom.

Girls badgered their mothers for dimity and gingham and Butterick dress patterns from the town dressmaker, then nagged their mothers to stitch up new dresses and shirtwaists and aprons. And Tillotsen's sweet shop enjoyed a surge in orders for milkshakes and ice cream sundaes, devoured by giggling girls in new dimity summer dresses.

At the mercantile, things went on as they had all year. Bushels of sweet corn and potatoes and peaches appeared in front of the store, and Leah was kept busy polishing so many fingerprints off the candy jars she wondered if the glass would wear down. Mr. Nanetti fussed and puttered up and down the aisles, straightening boys socks and belts and underdrawers and making sure the shovels and hoes and rakes stood upright and looked shiny and new.

Cal moved from the cabin behind the mercantile to his cherry farm outside town, but three afternoons a week he rode in to help Mr. Nanetti. He worked steadily, hoisting sacks of flour and coffee beans onto customers' freight wagons and watching them drive off in a cloud of dust. Leah noticed that he was unusually quiet and rarely smiled.

One day, Cal turned up at the mercantile in the early morning. Mr. Nanetti had just walked over to the livery stable, so Leah was there alone.

"I need a butter churn, Leah. You have one?"

"Well, yes, we do, but—"

"I finished up the cherry harvest last week, and I just bought a cow. She gives plenty of milk every day, but Mrs. Meyberg says she won't churn butter."

"Alma Meyberg is your housekeeper? Why, she's sixty if she's a day."

"Yeah. She keeps the place clean and gathers the eggs, but that's about it. She won't churn butter."

"She doesn't do the cooking?"

"Nope. Good thing Nina Nanetti taught me some

things, otherwise both Mrs. Meyberg and I would starve."

At that moment Mr. Nanetti stepped in through the back door. "Ah, Mister Cal! Why today you come in early?"

"I'm not here to work, Florio. Just buying a churn."

"Mrs. Meyberg, she work out okay?"

Cal hesitated. "Yeah, pretty much. She doesn't talk much, but she scrubs everything, even the ceiling."

"Is permanent, Mrs. Meyberg?"

Cal shrugged. "Guess so. She says she likes the place, and she didn't much like keeping house for Doc Holt. Too many bloody bandages."

When Cal left with his new churn, Mr. Nanetti stepped closer and studied Leah's face. "Mister Cal, he is happy?"

She hesitated. Was Cal happy? She couldn't tell. Ever since the wedding had been called off, Cal seemed distant and preoccupied, so she let him alone. She knew he wouldn't want to talk about Belle, and she also knew he wouldn't want sympathy. As for what he *did* want, she couldn't begin to guess, but right now she didn't want to poke at him.

"I don't know if Cal is happy, Mr. Nanetti. I know he likes living out on his farm, but whether he is happy or not, I couldn't say."

Her employer nodded. "What about you, Miss Leah? You are happy?"

Leah quickly turned away to hide her face. She was far from happy. She was so angry at Belle Fontaine for her dishonest, manipulative actions she could scarcely stand to look at her. Then there was the pain of watching Cal grow quieter and more withdrawn with every passing day. She couldn't possibly be happy when Cal was so obviously distressed.

"Miss Leah?" Mr. Nanetti laid a veined hand on her shoulder. "You come home with me and tell my Nina all about it."

Numbly, she nodded. The mercantile owner locked both the back and front doors, and Leah let him walk her over to the big white house on Spruce Street.

Nina took one look at her and drew her into the parlor. "You sit down, Leah. And Florio, bring some wine."

When he returned with two brimming glasses, Nina shooed her husband and the children out of the parlor and settled on the settee beside her. "Now, Leah, you tell me what make you sad."

Leah's throat closed. She took a sip of the wine and opened her mouth to speak but found she couldn't utter a single word.

Nina reached over to touch her hand. "Is all right, Leah. I know already what is problem. You drink your wine and then we have some lunch. We will talk about Cal later."

Leah nodded as tears stung into her eyes. She couldn't possibly talk about Cal. She had told no one, not even Sally, how she felt about him, though she suspected that Sally guessed far more than she ever let on.

She let Nina usher her to the big table in the dining room, where Mr. Nanetti and the children did their best to cheer her up over tomato and cheese sandwiches. But when daughter Sophia blushingly admitted that she fancied herself in love with Mister Cal and planned to marry him when she grew up, Leah laughed, and then she burst into tears.

Sophia stared at her with wide brown eyes. "Miss Leah, what did I say?"

"N-nothing, Sophia. I'm j-just having a h-hard time admitting something to myself."

"Oh, golly, Miss Leah. Is it something to do with—"

"Sophia!" her father interrupted. "That not our business, so you do not ask."

"A-all right, Papa. Sorry, Miss Leah."

Leah tried to smile at the girl, then gritted her teeth and finished her sandwich.

After lunch she made her excuses, and when Mr. Nanetti returned to the mercantile late that afternoon, she walked on back to the boardinghouse. She sat rocking in the porch swing until long past midnight when Sally arrived after her shift at the saloon.

"My goodness, Leah, whatever are you doing up so late?"

"Just…thinking, Sally."

The Irish woman nodded. "About what?"

"About how tired I am of everything."

"Tomorrow is the Fourth of July. The mercantile will be closed, so you can sleep in."

Leah groaned. It was July already? Half the summer had passed and she'd scarcely noticed. She felt as if a thick fog was enveloping her, and no matter how hard she tried, she couldn't see through it.

Chapter Forty-Two

Every year the townspeople of Maple Shade looked forward to the annual Fourth of July fireworks in the town park. Young boys managed to collect pockets full of firecrackers, and families gathered to picnic on the grass and wade in the river. At dusk, Leah walked slowly across the park, flanked by Sally and Martha and followed by Mrs. Swerdlow and one of the Nanetti girls, who danced along at the landlady's side.

Florio Nanetti, Nina, and the rest of their children sprawled on a blanket under a spreading maple tree. Mrs. Swerdlow and young Sofia Nanetti moved past them to a spot near Derrick and Ellen Crawley and their twin boys, the ones who had a yen for the mercantile's caramels. As they settled near the Crawley family, Sally touched Leah's arm. "Looks like Sofia is happy to sit near the Crawley boys."

Leah hid a smile. "Maybe Sofia is developing a fondness for Mr. Nanetti's candy jars," she murmured.

Mayor Grimes, standing at the podium in the latticework gazebo, launched his annual Independence Day speech. Mrs. Swerdlow settled on the quilt she spread on the grass and purposely turned her back on the mayor. Sofia plunked herself down and demurely folded her skirt around her legs. Martha joined Mrs. Swerdlow, keeping her back to the mayor as well.

Leah had just settled herself next to the landlady

when Sally touched her arm again. "Would you look at that!" the Irish woman breathed. She tipped her head in the direction of an odd trio just entering the park. Leah's gaze followed the direction Sally indicated, and it was all she could do to keep from laughing out loud.

Sauntering slowly across the grass was Belle Fontaine with her arms linked with that of the man on either side of her.

"Good gracious," Leah whispered, "That's Sheriff Mankewicz!"

"And Ted Dalrymple," Sally added.

"Doesn't Ted have a wife?"

"Not any more," Sally murmured. "His wife left him. Went back to her mother in Ohio."

"Oh, the poor man."

"Not so poor, *macushlah*. He owns the feed store and the bakery next door. Belle's not wasting any time, is she?"

Leah didn't answer. She watched Ted and the sheriff amble along beside Belle and tried not to smile. She'd known Morgan Mankewicz ever since she came to Maple Shade. He was a perfectly nice, respectable man, just a bit dull, and she felt a dart of sympathy for him. Morgan would be no match for Belle. At least Ted Dalrymple might be astute enough to see through Belle's wiles.

"It's all for show," Sally whispered. "Cal is sitting over there with Florio and Nina Nanetti."

Leah glanced behind her. Sure enough, Cal was absorbed in a game of mumble-t-peg with the two older Nanetti boys. He glanced up, nodded at Leah, and went back to the game.

Leah tried desperately to focus on Mayor Grimes's

speech. "…this great country, where our flag flutters high…"

Nobody seemed to be listening, and she let her attention drift back to Cal.

He was showing the boys how to flip the jackknife so the blade stuck in the ground, and she had to smile. She remembered Johnny practicing for hours flipping his jackknife. Often he would be so absorbed he would be late for supper. "I like to win," he had said. "Winning takes practice."

Her heart caught at the memory. She wondered if Johnny and Cal had played mumble-t-peg in prison.

The mayor droned on. His hypnotic, uninflected voice made Leah's eyelids heavy, and they finally drooped closed. But even with her eyes shut she was intensely aware of Cal. She hadn't seen much of him for the past two weeks while he was moving into his farmhouse and harvesting the last of his cherries. She missed him at the mercantile.

She missed him a *lot*.

At that moment the mayor ended his speech, and the first burst of fireworks bloomed overhead. Ooh's and aah's rose from the crowd, followed by more fireworks, bright red showers of stars dancing against the velvet-black sky. It went on and on, burst after burst of colored patterns that shimmered and pulsed overhead.

Sally leaned toward her. "Remind you of anything?" she murmured.

"What, you mean all those pretty red stars in the sky?"

"Yes, all those red stars."

Leah stared at her friend. "No. Should it?"

"Well…" Sally hesitated. "Maybe you're too

young."

"Too young for what?"

"For...being reminded of what explosions of pulsing color remind you of."

"Sally, you're not making any sense," Leah whispered.

"On the contrary, *macushlah*, I'm making a lot of sense. You seem to be missing a great deal of life."

Leah frowned, then her attention was again pulled skyward where a dazzling series of crimson pinwheels bloomed overhead. Entranced, she stretched out on her back and gazed up into the blackness, gasping along with the crowd as shower after shower of stars dazzled the onlookers.

The evening was lovely, the air soft and warm, punctuated by the happy cries of children. Everyone was happy here in the middle of the summer in Maple Shade, Oregon, Leah thought. Everyone but her.

Inside, in her deepest most private thoughts, she had to admit she was lonely. Something was missing. This subtle, insistent feeling of longing had been growing stronger over these past weeks. Well, months, really. She was restless at night and distracted at the mercantile, so distracted that Mr. Nanetti had started asking if she was ill. No, she wasn't ill. She was...lonely.

She missed her brother most during the warm summer months. When she and Johnny were young, after Mama and Papa were gone and it was just the two of them, they would gaze up at the stars at night and imagine their parents safe and happy somewhere in heaven. It had eased the sharp ache of loss. Of loneliness.

Lately she had been feeling the same way, and that was puzzling. She closed her eyes and tried to imagine

Johnny safe in heaven. Would he be playing mumble-t-peg? Or even poker?

A handle jostled her shoulder. "Wake up, sleepyhead," Sally whispered. "The fireworks are over. Everyone is going home."

"Oh!" Leah sat up and watched Martha and Mrs. Swerdlow fold up the quilt and start off across the grass.

"Mind if I go on ahead?" Sally asked. "You can catch up in a minute, when you're fully awake." She drifted off across the now quiet, moonlit park.

Leah was relieved in a way. She liked Sally, but at the moment she didn't feel like talking to anyone. She drew in a long breath of the soft, honeysuckle-scented air and closed her eyes again. All at once she found tears spilling out of her eyes and running down her cheeks. *What in the world is wrong with me?*

She heard footsteps move across the grass toward her, and she turned her back, hoping whoever it was would walk on by.

But they didn't. The steps slowed and came to a stop behind her, and then a strong, warm hand touched her shoulder. She opened her eyes and looked up.

Cal.

He didn't say anything, just extended his hand and closed his fingers around hers. Without a word he pulled her to her feet, and after a moment's hesitation he stepped in close and folded his arms around her. He smelled of pine soap and some kind of minty aftershave.

Suddenly she was so happy she felt she could fly. He didn't say anything. She raised her face to his and felt his warm breath against her cheek, and then his lips settled over hers.

A sweet, hot joy surged from her toes right to the top

of her head. His arms tightened around her, and when her hands crept around his neck, his arms tightened again. It was like the fireworks, a magical, unexpectedly beautiful moment. Her heart swelled until she felt it would burst into a shower of stars.

Cal's mouth moved slowly over hers, telling her something and asking her something at the same time. When he lifted his lips away she found she was shaking, and she felt his body tremble as well. She closed her eyes again. There were no words to describe this. All she knew was the happiness blooming inside her filled her heart and her head and washed over every inch of her.

Without speaking, he took her hand in his, turned her toward the edge of the park, and moved toward the lights of the town. When they reached the boardinghouse, he bent his head toward her and murmured something into her ear.

"Come to church tomorrow, Leah. My sermon will be for you."

Then he was gone, moving off down the sidewalk in his long-legged gait. She fought the urge to run after him, wind her arms about his tall form, and recapture the joy she felt just being near him.

Chapter Forty-Three

On Sunday morning Leah listened to her housemates rattle down the stairs on their way to church and tried not to think about Cal's sermon. It would be for her, he said. Whatever could he mean?

She thought about it for half an hour, and finally her curiosity triumphed over her reluctance. She climbed out of bed, splashed lukewarm water over her face, and put on her only church-going dress, the blue striped gingham with a ruffle at the hem. Curiosity, she reminded herself as she lifted her crocheted shawl off the chair, was what killed the cat.

She skimmed down the staircase into the kitchen, lifted a slice of cold cinnamon toast off the plate Mrs. Swerdlow had left for her, and crunched it up as she stepped off the porch.

She was late for church. By the time she arrived, the pews were crowded with women dressed in their best *goin'-to-meetin'* clothes and men who looked hot and uncomfortable in stiff shirt collars. Wriggly children kept busy squirming and playing with the hymnals.

She stood at the back of the church, as she had before. If she didn't like Cal's sermon, she could always leave. She reflected on her relationship with Cal over the months since he'd come to Maple Shade and felt a twinge of guilt. She had started out disliking him. Even on that desperate trip to Jason Halliday's Idaho ranch when Johnny was dying, she blew hot and cold about Callahan Zander.

She disliked him when he'd laughed at her campfire biscuits. But she had liked him when he'd shielded her from that frightening thunderstorm and when he'd rescued her from those three low-lifes at the mercantile in Idaho. She liked him when he made sure Mr. Nanetti wasn't lifting a sack of potatoes that was too heavy for him. And when he'd ridden for the doctor and helped deliver Nina Nanetti's twins. And when he'd danced with little Sofia Nanetti at Emer Janson's barn dance. And when he'd made supper at the Nanetti's when Nina was so tired after the birth. And...

And when he'd held her and let her cry all over his shirt after Johnny died. And when he'd worked half the night to fill Mr. Petrini's nine bushels of ripe cherries for his cherry cordial.

And when he'd kissed her on the way back to the boardinghouse that evening.

And, oh Lord, she liked Cal *enormously* when he had kissed her last night after the Fourth of July fireworks. More than enormously. She liked Cal Zander better than any man she'd ever known.

To think I once detested him, and now I am discovering that, far from detesting him, I like him. I even admire him. Maple Shade would not be the same without Cal Zander preaching his sermons to the townspeople every Sunday morning.

She was not the same person she'd been when Cal had come to Maple Shade. However, she acknowledged with a guilty start, that wasn't because of Cal's sermons. She would never be the same person because now she had come to know this capable, complicated man, and despite everything he had somehow touched her heart. She cared for Cal Zander.

The sound of his voice brought her back to the church where she now stood. He scanned the gathered congregation for a long moment without saying a word. When his gaze rested on her, standing against the back wall, he looked straight into her eyes and smiled.

A funny little buzz of recognition tugged at her, and she caught her breath.

At that moment Cal began to speak.

Chapter Forty-Four

"Today's sermon is gonna be a bit different, folks. Today I'm going to tell you about something I've learned, something that's been growing clearer and stronger ever since the day I rode into Maple Shade."

Leah noted the expectant quiet that settled over the congregation. Everyone sat up a little straighter. The children even stopped fidgeting.

"What I'm talking about this morning," Cal continued, "is something I bet some of you already know about. Something the rest of you might be searching for."

The silence that settled over the congregation was so thick Leah fancied she could hear them breathing. Her own breath felt fluttery with expectation.

"A man wants to belong," Cal said, his voice quiet. "To be useful. To be valued. A man also wants to be *connected* to someone. It's not primarily admiration, though admiration is a part of it. And it's not desire or passion, though that's part of it, too."

Leah waited, scarcely breathing.

"It's a feeling of being connected, a feeling that without a particular person in one's life—sharing the sunset, sharing one's innermost thoughts, sharing the beautiful and the difficult things we meet in life, there is something missing. It's the deep-down knowledge that another human being matters to you. *Really* matters."

Leah noticed a subtle movement at the front of the

church where Belle Fontaine, seated in the first row beside Sheriff Morgan Mankewicz, was slowly dropping her head onto his shoulder. For an instant Leah wanted to take Morgan aside and warn him, then she thought better of it. She knew Morgan well. She could stop by the sheriff's office in the morning and have a heart-to-heart talk with him, as a friend.

Cal's voice brought her back to his sermon. "Now," he said, "this thing we're all searching for is something pretty simple. It's a quiet, slow-growing feeling for another person, and when you find it, it changes your life. I call that feeling 'a Sunday kind of love.' "

Every bone in Leah's body came alive. *Oh.* She knew what Cal was talking about. Cal Zander was talking about exactly what she was feeling.

He looked up. His gray-green eyes locked with hers, and he smiled. *He is telling me something. Asking me something.*

Very slowly she inclined her head in a nod. *Yes, Cal, I feel it, too, that kind of love.*

Then he surprised her. "When you find that Sunday-kind-of-love person, you ask her an important question. You ask, 'Will you'?"

He paused and again held her gaze. Her heart stuttered. And then he spoke to the back of the church where she stood, and everything stopped.

"Will you, Leah? Will you?"

****

Leah Rydell and Callahan Zander were married the following Sunday afternoon by Reverend Strader, who arrived from Gillette Springs just an hour before the ceremony. Leah wore her best blue gingham dress, and at the last minute a teary-eyed Sally Flannigan pressed a bouquet of white Damask roses into her hand. Florio Nanetti stood up with Cal, surreptitiously swiping moisture off his cheeks, while Nina Nanetti beside him sniffled audibly into a lacy handkerchief.

After the ceremony, Mrs. Swerdlow served a four-layer applesauce-walnut wedding cake along with tiny glasses of cherry cordial provided by Andreas Petrini. Emer Janson strummed his banjo, and everyone sang "Drink to Me Only With Thine Eyes" and "Clementine."

Sally Flannigan kissed Cal on both cheeks and pronounced an Irish blessing, spoken in Gaelic, while Mr. Nanetti sang a Neapolitan love song in mellifluous Italian.

When Leah and Cal, tired and a little hazy from all the cherry cordial toasts to their happiness, finally departed for his cherry farm, the guests lined both sides of Mrs. Swerdlow's porch steps and tossed handfuls of rice at them for good luck.

And Mrs. Swerdlow spent the following spring plucking rice seedlings out of her front garden, with the help of Martha, Sally, and even, very reluctantly, Belle Fontaine.

A word about the author...

Lynna Banning combines a lifelong love of history and literature into a satisfying career as a writer. Born in Oregon, she graduated from Scripps College and embarked on a career as an editor and technical wrier and, after graduate work at UC Irvine, as a high school English teacher. She enjoys hearing from her readers. You may write to her directly at P.O. Box 324, Felton, CA 95018 USA. Email her at carowoolston@att.net or visit Lynna's website at lynnabanning.net. lynnabanning.net